THE CRIME AT BLACK DUDLEY

THE CRIME
AT BLACK DUDLEY

Margery Allingham

Felony & Mayhem Press • New York

All the characters and events portrayed in this work are fictitious.

THE CRIME AT BLACK DUDLEY

A Felony & Mayhem mystery

PRINTING HISTORY
First UK edition (Heinemann): 1929
First US edition (as The Black Dudley Murder) (Doubleday Doran): 1929
Felony & Mayhem edition: 2006

ISBN 978-1-933397-42-9

Manufactured in the United States of America

Library of Congress Cataloging-in-Publication Data

Allingham, Margery, 1904-1966.
  The crime at Black Dudley / Margery Allingham.
     p. cm.
  "A Felony & Mayhem mystery."
  ISBN 978-1-933397-42-9 (pbk.)
  1. Campion, Albert (Fictitious character)--Fiction. 2. Private investiga-
tors--England--Fiction. 3. London (England)--Fiction. I. Title.
  PR6001.L678C75 2008
  823'.912--dc22
                              2008046412

To
"THE GANG"

The icon above says you're holding a copy of a book in the Felony & Mayhem "Vintage" category. These books were originally published prior to about 1965, and feature the kind of twisty, ingenious puzzles beloved by fans of Agatha Christie and John Dickson Carr. If you enjoy this book, you may well like other "Vintage" titles from Felony & Mayhem Press, including:

MARGERY ALLINGHAM
Mystery Mile
Look to the Lady
Police at the Funeral
Sweet Danger
Death of a Ghost
Flowers for the Judge
Dancers in Mourning
The Case of the Late Pig
The Fashion in Shrouds
Black Plumes

EDMUND CRISPIN
The Case of the Gilded Fly
Holy Disorders
Swan Song
Love Lies Bleeding
Burried for Pleasure

ELIZABETH DALY
Murders in Volume 2
The House without the Door
Evidence of Things Seen
Nothing Can Rescue Me
Arrow Pointing Nowhere

MATTHEW HEAD
The Devil in the Bush

For more about these books, and other Felony & Mayhem titles, or to place an order, please visit our website at

www.FelonyAndMayhem.com

or contact us at

Felony and Mayhem Press
156 Waverly Place
New York, NY 10014

CONTENTS

THE CRIME AT BLACK DUDLEY

CHAPTER ONE

Candle-Light

THE VIEW FROM THE NARROW WINDOW was dreary and inexpressibly lonely. Miles of neglected park-land stretched in an unbroken plain to the horizon and the sea beyond. On all sides it was the same.

The grey-green stretches were hayed once a year, perhaps, but otherwise uncropped save by the herd of heavy-shouldered black cattle who wandered about them, their huge forms immense and grotesque in the fast-thickening twilight.

In the centre of this desolation, standing in a thousand acres of its own land, was the mansion, Black Dudley; a great grey building, bare and ugly as a fortress. No creepers hid its nakedness, and the long narrow windows were dark-curtained and uninviting.

The man in the old-fashioned bedroom turned away from the window and went on with his dressing.

"Gloomy old place," he remarked to his reflection in the mirror. "Thank God it's not mine."

He tweaked his black tie deftly as he spoke, and stood back to survey the effect.

George Abbershaw, although his appearance did not indicate it, was a minor celebrity.

He was a smallish man, chubby and solemn, with a choir-boy expression and a head of ridiculous bright-red curls which gave him a somewhat fantastic appearance. He was fastidiously tidy in his dress and there was an air of precision in everything he did or said which betrayed an amazingly orderly mind. Apart from this, however, there was nothing about him to suggest that he was particularly distinguished or even mildly interesting, yet in a small and exclusive circle of learned men Dr. George Abbershaw was an important person.

His book on pathology, treated with special reference to fatal wounds and the means of ascertaining their probable causes, was a standard work, and in view of his many services to the police in the past his name was well known and his opinion respected at the Yard.

At the moment he was on holiday, and the unusual care which he took over his toilet suggested that he had not come down to Black Dudley solely for the sake of recuperating in the Suffolk air.

Much to his own secret surprise and perplexity, he had fallen in love.

He recognized the symptoms at once and made no attempt at self-deception, but with his usual methodical thoroughness set himself to remove the disturbing emotion by one or other of the only two methods known to mankind—disillusionment or marriage. For that reason, therefore, when Wyatt Petrie had begged him to join a week-end party at his uncle's house in the country, he had been persuaded to accept by the promise that Margaret Oliphant should also be of the party.

Wyatt had managed it, and she was in the house.

George Abbershaw sighed, and let his thoughts run idly about his young host. A queer chap, Wyatt: Oxford turned out a lot of interesting young men with bees in their bonnets. Wyatt was a good lad, one of the best. He was profoundly grateful to Wyatt. Good Lord, what a profile she had, and there was brain there too, not empty prettiness. If only...! He pulled himself together and mentally rebuked himself.

This problem must be attacked like any other, decently and in order.

He must talk to her; get to know her better, find out what she liked, what she thought about. With his mind still on these things the booming of the dinner gong surprised him, and he hurried down the low-stepped Tudor staircase as nearly flurried as he had ever been in his life.

However bleak and forbidding was Black Dudley's exterior, the rooms within were none the less magnificent. Even here there were the same signs of neglect that were so evident in the Park, but there was a certain dusty majesty about the dark-panelled walls with the oil-paintings, hanging in their fast-blackening frames, and in the heavy, dark-oak furniture, elaborately carved and utterly devoid of polish, that was very impressive and pleasing.

The place had not been modernized at all. There were still candles in the iron sconces in the hall, and the soft light sent great shadows, like enormous ghostly hands, creeping up to the oak-beamed ceiling.

George sniffed as he ran down the staircase. The air was faintly clammy and the tallow smelt a little.

"Damp!" said he to himself. "These old places need a lot of looking after...shouldn't think the sanitary system was any too good. Very nice, but I'm glad it's not mine."

The dining-hall might have made him change his mind. All down one side of the long, low room was a row of stained-glass windows. In a great open fireplace a couple of faggots blazed whole, and on the long refectory table, which ran nearly the entire length of the flagged floor, eight seven-branched candlesticks held the only light. There were portraits on the walls, strangely differing in style, as the artists of the varying periods followed the fashions set by the masters of their time, but each face bearing a curious likeness to the next—the same straight noses, the same long thin lips, and above all, the same slightly rebellious expression.

Most of the party had already assembled when Abbershaw came in, and it struck him as incongruous to hear the babble of bright young conversation in this great tomb of a house with its faintly musty air and curiously archaic atmosphere.

As he caught sight of a gleam of copper-coloured hair on the other side of the table, however, he instantly forgot any sinister dampness or anything at all mysterious or unpleasant about the house.

Meggie Oliphant was one of those modern young women who manage to be fashionable without being ordinary in any way. She was a tall, slender youngster with a clean-cut white face, which was more interesting than pretty, and dark-brown eyes, slightly almond-shaped, which turned into slits of brilliance when she laughed. Her hair was her chief beauty, copper-coloured and very sleek; she wore it cut in a severe "John" bob, a straight thick fringe across her forehead.

George Abbershaw's prosaic mind quivered on the verge of poetry when he looked at her. To him she was exquisite. He found they were seated next to each other at table, and he blessed Wyatt for his thoughtfulness.

He glanced up the table at him now and thought what a good fellow he was.

The candle-light caught his clever, thoughtful face for an instant, and immediately the young scientist was struck by the resemblance to the portraits on the wall. There was the same straight nose, the same wide thin-lipped mouth.

Wyatt Petrie looked what he was, a scholar of the new type. There was a little careful disarrangement in his dress, his brown hair was not quite so sleek as his guests', but he was obviously a cultured, fastidious man: every shadow on his face, every line and crease of his clothes indicated as much in a subtle and elusive way.

Abbershaw regarded him thoughtfully and, to a certain degree, affectionately. He had the admiration for him that one first-rate scholar always has for another out of his own line. Idly he reviewed the other man's record. Head of a great public school, a First in Classics at Oxford, a recognized position as a minor poet, and above all a good fellow. He was a rich man, Abbershaw knew, but his tastes were simple and his charities many. He was a man with an urge, a man who took life, with its problems and its pleasures, very seriously. So far as the other man knew he had never betrayed the least interest in women in general or in one woman in particular. A month ago Abbershaw would have admired him for this attribute as much as for any other. Today, with Meggie at his side, he was not so sure that he did not pity him.

From the nephew, his glance passed slowly round to the uncle, Colonel Gordon Coombe, host of the week-end.

He sat at the head of the table, and Abbershaw glanced curiously at this old invalid who liked the society of young people so much that he persuaded his nephew to bring a houseful of young folk down to the gloomy old mansion at least half a dozen times a year.

He was a little man who sat huddled in his high-backed chair as if his backbone was not strong enough to support his frame upright. His crop of faded yellow hair was now almost white, and stood up like a hedge above a narrow forehead. But by far the most striking thing about him was the flesh-coloured plate with which clever doctors had repaired a war-mutilated face which must otherwise have been a horror too terrible to think upon. From where he sat, perhaps some fourteen feet away, Abbershaw could only just detect it, so skilfully was it fashioned. It was shaped roughly like a one-sided half-mask and covered almost all the top right-hand side of his face, and through it the Colonel's grey-green eyes peered out shrewd and interested at the tableful of chattering young people.

George looked away hastily. For a moment his curiosity had overcome his sense of delicacy, and a wave of embarrassment passed over him as he realized that the little grey-green eyes had rested upon him for an instant and had found him eyeing the plate.

He turned to Meggie with a faint twinge of unwanted colour in his round cherubic face, and was a little disconcerted to find her looking at him, a hint of a smile on her lips and a curious brightness in her intelligent, dark-brown eyes. Just for a moment he had the uncomfortable impression that she was laughing at him.

He looked at her suspiciously, but she was no longer smiling, and when she spoke there was no amusement or superiority in her tone.

"Isn't it a marvellous house?" she said.

He nodded.

"Wonderful," he agreed. "Very old, I should say. But it's very lonely," he added, his practical nature coming out in spite of himself. "Probably most inconvenient...I'm glad it's not mine."

The girl laughed softly.

"Unromantic soul," she said.

Abbershaw looked at her and reddened and coughed and changed the conversation.

"I say," he said, under the cover of the general prittle-prattle all around them, "do you know who everyone is? I only recognize Wyatt and young Michael Prenderby over there. Who are the others? I arrived too late to be introduced."

The girl shook her head.

"I don't know many myself," she murmured. "That's Anne Edgeware sitting next to Wyatt—she's rather pretty, don't you think? She's a Stage-cum-Society person; you must have heard of her."

Abbershaw glanced across the table, where a striking young woman in a pseudo-Victorian frock and side curls sat talking vivaciously to the young man at her side. Some of her conversation floated across the table to him. He turned away again.

"I don't think she's particularly pretty," he said with cheerful inconsequentialness. "Who's the lad?"

"That boy with black hair talking to her? That's Martin. I don't know his other name, he was only introduced to me in the hall. He's just a stray young man, I think." She paused and looked round the table.

"You know Michael, you say. The little round shy girl next to him is Jeanne, his fiancée; perhaps you've met her."

George shook his head.

"No," he said, "but I've wanted to; I take a personal interest in Michael"—he glanced at the fair, sharp-featured young man as he spoke— "he's only just qualified as an M.D., you know, but he'll go far. Nice chap, too…Who is the young prize-fighter on the girl's left?"

Meggie shook her sleek bronze head at him reprovingly as she followed his glance to the young giant a little higher up the table. "You mustn't say that," she whispered. "He's our star turn this party. That's Chris Kennedy, the Cambridge rugger blue."

"Is it?" said Abbershaw with growing respect. "Fine-looking man."

Meggie glanced at him sharply, and again the faint smile appeared on her lips and the brightness in her dark eyes. For all his psychology, his theorizing, and the seriousness with which he took himself, there was very little of George Abbershaw's mind that was not apparent to her, but for all that the light in her eyes was a happy one and the smile on her lips unusually tender.

"That," she said suddenly, following the direction of his gaze and answering his unspoken thought, "that's a lunatic."

George turned to her gravely.

"Really?" he said.

She had the grace to become a little confused.

"His name is Albert Campion," she said. "He came down in Anne Edgeware's car, and the first thing he did when he was introduced to me was to show me a conjuring trick with a two-headed penny—he's quite inoffensive, just a silly ass."

Abbershaw nodded and stared covertly at the fresh-faced young man with the tow-coloured hair and the foolish, pale-blue eyes behind tortoiseshell-rimmed spectacles, and wondered where he had seen him before.

The slightly receding chin and mouth so unnecessarily full of teeth was distinctly familiar. "Albert Campion?" he repeated under his breath. "Albert Campion? Campion? Campion?" But still his memory would not serve him, and he gave up calling on it and once more his inquisitive glance flickered round the table.

Since the uncomfortable little moment ten minutes ago when the Colonel had observed him scrutinizing his face, he had been careful to avoid the head of the table, but now his attention was caught by a man who sat next to his host, and for an instant he stared unashamedly.

The man was a foreigner, so much was evident at a glance; but that in itself was not sufficient to interest him so particularly.

The man was an arresting type. He was white-haired, very small and delicately made, with long graceful hands which he used a great deal in his conversation, making gestures, swaying his long, pale fingers gracefully, easily.

Under the sleek white hair which waved straight back from a high forehead his face was grey, vivacious, and peculiarly wicked.

George could think of no other word to describe the thin-lipped mouth that became one-sided and O-shaped in speech, the long thin nose, and more particularly the deep-set, round, black eyes which glistened and twinkled under enormous shaggy grey brows.

George touched Meggie's arm.

"Who is that?" he said.

The girl looked up and then dropped her eyes hurriedly.

"I don't know," she murmured, "save that his name is Gideon or something, and he is a guest of the Colonel's— nothing to do with our crowd."

"Weird-looking man," said Abbershaw.

"Terrible!" she said, so softly and with such earnestness that he glanced at her sharply and found her face quite grave.

She laughed as she saw his expression.

"I'm a fool," she said. "I didn't realize what an impression the man had made on me until I spoke. But he looks a wicked type, doesn't he? His friend, too, is rather startling, don't you think—the man sitting opposite to him?"

The repetition of the word "wicked," the epithet which had arisen in his own mind, surprised Abbershaw, and he glanced covertly up the table again.

The man seated opposite Gideon, on the other side of the Colonel, was striking enough indeed.

He was a foreigner, grossly fat, and heavily jowled, and there was something absurdly familiar about him. Suddenly it dawned upon George what it was. The man was the living image of the little busts of Beethoven which are sold at music shops. There were the same heavy-lidded eyes, the same broad nose, and to cap it all the same shock of hair, worn long and brushed straight back from the amazingly high forehead.

"Isn't it queer?" murmured Meggie's voice at his side. "See—he has no expression at all."

As soon as she had spoken George realized that it was true. Although he had been watching the man for the last few minutes he had not seen the least change in the heavy red face; not a muscle seemed to have moved, nor the eyelids to have flickered; and although he had been talking to the Colonel at the time, his lips seemed to have moved independently of the rest of his features. It was as if one watched a statue speak.

"I think his name is Dawlish—Benjamin Dawlish," said the girl. "We were introduced just before dinner."

Abbershaw nodded, and the conversation drifted on to other things, but all the time he was conscious of something faintly disturbing in the back of his mind, something which hung over his thoughts like a black shadow vaguely ugly and uncomfortable.

It was a new experience for him, but he recognized it immediately.

For the first time in his life he had a presentiment—a vague, unaccountable apprehension of trouble ahead.

He glanced at Meggie dubiously.

Love playing all sorts of tricks with a man's brain. It was very bewildering.

The next moment he had pulled himself together, telling himself soberly not to be a fool. But wriggle and twist as he might, always the black shadow sat behind his thoughts, and he was glad of the candle-light and the bright conversation and the laughter of the dinner-table.

CHAPTER TWO

The Ritual of the Dagger

AFTER DINNER, Abbershaw was one of the first to enter the great hall or drawing-room which, with the dining-room, took up the best part of the ground floor of the magnificent old mansion. It was an amazing room, vast as a barn and heavily panelled, with a magnificently carved fire-place at each end wherein two huge fires blazed. The floor was old oak and highly polished, and there was no covering save for two or three beautiful Shiraz rugs.

The furniture here was the same as in the other parts of the house, heavy, unpolished oak, carved and very old; and here, too, the faint atmosphere of mystery and dankness, with which the whole house was redolent, was apparent also.

Abbershaw noticed it immediately, and put it down to the fact that the light of the place came from a huge iron candlering which held some twenty or thirty thick wax candles suspended by an iron chain from the center beam of the ceiling, so that there were heavy shadows round the panelled walls and in the deep corners behind the great fire-places.

By far the most striking thing in the whole room was an enormous trophy which hung over the fire-place farthest from the door. It was a vast affair composed of some twenty or thirty lances arranged in a circle, heads to the centre, and surmounted by a feathered helm and a banner resplendent with the arms of the Petries.

Yet it was the actual centre-piece which commanded immediate interest. Mounted on a crimson plaque, at the point where the lance-heads made a narrow circle, was a long, fifteenth-century Italian dagger. The hilt was an exquisite piece of workmanship, beautifully chased and encrusted at the upper end with uncut jewels, but it was not this that first struck the onlooker. The blade of the Black Dudley Dagger was its most remarkable feature. Under a foot long, it was very slender and exquisitely graceful, fashioned from steel that had in it a curious greenish tinge which lent the whole weapon an unmistakably sinister appearance. It seemed to shine out of the dark background like a living and malignant thing.

No one entering the room for the first time could fail to remark upon it; in spite of its comparatively insignificant size it dominated the whole room like an idol in a temple.

George Abbershaw was struck by it as soon as he came in, and instantly the feeling of apprehension which had annoyed his prosaic soul so much in the other room returned, and he glanced round him sharply, seeking either reassurance or confirmation, he hardly knew which.

The house-party which had seemed so large round the dinner-table now looked amazingly small in this cathedral of a room.

Colonel Coombe had been wheeled into a corner just out of the firelight by a man-servant, and the old invalid now sat smiling benignly on the group of young people in the body of the room. Gideon and the man with the expressionless face sat one on either side of him, while a grey-haired, sallow-faced man whom Abbershaw understood was a Dr. White

Whitby, the Colonel's private attendant, hovered about them in nervous solicitude for his patient.

On closer inspection Gideon and the man who looked like Beethoven proved to be even more unattractive than Abbershaw had supposed from his first somewhat cursory glance.

The rest of the party was in high spirits. Anne Edgeware was illustrating the striking contrast between Victorian clothes and modern manners, and her vivacious air and somewhat outrageous conversation made her the centre of a laughing group. Wyatt Petrie stood amongst his guests, a graceful, lazy figure, and his well-modulated voice and slow laugh sounded pleasant and reassuring in the forbidding room.

It was Anne who first brought up the subject of the dagger, as someone was bound to do.

"What a perfectly revolting thing, Wyatt," she said, pointing at it. "I've been trying not to mention it ever since I came in here. I should toast your muffins with something else, my dear."

"Ssh!" Wyatt turned to her with mock solemnity. "You mustn't speak disrespectfully of the Black Dudley Dagger. The ghosts of a hundred dead Petries will haunt you out of sheer outraged family pride if you do."

The words were spoken lightly, and his voice had lost none of its quiet suavity, but whether it was the effect of the dagger itself or that of the ghostly old house upon the guests none could tell, but the girl's flippancy died away and she laughed nervously.

"I'm sorry," she said. "I should just loathe to be haunted. But quite seriously, then, if we mustn't laugh, what an incredible thing that dagger is."

The others had gathered round her, and she and Wyatt now stood in the centre of a group looking up at the trophy. Wyatt turned round to Abbershaw. "What do you think of it, George?" he said.

"Very interesting—very interesting indeed. It is very old, of course? I don't think I've ever seen one like it in my life." The little man spoke with genuine enthusiasm. "It's a curio, some old family relic, I suppose?"

Wyatt nodded, and his lazy grey eyes flickered with faint amusement.

"Well, yes, it is," he said. "My ancestors seem to have had high old times with it if family legends are true."

"Ah!" said Meggie, coming forward. "A ghost story?"

Wyatt glanced at her.

"Not a ghost," he said, "but a story."

"Let's have it." It was Chris Kennedy who spoke; the young rugger blue had more resignation than enthusiasm in his tone. Old family stories were not in his line. The rest of the party was considerably more keen, however, and Wyatt was pestered for the story.

"It's only a yarn, of course," he began. "I don't think I've ever told it to anyone else before. I don't think even my uncle knows it." He turned questioningly as he spoke, and the old man shook his head.

"I know nothing about it," he said. "My late wife brought me to this house," he explained. "It had been in the family for hundreds of years. She was a Petrie—Wyatt's aunt. He naturally knows more about the history of the house than I. I should like to hear it, Wyatt."

Wyatt smiled and shrugged his shoulders, then, moving forward, he climbed on to one of the high oak chairs by the fire-place, stepped up from one hidden foothold in the panelling to another, and stretching out his hand lifted the shimmering dagger off its plaque and carried it back to the group who pressed round to see it more closely.

The Black Dudley Dagger lost none of its sinister appearance by being removed from its setting. It lay there in Wyatt Petrie's long, cultured hands, the green shade in the steel blade more apparent than ever, and a red jewel in the hilt glowing in the candle-light.

"This," said Wyatt, displaying it to its full advantage, "is properly called the 'Black Dudley Ritual Dagger.' In the time of Quentin Petrie, somewhere about 1500, a distinguished guest was found murdered with this dagger sticking in his heart." He paused, and glanced round the circle of faces. From the corner by the fire-place Gideon was listening intently, his grey face livid with interest, and his little black eyes wide and unblinking. The man who looked like Beethoven had turned toward the speaker also, but there was no expression on his heavy red face.

Wyatt continued in his quiet voice, choosing his words carefully and speaking with a certain scholastic precision.

"I don't know if you know it," he said, "but earlier than that date there had been a superstition which persisted in outlying places like this that a body touched by the hands of the murderer would bleed afresh from the mortal wound; or, failing that, if the weapon with which the murder was committed were placed into the hand which struck the blow, it would become covered with blood as it had been at the time of the crime. You've heard of that, haven't you, Abbershaw?" he said, turning toward the scientist, and George Abbershaw nodded.

"Go on," he said briefly.

Wyatt returned to the dagger in his hand.

"Quentin Petrie believed in this superstition, it appears," he said, "for anyway it is recorded that on this occasion he closed the gates and summoned the entire household, the family, servants, labourers, herdsmen, and hangers-on, and the dagger was solemnly passed around. That was the beginning of it all. The ritual sprang up later—in the next generation, I think."

"But did it happen? Did the dagger spout blood and all that?" Anne Edgeware spoke eagerly, her round face alive with interest.

Wyatt smiled. "I'm afraid one of the family was beheaded for the murder," he said; "and the chronicles have it that the dagger betrayed him, but I fancy that there was a good deal of juggling in affairs of justice in those days."

"Yes, but where does the ritual come in?" said Albert Campion, in his absurd falsetto drawl. "It sounds most intriguing. I knew a fellow once who, when he went to bed, made a point of taking off everything else first before he removed his topper. He called that a ritual."

"It sounds more like a conjuring trick," said Abbershaw.

"It does, doesn't it?" agreed the irrepressible Albert. "But I don't suppose your family ritual was anything like that, was it, Petrie? Something more lurid, I expect."

"It was, a little, but nearly as absurd," said Wyatt, laughing. "Apparently it became a custom after that for the whole ceremony of the dagger to be repeated once a year—a sort of family rite as far as I can ascertain. That was only in the beginning, of course. In later years it degenerated into a sort of mixed hide-and-seek and relay race, played all over the house. I believe it was done at Christmas as late as my grandfather's time. The procedure was very simple. All the lights in the house were put out, and the head of the family, a Petrie by name and blood, handed the dagger to the first person he met in the darkness. Acceptance was of course compulsory, and that person had to hunt out someone else to pass the dagger on to, and the game continued in that fashion—each person striving to get rid of the dagger as soon as it was handed to him—for twenty minutes. Then the head of the house rang the dinner gong in the hall, the servants relit the lights, and the person discovered with the dagger lost the game and paid a forfeit which varied, I believe, from kisses to silver coins all round."

He stopped abruptly.

"That's all there is," he said, swinging the dagger in his fingers.

"What a perfectly wonderful story!"

Anne Edgeware turned to the others as she spoke. "Isn't it?" she continued. "It just sort of fits in with this house!"

"Let's play it." It was the bright young man with the teeth again, and he beamed round fatuously at the company as he spoke. "For sixpences if you like," he ventured as an added inducement, as no one enthused immediately.

Anne looked at Wyatt. "Could we?" she said.

"It wouldn't be a bad idea," remarked Chris Kennedy, who was willing to back up Anne in anything she chose to suggest. The rest of the party had also taken kindly to the idea, and Wyatt hesitated.

"There's no reason why we shouldn't," he said, and paused. Abbershaw was suddenly seized with a violent objection to the whole scheme. The story of the dagger ritual had impressed him strangely. He had seen the eyes of Gideon fixed upon the speaker with curious intensity, and had noticed the little huddled old man with the plate over his face harking to the barbarous story with avid enjoyment. Whether it was the great dank gloomy house or the disturbing effects of love upon his nervous system he did not know, but the idea of groping round in the dark with the malignant-looking dagger filled him with distaste more vigorous than anything he had ever felt before. He had an impression, also, that Wyatt was not too attracted by the idea, but in the face of the unanimous enthusiasm of the rest of the party he could do nothing but fall in with the scheme.

Wyatt looked at his uncle.

"But certainly, my dear boy, why should I?" The old man seemed to be replying to an unspoken question. "Let us consider it a blessing that so innocent and pleasing an entertainment can arise from something that must at one time have been very terrible."

Abbershaw glanced at him sharply. There had been a touch of something in the voice that did not ring quite true, something hypocritical—insincere. Colonel Coombe glanced at the men on either side of him.

"I don't know…" he began dubiously.

Gideon spoke at once: it was the first time Abbershaw had heard his voice, and it struck him unpleasantly. It was deep, liquid, and curiously caressing, like the purring of a cat.

"To take part in such an ancient ceremony would be a privilege," he said.

The man who had no expression bowed his head.

"I too," he said, a trace of foreign accent in his voice, "would be delighted."

Once the ritual had been decided upon, preparations went forward with all ceremony and youthful enthusiasm. The man-servant was called in, and his part in the proceedings explained carefully. He was to let down the great iron candle-ring, extinguish the lights, and haul it up to the ceiling again. The lights in the hall were to be put out also, and he was then to retire to the servants' quarters and wait there until the dinner-gong sounded, at which time he was to return with some of the other servants and relight the candles with all speed.

He was a big man with a chest like a prize-fighter and a heavy florid face with enormous pale-blue eyes which had in them an innately sullen expression. A man who could become very unpleasant if the occasion arose, Abbershaw reflected inconsequentially.

As head of the family, Wyatt the last of the Petries took command of the proceedings. He had the manner, Abbershaw considered, of one who did not altogether relish his position. There was a faintly unwilling air about everything he did, a certain over-deliberation in all his instructions which betrayed, the other thought, a distaste for his task.

At length the signal was given. With a melodramatic rattle of chains the great iron candle-ring was let down and the lights put out, so that the vast hall was in darkness save for the glowing fires at each end of the room. Gideon and the man with the face like Beethoven had joined the circle round the doorway to the corridors, and the last thing George Abbershaw saw before the candles were extinguished was the little wizened figure of Colonel Coombe sitting in his chair in the shadow of the fire-place smiling out upon the scene from behind the hideous flesh-coloured plate. Then he followed the others into the dim halls and corridors of the great eerie house, and the Black Dudley Ritual began.

CHAPTER THREE

In the Garage

THE WEIRDNESS OF THE GREAT stone staircase and unlit recesses was even more disquieting than Abbershaw had imagined it would be. There were flutterings in the dark, whisperings, and hurried footsteps. He was by no means a nervous man, and in the ordinary way an experience of this sort would probably have amused him faintly, had it not bored him. But on this particular night and in this house, which had impressed him with such a curious sense of foreboding ever since he had first seen it from the drive, he was distinctly uneasy.

To make matters worse, he had entirely lost sight of Meggie. He had missed her in the first blinding rush of darkness, and so, when by chance he found himself up against a door leading into the garden, he went out, shutting it softly behind him.

It was a fine night, and although there was no moon, the starlight made it possible for him to see his way about; he did not feel like wandering about the eerie grounds alone, and suddenly it occurred to him that he would go and inspect his A.C. two-seater which he had left in the big garage beside the drive.

He was a tidy man, and since he had no clear recollection of turning off the petrol before he left her, it struck him that now was a convenient opportunity to make sure.

He located the garage without much difficulty, and made his way to it, crossing over the broad, flagged drive to where the erstwhile barn loomed up against the starlight sky. The doors were still open and there was a certain amount of light from two hurricane lanterns hanging from a low beam in the roof. There were more than half a dozen cars lined up inside, and he reflected how very typical each was of its owner. The Rover coupé with the cream body and the black wings was obviously Anne Edgeware's; even had he not seen her smart black-and-white motoring kit he would have known it. The Salmson with the ridiculous mascot was patently Chris Kennedy's property; the magnificent Lanchester must be Gideon's, and the rest were simple also; a Bentley, a Buick, and a Swift proclaimed their owners.

As his eye passed from one to another, a smile flickered for an instant on his lips. There, in the corner, derelict and dignified as a maiden aunt, was one of the pioneers of motor traffic.

This must be the house car, he reflected, as he walked over to it, Colonel Coombe's own vehicle. It was extraordinary how well it matched the house, he thought as he reached it.

Made in the very beginning of the century, it belonged to the time when, as some brilliant American has said, cars were built, like cathedrals, with prayer. It was a brougham; coach-built and leathery, with a seating capacity in the back for six at least, and a tiny cab only in front for the driver. Abbershaw was interested in cars, and since he felt he had time to spare and there was nothing better to do, he lifted up the extraordinarily ponderous bonnet of the "museum-piece" and looked in.

For some moments he stood staring at the engine within,

and then, drawing a torch from his pocket, he examined it more closely.

Suddenly a smothered exclamation broke from his lips and he bent down and flashed the light on the underside of the car, peering under the ridiculously heavy running-boards and glancing at the axles and shaft. At last he stood up and shut down the bonnet, an expression of mingled amazement and curiosity on his cherubic face.

The absurd old body, which looked as if it belonged to a car which would be capable of twenty miles all out at most, was set upon the chassis and the engine of the latest "Phantom" type Rolls-Royce.

He had no time to reflect upon the possible motives of the owner of the strange hybrid for this inexplicable piece of eccentricity, for at that moment he was disturbed by the sounds of footsteps coming up the flagged drive. Instinctively he moved over to his own car, and was bending over it when a figure appeared in the doorway.

"Oh—er—hullo! Having a little potter—what?"

The words, uttered in an inoffensively idiotic voice, made Abbershaw glance up to find Albert Campion smiling fatuously in upon him.

"Hullo!" said Abbershaw, a little nettled to have his occupation so accurately described. "How's the Ritual going?"

Mr. Campion looked a trifle embarrassed.

"Oh, jogging along, I believe. Two hours' clean fun, don't you know."

"You seem to be missing yours," said Abbershaw pointedly.

The young man appeared to break out into a sort of Charleston, apparently to hide further embarrassment.

"Well, yes, as a matter of fact I got fed up with it in there," he said, still hopping up and down in a way Abbershaw found peculiarly irritating. "All this running about in the dark with daggers doesn't seem to me healthy.

I don't like knives, you know—people getting excited and all that. I came out to get away from it all."

For the first time Abbershaw began to feel a faint sympathy for him.

"Your car here?" he remarked casually.

This perfectly obvious question seemed to place Mr. Campion still less at ease.

"Well—er—no. As a matter of fact, it isn't. To be exact," he added in a sudden burst of confidence, "I haven't got one at all. I've always liked them, though," he continued hastily, "nice, useful things. I've always thought that. Get you where you want to go, you know. Better than a horse."

Abbershaw stared at him. He considered that the man was either a lunatic or drunk, and as he disliked both alternatives he suggested stiffly that they should return to the house. The young man did not greet the proposal with enthusiasm, but Abbershaw, who was a determined little man when roused, dragged him back to the side door through which he had come, without further ado.

As soon as they entered the great grey corridor and the faintly dank musty breath of the house came to meet them, it became evident that something had happened. There was a sound of many feet, echoing voices, and at the far end of the passage a light flickered and passed.

"Someone kicking up a row over the forfeit, what!" The idiotic voice of Albert Campion at his ear jarred upon Abbershaw strangely.

"We'll see," he said, and there was an underlying note of anxiety in his voice which he could not hide.

A light step sounded close at hand and there was a gleam of silk in the darkness ahead of them.

"Who's there?" said a voice he recognized as Meggie's.

"Oh, thank God, it's you!" she exclaimed, as he spoke to her.

Mr. Albert Campion then did the first intelligent thing

Abbershaw had observed in him. He obliterated himself and faded away up the passage, leaving them together.

"What's happened?" Abbershaw spoke apprehensively, as he felt her hand quiver as she caught his arm.

"Where have you been?" she said breathlessly. "Haven't you heard? Colonel Coombe had a heart atta ck right in the middle of the game. Dr. Whitby and Mr. Gideon have taken him up to his room. It was all very awkward for them, though. There weren't any lights. When they sounded the gong the servants didn't come. Apparently there's only one door leading from their quarters to the rest of the house and that seems to have been locked. They've the candles alight now, though," she added, and he noticed that she was oddly breathless.

Abbershaw looked down at her; he wished he could see her face.

"What's happening in there now?" he said. "Anything we can do?"

The girl shook her head. "I don't think so. They're just standing about talking. I heard Wyatt say that the news had come down that it was nothing serious, and he asked us all to go on as if nothing had happened. Apparently the Colonel often gets these attacks…" She hesitated and made no attempt to move.

Abbershaw felt her trembling by his side, and once again the curious fear which had been lurking at the back of his mind all the evening showed itself to him.

"Tell me," he said, with a sudden intuition that made his voice gentle and comforting in the darkness. "What is it?"

She started, and her voice sounded high and out of control.

"Not—not here. Can't we get outside? I'm frightened of this house." The admission in her tone made his heart leap painfully.

Something had happened, then.

He drew her arm through his.

"Why, yes, of course we can," he said. "It's a fine starlit night; we'll go on to the grass."

He led her out on to the roughly cut turf that had once been smooth lawns, and they walked together out of the shadows of the house into a little shrubbery where they were completely hidden from the windows.

"Now," he said, and his voice had unconsciously assumed a protective tone; "what is it?"

The girl looked up at him, and he could see her keen, clever face and narrow brown eyes in the faint light.

"It was horrible in there," she whispered. "When Colonel Coombe had his attack, I mean. I think Dr. Whitby found him. He and Mr. Gideon carried him up while the other man—the man with no expression on his face—rang the gong. No one knew what had happened, and there were no lights. Then Mr. Gideon came down and said that the Colonel had had a heart attack…" She stopped and looked steadily at him, and he was horrified to see that she was livid with terror.

"George," she said suddenly, "if I told you something would you think I—I was mad?"

"No, of course not," he assured her steadily. "What else happened?"

The girl swallowed hard. He saw she was striving to compose herself, and obeying a sudden impulse he slid his arm round her waist, so that she was encircled and supported by it.

"In the game," she said, speaking clearly and steadily as if it were an effort, "about five minutes before the gong rang, someone gave me the dagger. I don't know who it was—I think it was a woman, but I'm not sure. I was standing at the foot of the stone flight of stairs which leads down into the lower hall, when someone brushed past me in the dark and pushed the dagger into my hand. I suddenly felt frightened of it, and I ran down the corridor to find someone I could give it to."

She paused, and he felt her shudder in his arm.

"There is a window in the passage," she said, "and as I passed under it the faint light fell upon the dagger and—don't think I'm crazy, or dreaming, or imagining something—but I saw the blade was covered with something dark. I touched it, it was sticky. I knew it at once, it was blood!"

"Blood!" The full meaning of her words dawned slowly on the man and he stared at her, half-fascinated, half incredulous.

"Yes. You must believe me." Her voice was agonized and he felt her eyes on his face. "I stood there staring at it," she went on. "At first I thought I was going to faint. I knew I should scream in another moment, and then—quite suddenly and noiselessly—a hand came out of the shadows and took the knife. I was so frightened I felt I was going mad. Then, just when I felt my head was bursting, the gong rang."

Her voice died away in the silence, and she thrust something into his hand.

"Look," she said, "if you don't believe me. I wiped my hand with it."

Abbershaw flashed his torch upon the little crumpled scrap in his hand. It was a handkerchief, a little filmy wisp of a thing of lawn and lace, and on it, clear and unmistakable, was a dull red smear—dry blood.

CHAPTER FOUR

Murder

THEY WENT SLOWLY back to the house.

Meggie went straight up to her room, and Abbershaw joined the others in the hall.

The invalid's corner was empty, chair and all had disappeared.

Wyatt was doing his best to relieve any feeling of constraint amongst his guests, assuring them that his uncle's heart attacks were by no means infrequent and asking them to forget the incident if they could.

Nobody thought of the dagger. It seemed to have vanished completely. Abbershaw hesitated, wondering if he should mention it, but finally decided not to, and he joined in the halfhearted, fitful conversation.

By common consent everyone went to bed early. A depression had settled over the spirits of the company, and it was well before midnight when once again the great candle-ring was let down from the ceiling and the hall left again in darkness.

Up in his room Abbershaw removed his coat and waistcoat, and, attiring himself in a modestly luxurious dressinggown, settled down in the armchair before the fire to smoke a last cigarette before going to bed. The apprehension he had felt all along had been by no means lessened by the events of the last hour or so.

He believed Meggie's story implicitly: she was not the kind of girl to fabricate a story of that sort in any circumstances, and besides the whole atmosphere of the building after he had returned from the garage had been vaguely suggestive and mysterious.

There was something going on in the house that was not ordinary, something that as yet he did not understand, and once again the face of the absurd young man with the horn-rimmed spectacles flashed into his mind and he strove vainly to remember where he had seen it before.

His meditations were cut short by the sound of footsteps in the passage outside, and the next moment there was a discreet tap at his door.

Abbershaw rose and opened it, to discover Michael Prenderby, the young, newly qualified M.D., standing fully dressed in the doorway.

The boy looked worried, and came into the room quickly, shutting the door behind him after he had glanced up and down the corridor outside as if to make certain that he had not been followed.

"Forgive the melodrama," he said, "but there's something darn queer going on in this place. Have a cigarette?"

Abbershaw looked at him shrewdly. The hand that held the cigarette-case out to him was not too steady, and the facetiousness of the tone was belied by the expression of anxiety in his eyes.

Michael Prenderby was a fair, slight young man, with a sense of humour entirely unexpected.

To the casual observer he was an inoffensive, colourless individual, and his extraordinary spirit and strength of character were known only to his friends.

Abbershaw took a cigarette and indicated a chair.

"Let's have it," he said. "What's up?"

Prenderby lit a cigarette and pulled at it vigorously, then he spoke abruptly.

"In the first place," he said, "the old bird upstairs is dead."

Abbershaw's blue-grey eyes flickered, and the thought which had lurked at the back of his mind ever since Meggie's story in the garden suddenly grew into a certainty.

"Dead?" he said. "How do you know?"

"They told me." Prenderby's pale face flushed slightly. "The private medico fellow—Whitby, I think his name is—came up to me just as I was coming to bed; he asked me if I would go up with him and have a look at the old boy."

He paused awkwardly, and Abbershaw suddenly realized that it was a question of professional etiquette that was embarrassing him.

"I thought they'd be bound to have got you up there already," the boy continued, "so I chased up after the fellow and found the Colonel stretched out on the bed, face covered up and all that. Gideon was there too, and as soon as I got up in the room I grasped what it was they wanted me for. Mine was to be the signature on the cremation certificate."

"Cremation? They're in a bit of a hurry, aren't they?"

Prenderby nodded.

"That's what I thought, but Gideon explained that the old boy's last words were a wish that he should be cremated and the party should continue, so they didn't want to keep the body in the house a moment longer than was absolutely necessary."

"Wanted the party to go on?" repeated Abbershaw stupidly. "Absurd!"

The young doctor leant forward. "That's not all by any means," he said. "When I found what they wanted, naturally I pointed out that you were the senior man and should be first approached. That seemed to annoy them both. Old Whitby, who was very nervous, I thought, got very up-stage and talked a lot of rot about '*Practising* M.D.s,' but it was the foreigner who got me into the really unpleasant hole. He pointed out, in that disgustingly sticky voice he has, that I was a guest in the house and could hardly refuse such a simple request. It was all damn cheek and very awkward, but eventually I decided to rely on your decency to back me up and so…" He paused.

"Did you sign?" Abbershaw said quickly.

Prenderby shook his head. "No," he said with determination, adding explanatorily: "They wouldn't let me look at the body."

"What?" Abbershaw was startled. Everything was tending in the same direction. The situation was by no means a pleasant one.

"You refused?" he said.

"Rather." Prenderby was inclined to be angry. "Whitby talked a lot of the usual bilge—trotted out all the good old phrases. By the time he'd finished, the poor old bird on the bed must have been dead about a year and a half according to him. But he kept himself between me and the bed, and when I went to pull the sheet down, Gideon got in my way deliberately. Whitby seemed to take it as a personal insult that I should think even an ordinary examination necessary. And then I'm afraid I lost my temper and walked out."

He paused, and looked at the older man awkwardly. "You see," he said, with a sudden burst of confidence, "I've never signed a cremation certificate in my life, and I didn't feel like starting on an obviously fishy case. I only took my finals a few months ago, you know."

"Oh, quite right, quite right." Abbershaw spoke with conviction. "I wonder what they're doing?"

Prenderby grinned.

"You'll probably find out," he said dryly. "They'll come to you now. They thought I should be easier to manage, but having failed—and since they're in such a hurry—I should think you were for it. It occurred to me to nip down and warn you."

"Good of you. Thanks very much." Abbershaw spoke genuinely. "It's a most extraordinary business. Did it look like heart failure?"

Prenderby shrugged his shoulders.

"My dear fellow, I don't know," he said. "I didn't even see the face. If it was heart failure why shouldn't I examine him? It's more than fishy, you know, Abbershaw. Do you think we ought to do anything?"

"No. That is, not at the moment." George Abbershaw's round and chubby face had suddenly taken on an expression which immediately altered its entire character. His mouth was firm and decided, and there was confidence in his eyes. In an instant he had become the man of authority, eminently capable of dealing with any situation that might arise.

"Look here," he said, "if you've just left them they'll be round for me any moment. You'd better get out now, so that they don't find us together. You see," he went on quickly, "we don't want a row here, with women about and that sort of thing; besides, we couldn't do anything if they turned savage. As soon as I get to town I can trot along and see old Deadwood at the Yard and get everything looked into without much fuss. That is, of course, once I've satisfied myself that there is something tangible to go upon. So if they press me for that signature I think I shall give it 'em. You see, I can arrange an inquiry afterwards if it seems necessary. It's hardly likely they'll get the body cremated before we can get on to 'em. I shall go up to town first thing in the morning."

"That's the stuff," said Prenderby with enthusiasm. "If you don't mind, I'll drop down on you afterwards to hear how things have progressed. Hullo!"

He paused, listening. "There's someone coming down the passage now," he said. "Look here, if it's all the same to you I'll continue the melodrama and get into that press."

He slipped into the big wardrobe at the far end of the room and closed the carved door behind him just as the footsteps paused in the passage outside and someone knocked.

On opening the door, Abbershaw found, as he had expected, Dr. Whitby on the threshold. The man was in a pitiable state of nerves. His thin grey hair was damp and limp upon his forehead, and his hands twitched visibly.

"Dr. Abbershaw," he began, "I am sorry to trouble you so late at night, but I wonder if you would do something for us."

"My dear sir, of course." Abbershaw radiated good humour, and the other man warmed immediately.

"I think you know," he said, "I am Colonel Coombe's private physician. He has been an invalid for some years, as I dare say you are aware. In point of fact, a most unfortunate thing has happened, which although we have known for some time that it must come soon, is none the less a great shock. Colonel Coombe's seizure this evening has proved fatal."

Abbershaw's expression was a masterpiece: his eyebrows rose, his mouth opened.

"Dear, dear! How very distressing!" he said with that touch of pomposity which makes a young man look more foolish than anything else. "*Very* distressing," he repeated, as if another thought had suddenly struck him. "It'll break up the party, of course."

Dr. Whitby hesitated. "Well," he said, "we had hoped not."

"Not break up the party?" exclaimed Abbershaw, looking so profoundly shocked that the other hastened to explain.

"The deceased was a most eccentric man," he murmured confidentially. "His last words were a most urgently expressed desire for the party to continue."

"A little trying for all concerned," Abbershaw commented stiffly.

"Just so," said his visitor. "That is really why I came to you. It has always been the Colonel's wish that he should be cremated immediately after his decease, and, as a matter of fact, all preparations have been made for some time. There is just the formality of the certificate, and I wonder if I might bother you for the necessary signature."

He hesitated doubtfully, and shot a glance at the little red-haired man in the dressing-gown. But Abbershaw was ready for him.

"My dear sir, anything I can do, of course. Let's go up there now, shall we?"

All traces of nervousness had vanished from Whitby's face, and a sigh of relief escaped his lips as he escorted the obliging Dr. Abbershaw down the long, creaking corridor to the Colonel's room.

It was a vast old-fashioned apartment, high-ceilinged, and not too well lit. Panelled on one side, it was hung on the other with heavy curtains, ancient and dusty. Not at all the sort of room that appealed to Abbershaw as a bed-chamber for an invalid.

A huge four-poster bed took up all the farther end of the place, and upon it lay something very still and stiff, covered by a sheet. On a small table near the wide fire-place were pen and ink and a cremation certificate form; standing near it was Jesse Gideon, one beautiful hand shining like ivory upon the polished wood.

Abbershaw had made up his mind that the only way to establish or confute his suspicions was to act quickly, and assuming a brisk and officious manner he strode across the room rubbing his hands.

"Heart failure?" he said, in a tone that was on the verge of being cheerful. "A little unwonted excitement, perhaps—a slightly heavier meal—anything might do it. Most distressing— most distressing. Visitors in the house too."

He was striding up and down as he spoke, at every turn edging a little nearer the bed.

"Now let me see," he said suddenly. "Just as a matter of form, of course…" On the last word, moving with incredible swiftness, he reached the bedside and flicked the sheet from the dead man's face.

The effect was instantaneous. Whitby caught his arm and dragged him back from the bed, and from the shadows a figure that Abbershaw had not noticed before came out silently. The next moment he recognized Dawlish, the man who looked like Beethoven. His face was still expressionless, but there was no mistaking the menace in his attitude as he came forward, and the young scientist realized with a little thrill of excitement that the veneer was off and that he was up against an antagonistic force.

The moment passed, however, and in the next instant he had the situation in hand again, with added advantage of knowing exactly where he stood. He turned a mildly apologetic face to Whitby.

"Just as a matter of form," he repeated. "I like to make a point of seeing the body. Some of us are a little too lax, I feel, in a matter like this. After all, cremation is cremation. I'm not one of those men who insist on a thorough examination, but I just like to make sure that a corpse is a corpse, don't you know."

He laughed as he spoke, and stood with his hands in his pockets, looking down at the face of the man on the bed. The momentary tension in the room died down. The heavy-faced Dawlish returned to his corner, Gideon became suave again, and the doctor stood by Abbershaw a little less apprehensively.

"Death actually took place up here, I suppose?" Abbershaw remarked conversationally, and shot a quick sidelong glance at Whitby. The man was ready for it, however.

"Yes, just after we carried him in."

"I see." Abbershaw glanced round the room. "You brought

him up in his chair, I suppose? How wonderfully convenient those things are." He paused as if lost in thought, and Dawlish muttered impatiently.

Gideon interposed hastily.

"It is getting late," he said in his unnaturally gentle voice. "We must not keep Dr. Abbershaw—"

"Er—no, of course not," said Whitby, starting nervously.

Abbershaw took the hint.

"It is late. I bid you good night, gentlemen," he murmured, and moved towards the door.

Gideon slipped in front of it, pen in hand. He was suave as ever, and smiling, but the little round eyes beneath the enormous shaggy brows were bright and dangerous.

Abbershaw realized then that he was not going to be allowed to refuse to sign the certificate. The three men in the room were determined. Any objections he might raise would be confuted by force if need be. It was virtually a signature under compulsion.

He took the pen with a little impatient click of the tongue.

"How absurd of me, I had forgotten," he said, laughing as though to cover his oversight. "Now, let me look, where is it? Oh, I see—just here—you have attended to all these particulars, of course, Dr. Whitby."

"Yes, yes. They're all in order."

No one but the self-occupied type of fool that Abbershaw was pretending to be could possibly have failed to notice the man's wretched state of nervous tension. He was quivering and his voice was entirely out of control. Abbershaw wrote his signature with a flourish, and returned the pen. There was a distinct sigh of relief in the room as he moved towards the door.

On the threshold he turned and looked back.

"Poor young Petrie knows all about this, I suppose?" he inquired. "I trust he's not very cut up? Poor lad."

"Mr. Petrie has been informed, of course," Dr. Whitby said stiffly. "He felt the shock—naturally—but like the rest of us I fancy he must have expected it for some time. He was only a relative by his aunt's marriage, you know, and that took place after the war, I believe."

"Still," said Abbershaw, with a return of his old fussiness of manner, "very shocking and very distressing—very distressing. Good night, gentlemen."

On the last words he went out and closed the door of the great sombre room behind him. Once in the corridor, his expression changed. The fussy, pompous personality that he had assumed dropped from him like a cloak, and he became at once alert and purposeful. There were many things that puzzled him, but of one thing he was perfectly certain. Colonel Gordon Coombe had not died of heart disease.

CHAPTER FIVE

The Mask

Abbershaw MADE HIS WAY quietly down the corridor to Wyatt's room. The young man had taken him into it himself earlier in the day, and he found it without difficulty.

There was no light in the crack of the door, and he hesitated for a moment before he knocked, as if undecided whether he would disturb its occupant or not, but at length he raised his hand and tapped on the door.

There was no reply, and after waiting a few minutes he knocked again. Still no one answered him, and obeying a sudden impulse, he lifted the latch and went in.

He was in a long, narrow room with a tall window in the wall immediately facing him, giving out on to a balcony. The place was in darkness save for the faint light of a newly risen moon, which streamed in through the window.

He saw Wyatt at once. He was in his dressing-gown, standing in the window, his arms outstretched, his hands resting on either side of the frame.

Abbershaw spoke to him, and for a moment he did not move. Then he turned sharply, and for an instant the moonlight fell upon his face and the long slender lines of his sensitive hands. Then he turned round completely and came towards his friend.

But Abbershaw's mood had changed: he was no longer so determined. He seemed to have changed his mind.

"I've just heard," he said, with real sympathy in his tone. "I'm awfully sorry. It was a bit of a shock, coming now, I suppose? Anything I can do, of course..."

Wyatt shook his head.

"Thanks," he said, "but the old boy's doctor had been expecting it for years. I believe all the necessary arrangements have been made for some time. It may knock the life out of the party pretty thoroughly, though, I'm afraid."

"My dear man." Abbershaw spoke hastily. "We'll all sheer off first thing tomorrow morning, of course. Most people have got cars."

"Oh, don't do that." Wyatt spoke with sudden insistence. "I understand my uncle was very anxious that the party should go on," he said. "Really, you'd be doing me a great service if you'd stay on till Monday and persuade the others to do the same. After all, it isn't even as if it was his house, it's mine, you know. It passed to me on Aunt's death, but my uncle, her husband, was anxious to go on living here, so I rented it to him. I wish you'd stay. He would have liked it, and there's no point in my staying down here alone. He was no blood relative of mine, and he had no kin as far as I know." He paused, and added, as Abbershaw still looked dubious, "The funeral and cremation will take place in London. Gideon has arranged about that; he was his lawyer, you know, and a very close friend. Stay if you can, won't you? Good night. Thanks for coming down."

Abbershaw went slowly back to his room, a slightly puzzled expression in his eyes. He had meant to tell Wyatt his discoveries, and even now he did not know quite why he had not done so. Instinct told him to be cautious. He felt convinced that there were more secrets in Black Dudley that night than the old house had ever known. Secrets that would be dangerous if they were too suddenly brought to light.

He found Prenderby sitting up for him, the ash-tray at his side filled with cigarette-stubs.

"So you've turned up at last," he said peevishly. "I wondered if they'd done a sensational disappearing act with you. This house is such a ghostly old show I've been positively sweltering with terror up here. Anything transpired?"

Abbershaw sat down by the fire before he spoke.

"I signed the certificate," he said at last. "I was practically forced into it. They had the whole troupe there, old Uncle Tom Beethoven and all."

Prenderby leant forward, his pale face becoming suddenly keen again.

"They are up to something, aren't they?" he said.

"Oh, undoubtedly." Abbershaw spoke with authority. "I saw the corpse's face. There was no heart trouble there. He was murdered—stuck in the back, I should say." He paused, and hesitated as if debating something in his mind.

Prenderby looked at him curiously. "Of course, I guessed as much," he said, "but what's the other discovery? What's on your mind?"

Abbershaw looked up at him, and his round grey-blue eyes met the boy's for an instant.

"A darned queer thing, Prenderby," he said. "I don't understand it at all. There's more mystery here than you'd think. When I twitched back the sheet and looked at the dead man's face it was darkish in that four-poster, but there was light enough for me to see one thing. Extreme loss of blood had flattened the flesh down over his bones till he looked dead—very dead—and that plate he wore over the top of his face had slipped out of place and I saw something most extraordinary."

Prenderby raised his eyes inquiringly. "Very foul?" he said.

"Not at all. That was the amazing part of it."

Abbershaw leaned forward in his chair and his eyes were very grave and hard. "Prenderby, that man had no need to wear that plate. His face was as whole as yours or mine!"

"Good God!" The boy sat up, the truth slowly dawning on him. "Then it was simply—"

Abbershaw nodded.

"A mask," he said.

CHAPTER SIX

Mr. Campion Brings the House Down

ABBERSHAW SAT UP for some time, smoking, after Prenderby left him, and when at last he got into bed he did not sleep at once, but lay staring up into the darkness of the beamed ceiling—thinking.

He had just fallen into a doze in which the events of the evening formed themselves into a fantastic nightmare, when a terrific thud above his head and a shower of plaster upon his face brought him hurriedly to his senses.

He sat up in bed, every nerve alert and tingling, waiting for the next development.

It came almost immediately.

From the floor directly above his head came a series of extraordinary sounds. It seemed as if heavy pieces of furniture were being hurled about by some infuriated giant, and between the crashes Abbershaw fancied he could discern the steady murmur of someone cursing in a deep, unending stream.

After a second or so of this he decided that it was time to get up and investigate, and slipping on his dressing-gown he dashed out into the corridor, where the grey light of morning was just beginning to pierce the gloom.

Here the noise above was even more distinct. A tremendous upheaval seemed to be in progress.

Not only Abbershaw had been awakened by it; the whole house appeared to be stirring. He ran up the stair-case in the direction from which the noise was coming to discover that an old-time architect had not built another room above the one in which he slept but a wide gallery from which a second staircase descended. Here he was confronted by an extraordinary scene.

The man-servant he had noticed so particularly on the evening before was grappling with someone who was putting up a very stout resistance. The man was attacking his opponent with an amazing ferocity. Furniture was hurled in all directions, and as Abbershaw came up he caught a stream of oaths from the infuriated footman.

His first thought was that a burglar had been surprised redhanded, but as the two passed under a window in their violent passage round the place, the straggling light fell upon the face of the second combatant and Abbershaw started with surprise, for in that moment he had caught a glimpse of the vacant and peculiarly inoffensive features of Mr. Albert Campion.

By this time there were many steps on the stairs, and the next moment half the house-party came crowding round behind Abbershaw; Chris Kennedy in a resplendent dressing-gown was well to the fore.

"Hullo! A scrap?" he said, with something very near satisfaction in his voice, and threw himself upon the two without further preliminaries.

As the confusion increased with this new development Abbershaw darted forward and, stooping suddenly, picked up something off the floor by the head of the second staircase. It was very swiftly done, and no one noticed the incident.

Chris Kennedy's weight and enthusiasm brought the fight to an abrupt finish.

Mr. Campion picked himself up from the corner where he had been last hurled. He was half strangled, but still laughing idiotically. Meanwhile, Chris Kennedy inspected the butler, whose stream of rhetoric had become much louder but less coherent.

"The fellow's roaring tight," he announced, upon closer inspection. "Absolutely fighting-canned, but it's wearing off a bit now."

He pushed the man away from him contemptuously, and the erstwhile warrior reeled against the stair-head and staggered off down out of sight.

"What's happened? What's the trouble?" Wyatt Petrie came hurrying up the passage, his voice anxious and slightly annoyed.

Everybody looked at Mr. Campion. He was leaning up against the balustrade, his fair hair hanging over his eyes, and for the first time it dawned upon Abbershaw that he was fully dressed, and not, as might have been expected, in the dinner-jacket he had worn on the previous evening.

His explanation was characteristic

"Most extraordinary," he said, in his slightly high-pitched voice. "The fellow set on me. Picked me up and started doing exercises with me as if I were a dumb-bell. I thought it was one of you fellows joking at first, but when he began to jump on me it percolated through that I was being massacred. Butchered to make a butler's beano, in fact."

He paused and smiled fatuously.

"I began to hit back then," he continued. "The bird was tight, of course, but I'm glad you fellows turned up. I didn't like the idea of him chipping bits off the ancestral home with me."

"My dear fellow, I'm frightfully sorry this has happened. The man shall be discharged tomorrow. I'll see to it." Wyatt spoke with real concern, but Abbershaw was not nearly so easily satisfied.

"Where did he get at you?" he said, suddenly stepping forward. "Where were you?"

Mr. Campion met the question with charming ingenuousness.

"Just coming out of my room—that's the door, over there," he said. "I opened it and walked out into a war."

He was buttoning up his waistcoat, which had been ripped open in the fight, as he spoke.

Abbershaw glanced at the grandfather clock at the head of the staircase. It showed the hour at eight minutes past four. Mr. Campion followed the direction of his eyes.

"Yes," he said foolishly, "I—I always get up early."

"Amazingly early," said Abbershaw pointedly.

"I was, this morning," agreed Mr. Campion cheerfully, adding by way of explanation, "I'm one of those birds who can never sleep in a strange bed. And then, you know, I'm so afraid of ghosts. I didn't see any, of course," he went on hastily, "but I said to myself as I got into bed last night, 'Albert, this place smells of ghosts,' and somehow I couldn't get that idea out of my head all night. So as soon as it began to get light I thought a walk was indicated, so I got up, dressed, and sallied forth into the fray." He paused and yawned thoughtfully. "I do believe I shall go back to bed now," he remarked as they all stared at him. "I don't feel much like my walk now. In fact, I don't feel much like anything. Bung-ho, everybody, Uncle Albert is now closing down until nine-thirty, when the breakfast programme will begin, I hope." On the last word he waved his hand to them and disappeared into his own room, shutting the door firmly behind him.

As Abbershaw turned to go back to his bedroom he became aware of a slender figure in a dressing-gown at his side. It was Meggie. Seized by a sudden impulse, he spoke to her softly.

"Who brought Campion down?" She looked at him in surprise.

"Why, Anne," she said. "I told you. They arrived together about the same time that I did. Why the interest? Anything I can do?"

Abbershaw hesitated.

"Well, yes," he said at last. "She's a friend of yours, isn't she?"

Meggie nodded.

"Rather; I've known her for years."

"Good," said Abbershaw. "Look here, could you get her to come down into the garden? Meet me down there in half an hour in that shrubbery we found last night? There's one or two things I want to ask her. Can you manage that for me?"

"Of course." She looked up at him and smiled; then she added, "Anything happened?"

Abbershaw looked at her, and noticed for the first time that there was a faintly scared expression in her narrow brown eyes, and a sudden desire to comfort her assailed him. Had he been a little less precise, a little less timid in these matters, he would probably have kissed her. As it was, he contented himself by patting her hand rather foolishly and murmuring, "Nothing to get excited about," in a way which neither convinced her nor satisfied himself.

"In half an hour," she murmured and disappeared like a fragile ghost down the corridor.

CHAPTER SEVEN

Five o'clock in the Morning

GEORGE ABBERSHAW stood in front of the fire-place in his bedroom and looked down into the fast-greying embers amongst which some red sparks still glowed, and hesitated irresolutely. In ten minutes he was to meet Meggie and Anne Edgeware in the garden. He had until then to make up his mind.

He was not a man to do anything impulsively, and the problem which faced him now was an unusual one.

On the mantelpiece near his head lay a small leather wallet, the silk lining of which had been ripped open and something removed, leaving the whole limp and empty. Abbershaw looked down on a sheaf of paper which he held in one hand, and tapped it thoughtfully with the other.

If only, he reflected, he knew exactly what he was doing. The thought occurred to him, in parenthesis, that here arose the old vexed question as to whether it was permissible to destroy a work of art on any pretext whatsoever.

For five minutes he deliberated, and then, having made up his mind, he knelt down before the dying fire and fanned the embers into a flame, and after coolly preparing a small bonfire in the grate stood back to watch it burn.

The destruction of the leather case was a problem which presented more difficulties. For a moment or two he was at a loss, but then taking it up he considered it carefully.

It was of a usual pattern, a strip of red leather folded over at either end to form two inner pockets. He took out his own case and compared the two. His own was new; an aunt had sent it to him for his birthday, and in an excess of kindliness had caused a small gold monogram stud to be made for it, a circular fretted affair which fastened through the leather with a small clip. This stud Abbershaw removed, and, gouging a hole in the red wallet, effected an exchange.

A liberal splodging with ink from his fountain pen completed the disguise, and, satisfied that no one at a first or second glance would recognize it, he ripped out the rest of the lining, trimmed the edges with a pair of nail scissors, and calmly transferred his papers, with the exception of a letter or two, to it, and tucked it in his pocket. His own wallet he put carefully into the inner pocket of his dinner-jacket, hanging up in the wardrobe.

Then, content with his arrangements, he went softly down the wide staircase and let himself out into the garden.

Meggie was waiting for him. He caught a glimpse of her red-gold hair against the dark green of the shrubbery. She was dressed in green, and despite his preoccupation with the affairs on hand, he noticed how very much it suited her.

"Anne is just coming," she said, "I expect her any moment. I hope it's something important you want to ask her. I don't think she'll relish getting up just to see the sun rise."

Abbershaw looked dubious.

"I'm afraid that didn't occur to me," he said. "It is important, as it happens, although it may not sound so."

The girl moved a step closer to him.

"I told *you,*" she said, looking up into his face. "Tell me. What are the developments?"

"I don't know," he said, "...yet. There's only one thing I can tell you, and that will be common property by breakfast-time. Colonel Coombe is dead."

The girl caught her breath sharply, and looked at him with fear in her brown eyes.

"You don't mean he was...?" She broke off, not using the word.

Abbershaw looked at her steadily.

"Dr. Whitby has pronounced it heart failure," he said. The girl's eyes widened, and her expression became puzzled.

"Then—then the dagger—?" she began.

"Ssh!" Abbershaw raised his hand warningly, for in the house a door had creaked, and now Anne Edgeware, a heavily embroidered Chinese dressing-gown over her frivolous pyjamas, crossed the grass toward them.

"Here I am," she said. "I had to come like this. You don't mind, do you? I really couldn't bring myself to put on my clothes at the hour I usually take them off. What's all the fun about?"

Abbershaw coughed: this kind of girl invariably embarrassed him.

"It's awfully good of you to come down like this," he said awkwardly. "And I'm afraid what I am going to say will sound both absurd and impertinent, but if you would just take it as a personal favour to me I would be eternally grateful." He hesitated nervously, and then hurried on again. "I'm afraid I can't offer you any explanation at the moment, but if you would just answer one or two questions and then forget I ever asked them, you would be rendering me a great service."

The girl laughed.

"How thrilling!" she said. "It sounds just like a play! I've got just the right costume too, haven't I? I feel I shall break out into song at any moment. What is it?"

Abbershaw was still ill at ease, and he spoke with unwonted timidity.

"That's very good of you. As a matter of fact I wanted to ask you about Mr. Campion. I understood that he's a friend of yours. Excuse me, but have you known him long?"

"Albert Campion?" said Anne blankly. "Oh, he's not a friend of mine at all. I just gave him a lift down here in 'Fido'—that's my car."

Abbershaw looked puzzled.

"I'm sorry. I don't quite understand," he said. "Did you meet him at the station?"

"Oh no." The girl was amused. "I brought him all the way down. You see," she went on cheerfully, "I met him the night before we came down at the 'Goat on the Roof'—that's the new night-club in Jermyn Street, you know. I was with a party, and he sort of drifted into it. One of the lads knew him, I think. We were all talking, and quite suddenly it turned out that he was coming down here this week-end. He was fearfully upset, he said: he'd just run his bus into a lorry or something equally solid, so he couldn't come down in it. So I offered him a lift— naturally."

"Oh, er—naturally," said Abbershaw, who appeared to be still a little bewildered. "Wyatt invited him, of course."

The girl in pyjamas looked at him, and a puzzled expression appeared on her doll-like face.

"Oh no," she said. "I don't think so—in fact I'm sure he didn't, because I introduced them myself. Not properly, you know," she went on airily. "I just said, 'Hullo, Wyatt, this thing is Albert Campion,' and 'Albert, this is the man of the house,' but I could swear they didn't know each other. I think he's one of the Colonel's pals—how is the poor old boy, by the way?"

Neither Abbershaw nor Meggie spoke, but remained looking dubiously ahead of them, and Anne shivered.

"Here, I'm getting cold," she said. "Is that all you wanted to know? Because if it is, I'll get in, if you don't mind. Sunrises and dabbling in the dew aren't in my repertoire."

She laughed as she spoke, and Abbershaw thanked her. "Not a word, mind," he said hastily.

"Not a hint," she promised lightly, and went fluttering off across the lawn, the Chinese robe huddled about her.

As soon as she was out of earshot Meggie caught Abbershaw's arm.

"George," she said, "the Colonel didn't invite Albert Campion here."

He turned to her sharply.

"How do you know?" he demanded.

The girl spoke dryly.

"Because," she said, "the Colonel himself pointed Campion out to me and asked who he was. Why, George," she went on suddenly, as the idea occurred to her, "*nobody* asked him—he hasn't any business here at all!"

Abbershaw nodded.

"That's just exactly what had occurred to me," he said, and relapsed into silence.

They walked slowly back to the house together, Meggie quiet and perturbed, her brown eyes narrowed and thoughtful; Abbershaw walking with his hands clasped behind his back, his head bowed.

He had had, he supposed, as much association with crime and criminals as any man of his age, but never, in any of his previous experiences of crime mysteries, had he been placed in a position which required of him both initiative and action. On other occasions an incident had been repeated to him and he had explained it, a problem had been put before him and he had solved it. Now, for the first time in his life he had to pick out his own questions and answer them himself. Every instinct in him told him to do something, but what exactly he ought to do he did not know.

They had almost reached the heavy iron-studded door which led into the hall, when a smothered exclamation from the girl made him stop suddenly and look up. The next instant he had stepped back into the shadow of some overgrown laurels by the house and drawn the girl back after him.

Out of the garage, silent as a cloud of smoke, had come the incredible old car which Abbershaw had noticed on the previous evening.

The man-servant who had created the scene with Mr. Campion not an hour before was at the wheel, and Abbershaw noticed that for a man who had been murderously drunk so recently he was remarkably fresh and efficient.

The car drew up outside the main door of the mansion not ten paces from where they stood, hidden by the greenery. The man got out and opened the door of the car. For some minutes nothing happened, then Gideon appeared followed by Dawlish and Doctor Whitby, bearing between them a heavy burden.

They were all fully dressed, and appeared to be in a great hurry. So engrossed were they that not one of them so much as glanced in the direction of the laurel clump which hid the two onlookers. Whitby got into the back of the car and drew the blinds carefully over the windows, then Dawlish and Gideon lifted the long heavy bundle in after him and closed the door upon it.

The great car slid away down the drive, and the two men stepped back noiselessly into the house and disappeared.

The whole incident had taken perhaps three minutes, and it had been accomplished with perfect silence and precision.

Meggie looked up at Abbershaw fearfully.

"What was that?" she said.

The violence of his reply surprised her.

"Damn them!" he said explosively. "The only piece of real evidence there was against them. That was the body of Colonel Coombe."

CHAPTER EIGHT

Open Warfare

BREAKFAST THAT MORNING showed every promise of being a gloomy and uncomfortable meal.

Wyatt had discreetly announced his uncle's death, and the news had circulated amongst the guests with inevitable speed.

The general opinion was that a tactful farewell and a speedy departure was the obvious procedure of the day. The story of the old man's last wish had not tended greatly to alter anyone's decision, as it was clear that no party was likely to be a success, or even bearable in such circumstances. The wishes of the dead seemed more kindly in intention than in fact.

Wyatt seemed very crestfallen, and a great deal of sympathy was felt for him; events could not well have turned out more unfortunately for him. He sat at the end of the table, a little paler than usual, but otherwise the same graceful, courteous scholar as ever. He wore the coloured tie of one of the more obscure Oxford clubs, and had not attempted to show any outward signs of mourning.

Albert Campion, looking none the worse for his nocturnal adventure, sat next to Anne Edgeware. They were talking quietly together, and from the sullen look upon Chris Kennedy's handsome face it was evident to anybody who cared to see that the irrepressible young lady was indulging in the harmless feminine sport of encouraging one admirer in order to infuriate and thereby gain the interest of another more valued suitor—even though the occasion was so inauspicious. Mr. Campion was amazingly suited to his present role, and in low tones they planned their journey back to town together. Coming departures were indeed a subject for the general conversation of the rather dispirited assembly in the big sunlit hall.

Michael Prenderby was late for breakfast, and he came in, a trifle flushed and hurried, and took his place at the table between little Jeanne Dacre, his fiancée, and Martin Watt, the black-haired beaky youngster whom Meggie had described as "Just a stray young man." He was, in point of fact, a chartered accountant in his father's office, a pleasing youth with more brains than energy.

Neither Gideon nor Dawlish had appeared, nor had places been set for them, but the moment that Prenderby sat down and the number of guests was completed, the door opened and the two men who most interested Abbershaw in the house that day walked into the room.

Dawlish came first, and in the sunlight his face appeared more unprepossessing than it had seemed on the evening before. For the first time it became apparent what an enormous man he was.

He was fat to the point of grossness, but tall with it, and powerfully built. The shock of long grey hair, brushed straight back from the forehead, hung almost to his shoulders, and the eyes, which seemed to be the only live thing in his face, were bright now and peculiarly arresting.

Gideon, who came in behind him, looked small and insignificant by comparison. He was languid and sinuous as before, and he glanced over the group of young people round the table with a thoughtful, mildly appraising eye, as if he were estimating their combined weight—or strength.

Wyatt looked up as they came in and bade them a polite "Good Morning." To everyone's surprise they ignored him.

Dawlish moved ponderously to the top of the table, where he stood looking round at the astonished faces, with no expression on his own.

"Let there be silence," he said.

The words were so utterly unexpected and out of keeping with the situation that it is probable that a certain amount of amusement would have greeted them had not the tone in his deep Teutonic voice been singularly menacing.

As it was, the silence was complete, and the German went on, his expression still unchanged so that it seemed that his voice came to them through a mask.

"Something has been lost," he said, dividing the words up as he uttered them and giving equal emphasis to each. "It must be returned to me. There is no need to explain what it is. Whoever has stolen it will know of what I speak."

At this colossal piece of impudence a sensation ran round the table, and Wyatt sprang to his feet. He was livid with anger, but he kept his voice under perfect control, and the polished intensity of his icy tone contrasted sharply with the other's heavy rudeness.

"Mr. Dawlish," he said. "I think your anxiety to recover your property has upset your sense of proportion. Perhaps you are aware that you are a guest in a house that is mine, and that the people that you have just insulted are my guests also. If you will come to me after breakfast—before you go—I will do all I can to institute a proper search for the thing you have mislaid."

The German did not move. He stood at the head of the table and stared unblinkingly at the man before him.

"Until it is returned to me nobody leaves this house," he said, the same solid force behind his tone. Wyatt's snub he did not appear to have heard. A faint wave of colour passed over the young man's pale face, and he turned to the others, who were staring from one to the other in frank astonishment.

"I must apologize," he said. "I ask you to forgive this extraordinary display. My uncle's death appears to have turned this unfortunate man's brain."

Dawlish turned.

"That young man," he said. "Let him sit down and be quiet."

Gideon smiled at Wyatt, and the look on his grey decadent face was an insult in itself.

"My dear Mr. Petrie," he said, and his peculiarly oily voice was suave and ingratiating, "I don't think you quite realize the position you are in, you and your friends. Consider: this house is two miles from the public road. There is no telephone. We have two women servants and six men and a gate-keeper. All of these people are in Mr. Dawlish's employ. Your cars have been drained of petrol. I am afraid you are entirely helpless." He paused, and allowed his glance to take in the amazed expressions round the table.

"It would be better," he continued, "to listen rationally, for I must warn you, my friend Mr. Dawlish is not a man who is accustomed to any opposition to his wishes."

Wyatt remained on his feet; his face had grown slowly paler, and he was now rigid with barely controlled fury.

"Gentlemen, this farce has gone on long enough," he said, in a voice which quivered in spite of himself. "If you will please go away we will get on with our breakfast."

"Sit down!"

The words were uttered in a sudden titanic bellow, though but for the obvious fact that Gideon was incapable of producing so much noise there was nothing upon Benjamin Dawlish's face to betray that it was he who had shouted.

Wyatt started; the limit of his patience had come. He opened his mouth to speak, to assert his authority. Then, quite suddenly, he dropped back into his chair, his eyes dilating with as much surprise as fear. He was looking into the black barrel of a revolver.

The German stood stolidly, absolutely immobile, the dangerous little weapon levelled in one ponderous hand. "Here," he said in his unwieldy English, "there is one who has what I seek. To him I speak. When he returns to me what he has taken you shall all go free. Until then no one leaves this house—no one at all."

In the silence which followed this extraordinary announcement Jesse Gideon moved forward.

"If Mr. Dawlish were to receive his property immediately it would save us all a great deal of inconvenience," he murmured.

For several seconds there was no movement in the room, and the singing of the birds in the greenery outside the windows became suddenly very noticeable.

Then Albert Campion coughed discreetly and handed something wrapped up in his table napkin to the girl who sat next to him.

She passed it to her neighbor, and in utter stillness it went the whole length of the table until Gideon pounced on it avidly and set it before the German on the table. With a grunt of satisfaction the big man thrust the revolver into his coat pocket and threw aside the white napery. Then an exclamation of anger escaped him, and he drew back so that Mr. Campion's offering lay exposed.

It was a breakfast egg, the very one, in fact, which the fatuous young man had been on the verge of broaching when the extraordinary interruptions had occurred.

The effect was instantaneous; the reaction from the silent tension of a moment before complete.

The entire table shook with laughter.

The German stood stiffly as before. There was still no expression of any sort upon his face, and his little eyes became dull and lifeless.

Gideon, on the other hand, betrayed his anger vividly. His eyes were narrowed with fury and his long thin lips were drawn back over his teeth like an angry dog's. Gradually the laughter subsided. Benjamin Dawlish's personality was one that could not be ignored for long. When at last there was perfect silence in the room he put his hand in his pocket and drew out his revolver again.

"You laugh," he said heavily. "I do not laugh. And she, the little one," he tossed the gun in his hand with incredible delicacy for one who looked so clumsy, *"she does not laugh either."*

The last words were uttered with such amazing ferocity that his hearers started involuntarily, and for an instant there appeared upon the heavy face, which hitherto had seemed immovable, an expression of such animalic violence that not one at that table looked him in the eyes.

A moment later his features had relapsed into their usual stolidity, and followed by Jesse Gideon he walked slowly from the room.

As the door closed behind them, the silence became painful, and at last a fitful, uneasy conversation broke out.

"What an unpleasant old bird!" said Prenderby, looking at Abbershaw. He spoke lightly, but there was a worried expression in his eyes; one hand rested over his fiancée's, who sat very pale by his side apparently on the verge of tears. Even Anne Edgeware's magnificent sang-froid seemed a little shaken, and Meggie, although the least alarmed of the three girls, looked very white.

Wyatt was still angry. He gave up trying to apologize for the incident, however, and joined with the others in discussing it.

"He's loony, of course," said Martin Watt lazily. "Campion got his goat beautifully, I thought."

"Still, even if he is potty, if what he says is true, things are going to be pretty sportive," remarked Chris Kennedy cheerfully. "I fear I may be called upon to bash his head in."

Abbershaw rose to his feet.

"I don't know what you think, Wyatt," he said, "but it occurs to me that it might be an idea if we all went into the other room and talked this thing over. The servants won't disturb us there. I don't think there's any real danger," he went on reassuringly, "but perhaps we ought to find out if what Gideon says about the cars is true."

Chris Kennedy got up eagerly.

"I'll toddle down and discover, shall I?" he said. "Really—I should like to," he added, as Wyatt regarded him doubtfully, and he went off whistling.

The party adjourned to the next room as Abbershaw had suggested. They still talked lightly, but there was a distinctly constrained atmosphere among them. Jeanne was frankly scared, Anne Edgeware out of her depth, and the rest apprehensive.

Abbershaw was the last to step into the enormous hall that was now a blaze of sunlight. It poured in through long diamond-paned windows, glinted on the polished floor, and shone softly on Tudor rose and linenfold. But it was not these which caught his eye and made him start back with a half-concealed exclamation.

Over the far fire-place, set in the circle of lanceheads, its clear blade dazzling in the sun and gleaming as brightly as if it had never left its plaque, sinister and beautiful, was the Black Dudley Dagger.

CHAPTER NINE

Chris Kennedy Scores a Try Only

As soon as Abbershaw had recovered from his first surprise, he turned to Meggie. She was standing just beside him, the others having split up into little groups talking quietly together. "Did you come in here this morning," he said, "after we came in from the garden?"

She nodded, and he saw that she was trembling slightly. "Yes," she whispered, "and—and *it* was here then, hanging just where it is now. I—I couldn't help coming in to see. Someone must have put it back—in the night."

Her voice died away in a sob on the last word, and he laid a hand on her arm.

"Scared?" he said.

She met his eyes bravely.

"I'm glad you're here too," she said simply.

A wave of pleasure swept over Abbershaw, and he coloured, but he did not speak. The gravity of the situation was by no means lost to him. He was the eldest of the party, and, moreover, he knew more about the events of the last twelve hours than probably anyone else in the room.

Something told him to keep quiet about his discoveries,

however; he realized that they were up against dangerous men. Mr. Benjamin Dawlish, as he styled himself, was no ordinary individual, and, at the moment, he was angry.

The main idea now was to get away at all costs; Abbershaw was sure of it.

He had not dreamed that the late Colonel's extraordinary friends would dare to take this extreme course, but since they had done so, he was not fool enough to think that they would risk the possibility of being overpowered; their forces must be very strong.

Once out of the house he himself could get an immediate inquiry instituted by the highest authorities. If the police could be informed without their captors' knowledge, so much the better, but the principal problem was escape, and that, in the present circumstances, did not appear to be any too simple.

There was, of course, one way of obtaining freedom; he felt the battered red wallet in his pocket now, but he was loth to take that path, for it meant the escape of what he felt certain was a leader of one of the most skillful criminal organizations in the world. So far he had been working in the dark, and if he gave in now, that darkness would never be lightened. It would mean complete surrender. The mystery would remain a mystery.

He glanced down at Meggie.

"We'll lick 'em yet," he said.

She laughed at him.

"Or die in the attempt."

Abbershaw appeared vastly relieved.

"That's how I feel," he said.

It was at this moment that Mr. Campion made the entire party one group again by a single fatuous remark.

"Of course," he said affably, "I suppose nobody has pinched anything."

"I've got two bits of soap in my room," murmured Prenderby, "but I shouldn't think that's what the old bird's after by the look of him. And look here, Wyatt," he added suddenly, "there's something damned queer about something else! I suppose you know—"

Abbershaw interposed hastily.

"The whole thing is a bit queer, Michael," he said, fixing the boy with his eyes. Prenderby took the hint, and was silent, but Wyatt turned to him.

"I'm beyond apologizing," he said. "The whole business is quite out of my experience. My uncle asked me to bring a party down for this week-end. He had often done so before. I have met Gideon here before, but never exchanged more than half a dozen words with him. As for that Hun, Dawlish, he's a complete stranger."

Prenderby, to whom the words had sounded like a reproach, coloured, and what might have been an uncomfortable pause was covered by the sudden return of Chris Kennedy. He was in high good humour. His handsome young face was flushed with excitement, and the others could not banish the suspicion that he was enjoying the situation thoroughly.

"They *have*, the blighters!" he said, bursting into the group. "Not a drain of juice in any of the buses. Otherwise they're all right, though. 'Exhibit A' has vanished, by the way—crumbled into dust, I should think—but apart from that they're all there."

"Meet anyone?" said Martin.

"Not a soul," said Kennedy cheerfully, "and little Christopher Robin has an idea. If I asked you for a drink, Petrie, would you give me ginger-beer?" There was an air of suppressed jubilation in his tone as he spoke.

"My dear fellow..." Wyatt started forward. "I think you'll find all you want here," he said, and led the way to a cupboard set in the panelling of the fire-place. Kennedy stuck his head in it, and came out flushed and triumphant. "Two Scotch and a 'Three Star' Brandy," he said, tucking the bottles under his arm. "It's blasphemy, but there's no other way. Get to the window, chicks, and Uncle Christopher will now produce the rabbit."

"What are you going to do with that stuff?" said Watt, who was not an admirer of the athletic type. "Fill yourself up with it and run amok?"

Kennedy grinned at him over his shoulder; he was already half out of the room.

"No fear!" he said, pausing with his hand on the door-handle. "But the Salmson is. Watch the garage. Keep your eyes upon the performance, ladies and gentlemen. This trick cannot be repeated."

The somewhat bewildered little group regarded him doubtfully.

"I'm afraid I don't follow you even now," said Martin, still coldly. "I'm probably infernally thick, but I don't get your drift."

Michael Prenderby suddenly lifted his head.

"Good Lord!" he said. "I do believe you might do it. What a stunt!"

"That's what I thought," said Kennedy.

He went out, and they heard him racing down the corridor.

Abbershaw turned to Michael.

"What's the idea?" he said.

Prenderby grinned.

"He's going to use the booze as juice," he said. "Rather an idea, don't you think? A car like that ought to run on pure spirit, I suppose. Let's watch him."

He led the way to the windows and the others followed him. By craning their necks they could just see the doors of the barn, both of which stood open.

For some minutes nothing happened, and Martin Watt was just beginning to assure himself that his first impression of Kennedy's ideas in general was going to be justified when a terrific back-fire sounded from the garage.

"Good heavens!" said Abbershaw. "He's going to do it."

Someone began to laugh.

"What a pack of fools they'll look," said Prenderby.

Another small explosion sounded from the garage, and the next moment the little car appeared in a cloud of blue smoke, with Mr. Kennedy at the wheel. It was moving slowly but triumphantly, and emitting a stream of backfires like a machine-gun.

"Isn't he marvellous?"

Anne Edgeware clasped her hands as she spoke, and even Martin Watt admitted grudgingly that "the lad had initiative." Kennedy waved to them, and they saw his face flushed and excited as a child's. As he changed gear the car jerked forward and set off down the drive at an uneven but ever-increasing pace.

"That'll show 'em," said Prenderby with a chuckle.

"They haven't even tried to stop him," said little Jeanne Dacre.

At that moment Mr. Kennedy changed into top gear with a roar, and immediately there was a sharp report, followed by a second, which seemed to come from a window above their heads. Instantly, even as they watched it, the Salmson swerved violently, skidded drunkenly across the drive and turned over, pitching its occupant out upon the grass beside the path.

"Good God!"

Michael Prenderby's voice was hoarse in the silence.

Martin Watt spoke quickly.

"Dawlish's gun. They've got him. The Hun was in earnest. Come on, you fellows."

He thrust open the window and leapt out upon the lawn, the men following him.

Chris Kennedy was already picking himself up when they reached him. He was very white, and his left hand grasped his other wrist, from which the blood was streaming.

"They got my near-side front wheel and my driving arm," he gasped, as they came up. "There's a bloke somewhere about who can shoot like hell."

He swayed a little on the last word, and smiled valiantly. "Do you mind if we get in?" he murmured. "This thing is turning me sick."

They got him back to the house and into the room where they had all been standing. As they crossed the lawn, Abbershaw, glancing up at the second-floor windows, fancied he saw a heavy expressionless face peering out at them from behind the dark curtains.

The rescue party was considerably subdued. They were beginning to believe in the sincerity of Mr. Benjamin Dawlish's remarks.

Kennedy collapsed into a chair, and, after saving him from the tender ministrations of Anne Edgeware, Abbershaw was just about to set out in search of warm water and a dress shirt to tear up as a bandage, when there was a discreet tap on the door and a man-servant entered bearing a complete surgical outfit together with antiseptic bandages and hot water.

"With Mr. Gideon's compliments," he said gravely, and went out.

Kennedy smiled weakly.

"Curse their dirty politeness," he said, and bowed his head over his injured wrist.

Abbershaw removed his coat and went over to the tray which the man had brought.

"Hullo!" he said. "There's a note. Read it, Wyatt, will you, while I get on with this. These are Whitby's things, I suppose. It almost looks as if he was expecting trouble."

Wyatt took the slip of paper off the tray and read the message aloud in his clear even voice.

"We are not joking. No one leaves this house until we have what we want."

"There's no signature," he added, and handed the note to Prenderby, who looked at it curiously.

"Looks as if they *have* lost something," he said. "What the devil is it? We can't help 'em much till we know what it is."

No one spoke for a moment.

"Yes, that's true," said Martin Watt at last, "and the only thing we know about it is that it isn't an egg."

There was a faint titter of laughter at this, but it soon died down; the party was beginning to realize the seriousness of their position.

"It must be something pretty fishy, anyway," said Chris Kennedy, still white with the pain of his wound which Abbershaw was now bandaging. "Else why don't they describe it so that we can all have a hunt round? Look here, let's go to them and tell them that we don't know what their infernal property is. They can search us if they like, and when they find we haven't got it they can let us go, and by God, when they do I'll raise hell!"

"It is precisely for that reason that I'm not inclined to endorse that suggestion, Kennedy," said Abbershaw without looking up from the bandage he was winding. "Our friends upstairs are very determined, and they're not likely to risk a possible visit from the police before they have got what they want and have had reasonable time to make a good getaway."

Martin Watt raised his hand.

"One moment," he said, "let us do a spot of neat detective work. What the German gentleman with no manners has lost must be very small. 'And why, my dear Sherlock?' you ask. Because, my little Watsons, when our obliging young comrade, Campion, offered them an egg wrapped up in a table napkin they thought they'd holed in one. It isn't the Black Dudley diamonds, I suppose, Petrie?"

"There aren't any," said Wyatt shortly. "Damn it all!" he burst out with a sudden violence. "I never felt so helpless in my life."

"If only we had a few guns," mourned Chris Kennedy, whose wound even had not slaked his thirst for a scrap. "Then we might make an attempt to rush 'em. But unarmed against birds who shoot like that we shouldn't have an earthly."

"It's not such a bad thing for you that we're not armed, my lad," said Abbershaw, straightening his shoulders and stepping back from the table. "You don't want too much excitement with an arm like that. You've lost enough blood already. If I were you, I'd try and get a spot of sleep. What's your opinion, Prenderby?"

"Oh, sleep, by all means," said Michael, grinning, "if he can get it, which doesn't seem likely."

They were all standing round the patient on the hearth-rug, with their backs to the fire-place, and for the moment Kennedy was the center of interest.

Hardly were the words out of Prenderby's mouth when they were suddenly and startlingly confirmed by an hysterical scream from Anne Edgeware.

"He's gone!" she said wildly, as they turned to her. Her dark eyes were dilated with fear, and every trace of her usual sophisticated and slightly blasé manner had disappeared.

"He was standing here—just beside me. He spoke to me a second ago. He couldn't have got past me to the door—I was directly in his way. He's just vanished. Oh, God—I'm going potty! I think—I…"She screamed again.

"My dear girl!"

Abbershaw moved to her side. "What's the matter? Who's vanished?"

The girl looked at him in stupid amazement. "He went from my side just as if he had disappeared into the air," she repeated. "I was just talking to him—I turned away to look at Chris for a moment—I heard a sort of thud, and when I turned round he'd gone."

She began to cry noisily.

"Yes, but who? Who?" said Wyatt impatiently. "Who has vanished?"

Anne peered at him through her tears.

"Why, *Albert*!" she said, and burst into louder sobbing. "Albert Campion. They've got him because he made fun of them!"

CHAPTER TEN

The Impetuous Mr. Abbershaw

A HASTY SEARCH revealed the fact that Mr. Campion had indeed disappeared, and the discovery, coupled with Chris Kennedy's experience of the morning, reduced the entire company to an unpleasant state of nerves. The terrified Anne Edgeware and the wounded rugby blue comforted each other in a corner by the fire. Prenderby's little fiancée clung to his hand as a frightened child might have done. The others talked volubly, but every minute the general gloom deepened.

In the midst of this the lunch gong in the outer hall sounded, as if nothing untoward had happened. For some moments nobody moved. Then Wyatt got up. "Well, anyway," he said, "they seem to intend to feed us—let's go in, shall we?"

They followed him dubiously into the other room, where a cold luncheon had been prepared at the long table. Two men-servants waited on them, silent and surly, and the meal was a quiet one. No one felt in the mood for trivialities, and Mr. Campion was not there to provide his usual harmless entertainment.

There was a certain amount of apprehension, also, lest Mr. Dawlish might reappear and the experience of breakfast be repeated. Everyone felt a little relieved, therefore, when the meal ended without a visitation. The explanation of this apparent neglect came ten minutes or so later, when Martin Watt, who had gone up to his room to replenish his cigarette-case, came dashing into the hall where they were all sitting, the lazy expression for once startled out of his grey eyes.

"I say," he said, "the blighters have searched my room! Had a real old beano up there by the look of it. Clothes all over the place—half the floor boards up. I should say the Hun had done it himself—it looks as if an elephant had run amok there. If I were you people I'd trot up to your rooms and see if they've done the thing thoroughly."

This announcement brought everybody to their feet. Wyatt, who still considered himself the host of the party, fumed impotently. Chris Kennedy swore lurid deeds of revenge under his breath, and Prenderby and Abbershaw exchanged glances. Abbershaw smiled grimly. "I think perhaps we had better take Watt's suggestion," he said, and led the way out of the hall.

Once in his room he found that their fears had been justified. His belongings had been ransacked, his meticulously arranged suitcase lying open on its side, and his clothes strewn in all directions. The door of the big oak press with the carved front, which was built into the wall and took up all one end of the room, stood open, its contents all over the floor.

A wave of uncontrollable anger passed over him, and with that peculiarly precise tidiness which was one of his most marked characteristics he began methodically to put the room straight again.

Prisoners they might be, shots could be fired, and

people could disappear apparently into thin air, none of these could shake him, but the sight of his belongings jumbled into this appalling confusion all but unnerved him completely.

He packed up everything he possessed very neatly, and stowed it in the press, then slamming the heavy oaken door, he turned the key and thrust it into his pocket.

It was at this precise moment that an extraordinary mental revolution took place in Abbershaw.

It happened as he put the cupboard key in his pocket; during the actual movement he suddenly saw himself from the outside. He was naturally a man of thought, not of action, and now for the first time in his life he was thrust into a position where quick decisions and impulsive actions were forced from him. So far, he realized suddenly, he had always been a little late in grasping the significance of each situation as it had arisen. This discovery horrified him, and in that moment of enlightenment Dr. George Abbershaw, the sober, deliberate man of science, stepped into the background, and George Abbershaw the impulsive, energetic enthusiast came forward to meet the case.

He did not lose his head, however. He realized that at the present juncture infinite caution was vital. The next move must come from Dawlish. Until that came they must wait patiently, ready to grasp at the first chance of freedom. The present state of siege was only tenable for a short time. For a week-end Black Dudley might be safe from visitors, tradespeople, and the like, but after Monday inquiries must inevitably be made. Dawlish would have to act soon.

There was the affair of Albert Campion. Wyatt had been peculiarly silent about him, and Abbershaw did not know what to make of it at all. His impulse was to get the idiot back into their own circle at all costs, but there was no telling if he had been removed or if he had vanished of his own free will. No one knew anything about him.

Abbershaw went slowly out of the room and down the corridor to the staircase, and was just about to descend when he heard the unmistakable sound of a woman crying.

He paused to listen, and discovered that the noise came from behind a door on his left.

He hesitated.

Half an hour before, a fear of being intrusive would have prevented him from doing anything, but a very considerable change had taken place in him in that time, and he listened again.

The sound continued.

The thought dawned upon him that it was Meggie; he fancied that this was her room, and the idea of her alone and in distress banished his last vestige of timidity and caution. He knocked at the door.

Her voice answered him.

"It's George," he said, almost defiantly. "Anything the matter?"

She was some seconds opening the door, and when at last she came he saw that although she had hastily powdered her face the tear-stains were still visible upon it.

For one moment Abbershaw felt that he was going to have a relapse into his old staid self, but he overcame it and there was an expression of fiery determination in his chubby round face which astonished the girl so much that her surprise showed in her eyes. Abbershaw recognized it, and it annoyed him.

In a flash he saw himself as she must have seen him all along, a round, self-important little man, old for his years, inclined to be pompous, perhaps—terrible thought—even fussy. A horrible sense of humiliation swept over him and at the same time a growing desire to teach her she was wrong, to show her that she had been mistaken, to prove to her that he was a man to be reckoned with, a personality, a man of action, vigorous, resourceful, a he-man, a...!

He drew a deep breath.

"I can't have you crying like this," he said, and picked her up and kissed her.

Meggie could not have responded more gracefully. Whether it was relief, shock, or simply the last blow to her tortured nerves, he never knew, but she collapsed into his arms; at first he almost thought she had fainted.

He led her firmly down the long corridor to the wide window-seat at the far end. It was recessed, and hung with heavy curtains. He sat down and drew her beside him, her head on his shoulders.

"Now," he said, still bristling with his newly discovered confidence, "you're going to escape from here tomorrow certainly, if not tonight, and you're going to marry me because I love you! I love you! I love you!"

He paused breathlessly and waited, his heart thumping against his side like a schoolboy's.

Her face was hidden from him and she did not speak. For a moment the awful thought occurred to him that she might be angry with him, or even—laughing.

"You—er—you will marry me?" he said, a momentary anxiety creeping into his tone. "I'm sorry if I startled you," he went on, with a faint return of his old primness. "I didn't mean to, but I—I'm an impetuous sort of fellow."

Meggie stirred at his side, and as she lifted her face to him he saw that she was flushed with laughter, but there was more than mere amusement in her brown eyes. She put her arm round his neck and drew his head down.

"George, you're adorable," she said. "I love you ridiculously, my dear."

A slow, warm glow spread all over Abbershaw. His heart lolloped in his side, and his eyes danced.

He kissed her again. She lay against his breast very quiet, very happy, but still a little scared.

He felt like a giant refreshed—after all, he reflected, his first essay in his new role had been an unparalleled success.

CHAPTER ELEVEN

One Explanation

THAT EVENING, after tea had been served in ominous silence by the same two men-servants who had waited at lunch, Michael Prenderby crossed the room and spoke confidentially to Abbershaw.

"I say," he said awkwardly, "poor old Jeanne has got the wind up pretty badly. Do you think we've got an earthly chance of making a bolt for it?" He paused, and then went on again quickly, "Can't we hatch out a scheme of some sort? Between you and me, I'm feeling a bit desperate."

Abbershaw frowned.

"We can't do much at the moment, I'm afraid," he said slowly; but added, as the boy's expression grew more and more perturbed, "Look here, come up and smoke a cigarette with me in my room and we'll talk it over."

"I'd like to." Prenderby spoke eagerly, and the two men slipped away from the others and went quietly up to Abbershaw's room.

As far as they could ascertain, Dawlish and the others had their headquarters in the vast old apartment which had been Colonel Coombe's bedroom and the rooms immediately above and below it, into which there seemed no entrance from any part of the house that they knew.

Even Wyatt could not help them with the geography of Black Dudley. The old house had been first monastery, then farmstead, and finally a dwelling-house, and in each period different alterations had been made.

Besides, before the second marriage of his aunt, the enormous old place had been shut up, and it was not until shortly before her death that Wyatt first stayed at the place. Since then his visits had been infrequent and never of a long enough duration to allow him to become familiar with the numberless rooms, galleries, passages, and staircases of which the place was composed.

Prenderby was getting nerves, his fiancée's terror was telling on him, and, of course, he knew considerably more of the ugly facts of the situation than any one of the party save Abbershaw himself.

"The whole thing seemed almost a joke this morning," he said petulantly. "That old Hun might have been a music-hall turn then, but I don't mind confessing that I've got the wind up now. Hang it all," he went on bitterly, "we're as far away from civilization here as we should be if this was the seventeenth century. The modern 'Majesty of the Law' and all has made us so certain of our own safety that when a trap like this springs we're fairly caught. Damn it, Abbershaw, brute force is the only real power, anyway."

"Perhaps," said Abbershaw guardedly, "but it's early yet. Some opportunity is bound to crop up within the next twelve hours. I think we shall see our two troublesome friends in gaol before we're finished."

Prenderby glanced at him sharply.

"You're very optimistic, aren't you?" he said. "You talk as if something distinctly promising had happened. Has it?"

George Abbershaw coughed.

"In a way, yes," he said, and was silent. Now, he felt, was not the moment to announce his engagement to Meggie.

They had reached the door of the bedroom by this time, and further inquiries on Prenderby's part were cut short by a sudden and arresting phenomenon.

From inside the room came a series of extraordinary sounds—long, high-pitched murmurs, intermingled with howls and curses, and accompanied now and then by a sound of scuffling.

"My God!" said Prenderby. "What in the name of good fortune is that?"

Abbershaw did not answer him.

Clearly the move which he had been expecting had been made.

With all his new temerity he seized the door-latch and was about to fling it up, when Prenderby caught his arm.

"Go carefully! Go carefully!" he said, with a touch of indignation in his voice. "You don't want to shove your head in it, whatever it is. They're armed, remember."

The other nodded, and raising the latch very cautiously he thrust the door gently open.

Prenderby followed him; both men were alert and tingling with expectation.

The noise continued; it was louder than before, and sounded peculiarly unearthly in that ghostly house.

Abbershaw was the first to peer round the door and look in.

"Good Lord!" he said at last, glancing back over his shoulder at Prenderby, "there's not a soul here."

The two men burst into the room, and the noise, although muffled, became louder still.

"I say!" said Prenderby, suddenly startled out of his annoyance, "it's in *there*!"

Abbershaw followed the direction of his hand and gasped.

The extraordinary sounds were indubitably proceeding

from the great oak press at the far end of the room—the wardrobe which he had locked himself not two hours before and the key of which was still heavy in his pocket. He turned to Michael.

"Shut the door," he said. "Lock it, and take the key." Then he advanced towards the cupboard.

Michael Prenderby stood with his back against the door of the room, waiting.

Very gingerly Abbershaw fitted the huge iron key into the cupboard, turned over the lock, and wrenched the door open, starting back instantly.

The noise stopped abruptly.

There was a smothered exclamation from Prenderby and both men stood back in utter amazement.

There, seated upon a heavy oaken shelf in a square cavity just large enough to contain him, his hair over his eyes, his clothes dishevelled, his inane face barely recognizable, was Mr. Albert Campion.

For several seconds he did not move, but sat blinking at them through the lank strands of yellow hair over his eyes. Then it was that Abbershaw's memory revived.

In a flash it came to him where he had seen that vacuous, inoffensive face before, and a slow expression of wonderment came into his eyes.

He did not speak, however, for at that moment Campion stirred, and climbed stiffly out into the room.

"No deception, ladies and gentlemen," he said, with a wan attempt at his own facetiousness. "All my own work."

"How the devil did you get in there?" The words were Prenderby's; he had come forward, his eyes fixed upon the forlorn figure in child-like astonishment.

"Oh—influence, mostly," said Campion, and dropped into a chair. But it was evident that a great deal of his spirit had left him. Obviously he had been badly handled, there were crimson marks round his wrists, and his shirt showed ragged beneath his jacket.

Prenderby opened his mouth to speak again, but a sign from Abbershaw silenced him.

"Dawlish got you, of course?" he said, with an unwonted touch of severity in his tone.

Mr. Campion nodded.

"Did they search you?" Abbershaw persisted.

"Search me?" said he. A faintly weary expression came into the pale eyes behind the large spectacles. "My dear sir, they almost had my skin off in their investigations. That Hun talks like comic opera but behaves like the Lord High Executioner. He nearly killed me." He took his coat off as he spoke, and showed them a shirt cut to ribbons and stained with blood from great weals across his back.

"Good God!" said Abbershaw. "Thrashed!" Instantly his magisterial manner vanished and he became the professional man with a case to attend to.

"Michael," he said, "there's a white shirt amongst my things in that cupboard, and water and boracic on the washstand. What happened?" he continued briefly, as Prenderby hurried to make all preparations for dressing the man's injuries.

Mr. Campion stirred painfully.

"As far as I can remember," he said weakly, "about four hundred years ago I was standing by the fire-place talking to Anne What's-her-name, when suddenly the panel I was leaning against gave way, and the next moment I was in the dark with a lump of sacking in my mouth." He paused. "That was the beginning," he said. "Then I was hauled up before old Boanerges and he put me through it pretty thoroughly; I couldn't convince him that I hadn't got his packet of love-letters or whatever it is that he's making such a stink about. A more thorough old bird in the questioning line I never met."

"So I should think," murmured Prenderby, who had now got Campion's shirt off and was examining his back.

"When they convinced themselves that I was as innocent as a new-born babe," continued the casualty, some of his old cheerfulness returning, "they gave up jumping on me and put me into a box-room and locked the door." He sighed. "I sleuthed round for a bit," he went on, while they listened to him eagerly. "The window was about two thousand feet from the ground with a lot of natty ironwork on it—and finally, looking round for a spot soft enough for me to lie down without yowling, I perceived an ancient chest, under the other cardboard whatnots and fancy basketwork about the place, and I opened it." He paused, and drank the tooth-glass of water which Prenderby handed him.

"I thought some grandmotherly garment might be there," he continued. "Something I could make a bed of. All I found, however, was something that I took to be a portion of an ancient bicycle—most unsuitable for my purpose. I was so peeved that I jumped on it with malicious intent, and immediately the whole show gave way and I made a neat but effective exit through the floor. When I got the old brain working again, I discovered that I was standing on the top of a flight of steps, my head still half out of the chest. The machinery was the ancients' idea of a blind, I suppose. So I shut the lid of the trunk behind me, and lighting a match toddled down the steps."

He stopped again. The two men were listening to him intently.

"I don't see how you got into the cupboard, all the same," said Prenderby.

"Nor do I, frankly," said Mr. Campion. "The steps stopped after a bit and I was in a sort of tunnel—a ratty kind of place; the little animals put the wind up me a bit—but eventually I crawled along and came up against a door which opened inwards, got it open, and sneaked out into your cupboard. That didn't help me much," he added dryly. "I didn't know where I was, so I just sat there reciting 'The Mistletoe Bough' to myself, and confessing my past life—such sport!" He grinned at them and stopped. "That's all," he said.

Abbershaw, who had been watching him steadily as he talked, came slowly down the room and stood before him.

"I'm sorry you had such a bad time," he said, and added very clearly and distinctly, "but there's really no need to keep up this bright conversation, *Mr. Mornington Dodd.*"

For some seconds Mr. Campion's pale eyes regarded Abbershaw blankly. Then he started almost imperceptibly, and a slow smile spread over his face.

"So you've spotted me," he said, and, to Abbershaw's utter amazement, chuckled inanely. "But," went on Mr. Campion cheerfully, "I assure you you're wrong about my magnetic personality being a disguise. There is *absolutely no fraud.* I'm like this—always like this—my best friends could tell me."

This announcement took the wind out of Abbershaw's sails; he had certainly not expected it.

Mr. Campion's personality was a difficult one to take seriously; it was not easy, for instance, to decide when he was lying and when he was not. Abbershaw had reckoned upon his thrust going home, and although it had obviously done so he did not seem to have gained any advantage by it.

Prenderby, however, was entirely in the dark, and now he broke in upon the conversation with curiosity.

"Here, I say, I don't get this," he said. "Who and what is Mr. Mornington Dodd?"

Abbershaw threw out his hand, indicating Mr. Albert Campion.

"That gentleman," he said, "is Mornington Dodd."

Albert Campion smiled modestly. In spite of his obvious pain he was still lively.

"In a way yes, and in a way no," he said, fixing his eyes on Abbershaw. "Mornington Dodd is one of my names. I have also been called the 'Honourable Tootles Ash,' which I thought was rather neat when it occurred to me. Then there was a girl who used to call me 'Cuddles' and a man at the Guards Club called me something quite different—"

"Campion, this is not a joke." Abbershaw spoke sternly. "However many and varied your aliases have been, now isn't the time to boast of them. We are up against something pretty serious now."

"My dear man, don't I know it?" said Mr. Campion peevishly, indicating the state of his shoulders. "Even better than you do, I should think," he said dryly.

"Now look here," said Abbershaw, whose animosity could not but be mollified by this extraordinary naïveté, "you know something about this business, Campion—that is your name, I suppose?"

"Well—er—no," said the irrepressible young man. "But," he added, dropping his voice a tone, "my own is rather aristocratic, and I never use it in business. Campion will do quite well."

Abbershaw smiled in spite of himself.

"Very well, then, Mr. Campion," he said, "as I remarked before, you know something about this business, and you're going to tell us here and now. But my dear lad, consider," he went on as the other hesitated, "we're all in the same boat. You, I presume, are as anxious to get away as anyone. And whereas I am intensely interested in bringing Dawlish and his confederates to justice, there is no other delinquency that I am concerned with. I am not a policeman."

Mr. Campion beamed. "Is that so?" he inquired.

"Certainly it is," said Abbershaw. "I am a consultant only as far as the Yard is concerned."

Mr. Campion looked vastly relieved.

"That's rather cheered me up," he said. "I liked you. When I saw you pottering with your car I thought, 'There's a little joss who might be quite good fun if he once got off the lead,' and when you mentioned Scotland Yard just now all that good impression just faded away."

He paused, and Abbershaw cut in quickly.

"This doesn't get us very far," he said quietly, "does it? You know the explanation of this extraordinary outrage. Let's have it."

Mr. Campion regarded him frankly.

"You may not believe me," he said, "but I don't know quite what they're driving at even now. But there's something pretty serious afoot, I can tell you that."

It was obvious that he was telling the truth, but Abbershaw was not satisfied.

"Well, anyway, you know one thing," he said. "Why are you here? You just admitted yourself it was on business."

"Oh, it was," agreed Campion, "most decidedly. But not my business. Let me explain."

"I wish to God you would," said Prenderby, who was utterly out of his depth.

"Well then, chicks, Uncle Albert speaking." Campion leant forward, his expression more serious than his words. "Perhaps I ought to give you some little idea of my profession. I live, like all intelligent people, by my wits, and although I have often done things that mother wouldn't like, I have remembered her parting words and have never been vulgar. To cut it short, in fact, I do almost anything within reason—for a reasonable sum, but nothing sordid or vulgar—quite definitely nothing vulgar."

He glanced at Abbershaw, who nodded, and then went on.

"In this particular case," he said, "I was approached in London last week by a man who offered me a very decent sum to get myself included as unobtrusively as possible into the house-party this week-end and then to seize the first opportunity I could get to speaking to my host, the Colonel, alone. I was to make sure that we were alone. Then I was to go up to him, murmur a password in his ear, and receive from him a package which I was to bring to London immediately—unopened. I was warned, of course," he continued, looking up at Abbershaw. "They told me I was up against men who would have no compunction in killing me to prevent me getting away with the package, but I had no idea who the birds were going to be or I shouldn't have come for any money. In fact when I saw them at dinner on the first night I nearly cut the whole job right out and bunked back to town."

"Why? Who are they?" said Abbershaw.

Mr. Campion looked surprised.

"Good Lord, don't you know?" he demanded. "And little George a Scotland Yard expert, too. Jesse Gideon calls himself a solicitor. As a matter of fact he's rather a clever fence. And the Hun is no one else but Eberhard von Faber himself."

Prenderby still looked blank, but Abbershaw started.

"The '*Trois Pays*' man?" he said quickly.

"And '*Der Schwarzbund.*' And 'The Chicago Junker,' and now our own little '0072' at the Yard," said Mr. Campion, and there was no facetiousness in his tone.

"This means nothing to me," said Prenderby.

Mr. Campion opened his mouth to speak, but Abbershaw was before him.

"It means, Michael," he said, with an inflection in his voice which betrayed the gravity in which he viewed the situation, "that this man controls organized gangs of crooks all over Europe and America, and he has the reputation of being utterly ruthless and diabolically clever. It means we are up against the most dangerous and notorious criminal of modern times.

CHAPTER TWELVE

"Furthermore..." Said Mr. Campion

AFTER THE LITTLE SILENCE that followed Abbershaw's announcement, Prenderby spoke.

"What's in this mysterious package they've lost?" he said.

Abbershaw looked at Mr. Campion inquiringly.

"Perhaps you could tell us that," he said pointedly.

Albert Campion's vacuous face became even more blank than usual.

"I don't know much about it," he said. "My client didn't go into all that, naturally. But I can tell you this much, it's something sewn in the lining of a red leather wallet. It felt to me like paper—might have been a couple of fivers, of course—but I shouldn't think so."

"How do you know?" said Prenderby quietly.

Mr. Campion turned to him cheerfully.

"Oh, I collected the doings all right," he said, "and I should have got away with them if little George here hadn't been a car fiend."

Abbershaw frowned.

"I think you'd better explain," he said.

"Explain?" said Mr. Campion. "My dear chicks, there

was nothing in it. As soon as I saw old Uncle Ben and his friends at the table my idea was to get the package and then beat it, manners or no manners, so when the story of the Ritual came up I thought 'and very nice too' and suggested the game. Then while all you people were playing 'Bats in the Belfry' with the ancestral skewer, I toddled over to the old boy, whispered 'Inky-Pinky' in his ear, got the wallet, and made a beeline for the garage."

He paused and sighed.

"It was all very exhilarating," he went on easily. "My only trouble was that I was afraid that the wretched game would come to an end before I got away. With great presence of mind, therefore, I locked the door leading to the servants' quarters so that any serenade on the dinner gong would not bring out the torchlight procession immediately. Then I toddled off down the passage, out of the side door, across the garden, and arrived all girlish with triumph at the garage and walked slap-bang into our Georgie looking like an illustration out of *How to Drive in Three Parts, Send No Money.*"

He stopped and eyed Abbershaw thoughtfully.

"I got the mental machinery to function with a great effort," he continued, "and when I had it ticking over nicely I said to myself, 'Shall I tonk this little cove on the cranium, and stuff him under the seat? Or shall I leap past him, seize the car, and go home on it?' And neither stunt seemed really promising. If I bunked, I reasoned, George would rouse the house or chase me in one of the other cars. I couldn't afford to risk either just then. The only other expedient therefore was to tonk him, and the more I looked at him the less I liked the notion. Georgie is a sturdy little fellow, a pugnacious little cove, who might quite easily turn out to be a fly-weight champ, somewhere or other. If I was licked I was absolutely sunk, and even if I won we were bound to make a hell of a noise and I was most anxious not to have any attention focused on me while I had that pocketbook."

"So you came back to the house with me meaning to slip out later?" said Abbershaw.

"George has made the bell ring—three more shots or a packet of Gold Flake," said Mr. Campion facetiously. "Of course I did; and I should have got away. All would have been as merry as a wedding bell, in fact," he went on more sadly, "if that Anne woman had not decided that I was just the sort of harmless mutt to arouse jealousy safely with Mr. Kennedy without giving trouble myself. I couldn't escape her—she clung. So I had to wait until I thought everyone would be asleep, and then, just as I was sneaking out of my room, that precious mock butler of theirs came for me with a gun. I knocked it out of his hand, and then he started to jump on me. They must have rumbled by that time that the old boy had got rid of the packet, and were on the look-out for anyone trying a moonlight flit."

He paused, a faintly puzzled expression passed over his face. "I could have sworn he got the packet," he said; "anyway, in the fight I lost it. And that's the one thing that's really worrying me at the moment—what has happened to that wallet? For if the man who calls himself Dawlish doesn't get what he wants, I think we are all of us for a pretty parroty time."

He stopped and looked at Abbershaw steadily.

"It doesn't seem to be of any negotiable value," he said, "and as far as I can see, the only people who are interested in it are my client and Dawlish, but I can tell you one thing. It does interest them very much, and to get hold of it I don't believe they'd stick at anything."

"But what was it?" persisted Prenderby, who was more puzzled than ever by these explanations.

Campion shook his head.

"I don't know," he said, "unless it was the Chart of the Buried Treasure, don't you know."

Abbershaw got up from his chair and paced slowly up and down the room.

"There's only one weak spot in your story, Campion," he said suddenly. "It sounds like Gospel apart from that. But there is one thing I don't understand. It's this: Why didn't you have a revolver on you when you came out into the garage?"

"Answered in one," said Mr. Campion. "Because I hadn't one: I never carry guns."

"Do you mean to say that you set out on an infernally dangerous game like this without one?" Abbershaw's voice was incredulous.

Mr. Campion became momentarily grave.

"It's a fact," he said simply. "I'm afraid of them. Horrible things—guns. Always feel they might go off in a fit of temper and I should be left with the body. And no bag to put it in either. Then poor little Albert would be in the soup." He shuddered slightly.

"Let's talk about something else," he said. "I can keep up my pecker in the face of anything else but a corpse."

Prenderby and Abbershaw exchanged glances, and Abbershaw turned to where the young man with the tow-coloured hair and the unintelligent smile sat beaming at them through his glasses.

"Campion," he said, "you know, of course, that Colonel Coombe died last night? Do you know how he died?"

Mr. Campion looked surprised.

"Heart, wasn't it?" he said. "I thought the old bird had been scratching round the grave for the last year or so."

Abbershaw's expression did not change.

"Oh," he said, "if that is all you know it may surprise you to hear that he was murdered—while the Dagger Ritual was going on."

"Murdered!"

Every trace of frivolity had vanished from Albert Campion's face. There was no mistaking the fact that the news had appalled him, and he looked at Abbershaw with undisguised horror in his pale eyes.

"Murdered?" he repeated. "How do you know?"

"I saw him," said Abbershaw simply. "They wanted a signature on the cremation certificate, and got me in for it. They wouldn't let me examine the body, but I saw the face and neck and I also saw his invalid chair." His eyes were fixed on Campion the whole time he was speaking. "Then there was the dagger itself," he said. "There was blood on the dagger, and blood on the cushions of the chair, but even if I had not known of these, the body, though I saw so little of it, would have convinced me that he had been murdered. As perhaps you know," he went on, "it is my job to explain how men die, and as soon as I saw that dead grey face with the depleted veins I knew that he had died of some wound. Something that would bleed very freely. I should say it was a stab in the back, myself."

The change in Mr. Campion was extraordinary; he pulled himself together with an effort.

"This is horrible," he said. "I suppose they got him when they discovered that he had parted with the package. Pretty quick work," he added thoughtfully. "I wonder how they rumbled him so soon."

There was silence for a moment or two after he had spoken, then Prenderby looked up.

"The store they set by that package must be enormous, on the face of it," he said. "Clearly they'll do anything for it. I wonder what their next move will be?"

"He's searched our rooms," said Abbershaw, "and I believe he intended to lock us in the dining-room and search us immediately after, but his experiences in the bedrooms taught him the utter impossibility of ever making a thorough search of a house like this. It couldn't be done in the time he had at his disposal. I think he realizes that his only chance of getting hold of what he wants is to terrorize us until someone hands it over."

"Then I hope to goodness whoever has got it gets the wind up soon," said Prenderby.

Campion nodded and sat down gingerly on the edge of the bed. "I expect he'll have you people up one at a time and bully the truth out of you until he gets what he wants," he said.

"For a great crook he hasn't proved very methodical, so far," said Abbershaw. "He might have known from the first that there'd be no point in churning everybody's clothes up."

Albert Campion leaned forward. "You know, you fellows don't understand this bright specimen of German culture," he said, with more gravity than was usual in his falsetto voice. "He's not used to little details of this sort. He's the laddie at the top—the big fellow. He just chooses his men carefully and then says, 'You do this,' and they do it. He doesn't go chasing round the country opening safes or pinching motor-cars. I don't believe he even plans the *coups* himself. He just buys criminal brains, supplies the finance, and takes the profits. That's why I can't understand him being here. There must have been something pretty big afoot, or he'd have had a minion in for it. Gosh! I wish I was well out of it."

Abbershaw and Prenderby echoed his wish devoutly in their hearts, and Prenderby was the first to speak.

"I wonder whom he'll start on first," he said thoughtfully.

Campion's pale eyes flickered.

"I fancy I could tell you that," he said. "You see, when they couldn't get anything out of me, except banalities, they decided that I was about the fool I looked, and just before a couple of thugs, armed to the teeth, bundled me off to the box-room, I heard a certain amount of what they said. Jesse Gideon had apparently gone carefully over the crowd, and prepared a dossier about each one of us. I came first on the list of people about which nothing was known, and the next was a girl. She wasn't a friend of Petrie's apparently, and the enemy couldn't place her at all."

"Who—who was that?"

Abbershaw was staring at the speaker, his eyes grown suddenly hard. A terrible apprehension had sent the colour to his face. Campion glanced at him curiously.

"That red-haired girl who met us in the passage when we came back from the garage. What's her name—Oliphant, isn't it? Meggie Oliphant. She's the next to be for it, I believe."

CHAPTER THIRTEEN

Abbershaw Sees Red

"MY GOD, Abbershaw, he was right! They've got her!"

Ten minutes after Mr. Campion had first suggested that Meggie might be the next victim, Prenderby ran into Abbershaw in the corridor outside the girl's room. "I've been all over the house," he said. "The girls say that she went up to her room an hour ago to lie down. Now there's not a sign of her about."

Abbershaw did not speak.

In the last few minutes his face had lost much of its cherubic calm. An entirely new emotion had taken possession of him. He was wildly, unimaginably angry.

Never, in all his life before, had he experienced anything that could compare with it, and even as Prenderby watched him he saw the last traces of the cautious methodical expert vanish and the new, impulsive, pugnacious fighter come into being.

"Michael," he said suddenly, "keep an eye on Campion. His story may be absolutely true—it sounds like it—but we can't afford to risk anything. Keep him up in my room so that he can hide in the passage if need be. You'll have to smuggle food up to him somehow. Cheer the others up if you can." Prenderby looked at him anxiously.

"What are you going to do?" he said.

Abbershaw set his teeth.

"I'm going to see them," he said. "There's been enough of this mucking about. There is going to be some sort of understanding, anyway. Damn it all! They've got my girl!" Turning on his heel he strode off down the passage.

A green-baize door cut off that portion of the house where Dawlish had established his headquarters. He passed through it without any interruption, and reached the door of the room that had once been Colonel Coombe's bedchamber.

He tapped on it loudly, and it was opened immediately by a man he had never seen before, a heavy bull of a fellow whom he guessed to be one of the servants.

"What do you want?" he demanded suspiciously.

"Mr. Dawlish," said Abbershaw, and attempted to push past him.

A single blow, violent as a mule kick, sent him flying back against the opposite wall of the corridor, and the giant glowered at him.

"Nobody comes in 'ere," he said. "Mr. Dawlish isn't seeing anybody for another hour at least," he added with a laugh that sent Abbershaw cold as he grasped its inference.

"Look here," he said, "this is very important. I must get in to Mr. Dawlish. Does this interest you?"

He drew a notecase from his pocket as he spoke. The man advanced towards him and stood glaring down at him, his heavy red face darker than ever with anger.

Suddenly his hand shot out and Abbershaw's throat was encased in a band of steel.

"You just 'aven't realized, you and your lot downstairs, what you're playing about wiv," he said. "This 'ere isn't no Sunday School hunt-the-thimble-set-out. There's nine of us, we're armed, and *he* isn't jokin'." The hand round Abbershaw's throat tightened as the thug thrust his face close against his victim's.

" 'E ain't ordered about by nobody. Makes 'is own laws, 'e does. *As* you'll soon find out. At the moment 'e's busy—talking to a lady. And when 'e's done wiv 'er I'll take your message in to 'im and not before. Now get out—if I 'aven't killed yer."

On the last words he flung the half-strangled Abbershaw away from him as if he had been a terrier, and, re-entering the room, slammed the door behind him, shooting home the bolts.

Abbershaw scrambled to his feet, flung himself against the door, beating it with his hands, in a paroxysm of fury.

At last he paused in despair: the heavy oak would have withstood a battering ram. He stood back, helpless and half-maddened with apprehension for Meggie's safety.

Then from somewhere far away he fancied he heard a muffled cry.

The effect upon him was instantaneous. His impotent fury vanished and he became once more cold and reasoning. His one chance of saving her was to get round the other way: to break in upon Dawlish's inquisition from an unguarded point, and, once there, declare all he knew about the red wallet and the fate of its contents, regardless of the revenge the German would inevitably take.

Campion had been imprisoned conceivably somewhere near the room where Dawlish had dealt with him. It was just possible, therefore, that the passage through the cupboard would lead him to Meggie.

He turned quickly: there was no time to be lost; even now Dawlish might be trying some of the same methods of urging a confession as he had employed upon Campion earlier in the day. The thought sickened him and he dashed down the passage into his own room.

Brushing the astonished Campion aside, he threw open the cupboard door and pressed against the back of the shelf steadily.

It gave before his weight and swung open, revealing a dark cavity behind.

He took out his pocket torch and flashed it in front of him. The passage was wood-lined and very dusty. Doubtless it had not been used for years before Campion stumbled upon it by chance that afternoon.

It was narrow also, admitting only just enough space for a man to pass along it, crawling on his hands and knees. But Abbershaw set off down it eagerly.

The air was almost unbearably musty, and there was a scuttling of rats in front of him as he crawled on, shining the torch ahead of him as he went. At length he reached the steps of which Campion had spoken. They were steep and solid, leading straight up into the darkness which had opened above his head.

He mounted them cautiously, and a moment later found himself cut off by an apparently solid floor over him.

A closer examination, however, showed a catch, which, upon being released, allowed the trap to drop slowly open, so that he had to retreat some steps in order to avoid its catching him.

The machinery which Campion had referred to as a "piece of old bicycle" was in fact an ancient iron device, worked with a pedal, for opening the trap. As soon as he had lifted this hatch, Abbershaw hauled himself into the open space above it which he knew must be the chest itself. The lid was down, and he waited for some moments, breathless, listening. He could hear nothing, however, save the scuffling of the rats behind him, and at length, very cautiously, he put his hands above his head, pressed the lid up an inch or two, and peered out.

No one appeared to be about, and he climbed silently out of the box. He was in a longish vaulted room, one of the relics of the days when Black Dudley had been a monastery. Its stone walls were unpanelled, and a small window high up was closely barred. It was, as Campion had said, used as a box-room, and filled with lumber of every description.

Abbershaw looked round eagerly for a door, and saw it built almost next door to the fire-place in the wall opposite him.

It was small, iron, hinged, and very heavy.

He tried it cautiously, and found to his relief that it was unlocked. So Campion's escape had been discovered, he reflected, and went warily. He let himself out cautiously; he had no desire to be apprehended before he reached Dawlish himself.

The door opened out on to a small stone landing in which were two similar doors. A steep spiral staircase descended almost at his feet.

He listened attentively, but there was no sound, and he decided that Dawlish's inquisition could not be taking place on that floor. He turned down the steps, therefore, treading softly and hugging the wall. Once round the first bend, he heard a sound which made him stiffen and catch his breath—the muffled murmur of voices somewhere quite close. He went on eagerly, his ears strained to catch the first recognizable words.

The stairs ended abruptly in a small oak door to the right of which a narrow passage led off into the darkness.

Through the door he could hear clearly Dawlish's deep German voice raised menacingly.

Abbershaw took a deep breath, and pressing up the latch, carefully pushed the door open. It swung silently on well-greased hinges, and he passed through it expecting to find himself in the Colonel's bedroom.

To his surprise he came out into what appeared to be a large cupboard. The air in it was insufferably hot, and it dawned upon him that he was in one of those hiding-places that are so often to be found in the sides of ancient fire-places. Doubtless it was just such another cache that had swallowed up Campion when he disappeared off the hearth-rug in the hall. Perhaps the mysterious passage behind him led directly down to that great sombre room.

From where he stood, every sound in the room without was distinctly audible.

Dawlish's voice, bellowing with anger, sounded suddenly quite near to where he stood.

"Speak!" it said. "What do you know? All of it—all of it. Keep nothing back." And then, explosively, as if he had turned back to someone else in the room—"Stop her crying—make her speak."

There was a soft, short, unmistakable sound, and Meggie screamed. A blinding flash of red passed before Abbershaw's eyes, and he hurled himself against the wooden panel nearest him. It gave way before him, and he shot out into the midst of Dawlish's inquiry like a hand grenade.

CHAPTER FOURTEEN

Abbershaw Gets His Interview

WHEN ABBERSHAW PICKED HIMSELF UP he discovered that he was not in Colonel Coombe's bedroom as he had supposed, but in a smaller and more luxurious apartment presumably leading off it.

It was lined with books, and had been used apparently as a study or library.

At a heavy oak table-desk set across one end sat Dawlish, his face mask-like as ever, and his ponderous hands resting among the papers in front of him.

Before him stood Jesse Gideon, looking down at Meggie, who sat on a chair; a man Abbershaw had never seen before leaning over her.

She had been crying, but in spite of her evident terror there was a vestige of spirit in her narrow brown eyes, and she held herself superbly.

Abbershaw's somewhat precipitate entrance startled everybody, and he was on his feet again before Dawlish spoke.

The German's dull, expressionless eyes rested on his face.

"You," he said, in his peculiarly stilted English. "How

foolish you are. Since you have come out of your turn you may stay. Sit down."

As the young man stared at him he repeated the last words violently, but without any movement or gesture.

The man was almost unbelievably immobile.

Abbershaw remained where he was.

His anger was slowly getting the better of him, and he stood there stiffly, his flaming red hair on end and his round face white and set.

"I insist that you listen to me," he said. "This terrorizing of women has got to stop. What are you gaining by it, anyway? Have you learnt anything of value to you from this girl?" His voice rose contemptuously. "Of course you haven't. You're making fools of yourselves."

The German looked at him steadily, unblinkingly, not a muscle of his face moved.

"Gideon," he said, "tell me, who is this foolish redheaded young man who so loves to hear his own voice?"

Gideon glided forward obsequiously and stood beside the desk, his grey face and glittering eyes hideous beneath his white hair. He used his hands as he talked, emphasizing his words with graceful fluttering gestures.

"His name is George Abbershaw," he said. "He is a doctor of medicine, a pathologist, an expert upon external wounds and abrasions with especial regard to their causes. In this capacity he has been often consulted by Scotland Yard. As a university friend of Wyatt Petrie's, there is no reason to suppose that he came here with any ulterior motive."

The German continued to regard Abbershaw steadily.

"He is not a detective, *ja*?"

"No." Gideon spoke emphatically. "That is obvious. English detectives are a race apart. They are evident at the first glance. No one who knew anything about the English Police Force could possibly suspect Dr. Abbershaw of holding any rank in it."

The German grunted.

"So," he said, and returned to Abbershaw, "you are just an ordinary headstrong young man who, like the others downstairs, is under the impression that this affair is a melodrama which has been especially devised in order that they may have the opportunity of posing heroically before the young ladies of your party. This is an old house, suitable for such gaming, but I, one of the chief actors in your theatre, I am not playing."

He paused, and Abbershaw was conscious of a faint change in his face, although he did not appear to have moved a muscle.

"What does it matter to me," he continued, "if you hide yourselves in priestholes or spring upon me out of cupboards? Climb from one room to another, my friend, make yourself dusty in disused passages, attempt to run your motor-cars upon alcohol: it does me no harm. My only interest is in a package I have lost—a thing that can be of no use to anyone but myself and possibly one other man in the world. It is because I believe that there is in this house someone who is in the employ of that other man that I am keeping you all here until I recover my property."

The dull, rasping voice stopped for a moment, and Abbershaw was about to speak when Dawlish again silenced him.

"To recover that property," he repeated, "at *whatever cost*. I am not playing a game. I am not jumping out of cupboards in an attempt to be heroic. I am not pretending. I think the boy who attempted to drive off in his motor-car and the madman who escaped from the room upstairs where I had locked him understood me. The girl here, too, should begin to understand by now. And the rest of you shall be convinced even as they have been."

Abbershaw's anger had by no means died down under this harangue, and when he spoke his voice was frigid and very formal.

"If you carry out those threats, Herr Eberhard von Faber," he said, "you will be wasting your time."

Gideon started violently at the name, but the German did not appear even to have heard.

"I had your packet," Abbershaw continued bitingly.

They were listening intently, and he fancied he discerned a change in Dawlish's dull eyes.

"And in the morning before you had the audacity to place us under this restraint I destroyed it in the grate of my bedroom." He paused, breathless; the truth was out now, they could do what they liked with him.

The German's reply came, very cold and as contemptuous as his own.

"In the present situation you cannot expect to be believed," he said. "Do not they tell me after every crime in which great public interest is taken at least four or five imbeciles approach the police, confessing to it? Forgive me if I say that you remind me of one of those imbeciles, Dr. Abbershaw."

He laughed on the last word, and the effect of the deep-throated chuckle emerging from that still expressionless face was curiously inhuman.

Abbershaw thrust his hand into his pocket and drew out the red wallet. To his astonishment neither Dawlish nor his two subordinates betrayed any sign of recognition, and with a feeling approaching dismay he realized that this was not what they had visualized as the container of the thing they sought. He opened it, drew out his own papers, and laid the case upon the desk in front of the German.

"The papers you were looking for were sewn inside the lining of this wallet," he said. "I ripped them out and destroyed them."

There was silence for a moment after he had spoken, and Gideon leant forward and picked up the case in his pale, exquisitely tapering fingers.

"It is too small," he pronounced at last, turning to the German.

Dawlish spoke without taking his eyes off Abbershaw. It was impossible to tell what he was thinking.

"If you are not lying, young man with red hair," he said, "will you explain to me why you saw fit to destroy the papers that were concealed in that pocket-case? Did you read them?"

"They were in code," said Abbershaw sullenly.

Gideon shot a swift glance at him under his bushy eyebrows, and then turned to Dawlish.

"Code?" he said. Still the German did not look at him, but remained staring at Abbershaw unblinkingly.

"There may have been a code message in the wallet," he said, "and you may have destroyed it. But I do not think it is likely that it had anything to do with my business down here; unless…"

For the first time during that conversation he turned to Gideon. "Coombe," he said, and there was sullen ferocity in his tone, "he may have succeeded at last."

Gideon stared.

"Double-crossed?" he said, and his voice died away in a question.

"We don't know."

The German spoke fiercely. "I have no faith in this young fool's story—he's only concerned with the girl. Is Whitby back yet?"

"No," said Gideon. "We can't expect him yet."

"So." Dawlish nodded. "We must keep them till he comes. He may be able to recognize this case. Whose initials are these?"

"Mine," said Abbershaw. "You'll find that they are clipped on at the back. I put them on myself."

Gideon smiled.

"A very singular thing to do, Dr. Abbershaw," he said. "And may I ask where you got this wallet?"

Abbershaw hesitated. For the moment he was in a quandary. If he told the truth he could hardly help incriminating Campion, and in view of that young man's present condition it was inhuman to betray him.

"I found it," he said at last, realizing at once how lame the explanation must sound. Gideon shrugged his shoulders. "This man is wasting our time," he said. "No, it is Petrie you should examine, as I have told you all along. He's just the type *they* would choose. What shall we do with these two?"

"Put them in the other room—not the one the young lunatic got out of," said Dawlish. "You came through the passage from the fire-place in the hall, I suppose," he added, turning heavily to Abbershaw, who nodded. "We must wait for Whitby to see this case," he continued, "then we will consider what is to be done."

The stranger who had been standing at Meggie's side laid a hand on her shoulder.

"Come," he said, jerking her to her feet.

Abbershaw turned on him furiously, only to find a revolver pressed against his ribs. They were headed towards the staircase behind the fire-place by which he had come, but when they reached the threshold Dawlish spoke again.

"Dr. Abbershaw," he said, "come here."

Unwillingly, the young man turned and stood before the desk, looking down at the florid Teutonic face with the dull corpse-like eyes.

"So you are an expert often referred to by Scotland Yard."

The German spoke with curious deliberation.

"I have heard of you. Your name has been mentioned in several cases which have interested me deeply. You gave evidence in the Waterside-Birbeck murder, didn't you?"

Abbershaw nodded.

"And in the Sturges affair?"

"Yes."

"Had it not been for you, Newman would never have been hanged?"

"Very probably not."

A slightly deeper colour seemed to flood the expressionless face.

"Three of my best men," he said. "I am very glad to have met you, Dr. Abbershaw. Put them in the small room, Wendon, and lock the door very carefully. When I have a little more time to speak I have promised myself another interview with you, Dr. Abbershaw."

CHAPTER FIFTEEN

Doctor Abbershaw's Deductions

THE ROOM into which Meggie and Abbershaw were thrust so unceremoniously in the middle of the night was one of the three which opened out on to the small winding staircase leading down to Colonel Coombe's study.

It was comparatively empty, containing only a pile of disused tapestries and old curtains, two or three travelling trunks and a chair.

Here, as in the other room, the window was high up in the wall and iron-barred. There was a second door in the room but it appeared to be heavily bolted on the other side. Abbershaw made a thorough investigation of the room with his torch, and then decided that escape was impossible, and they sat down on the tapestry in silence.

Until now they had not spoken very much, save for a brief account from Abbershaw of his interview with Campion and his journey through the passage from his cupboard. Meggie's story was simpler. She had been seized on her way up to her room and dragged off through the green-baize door to be questioned.

Neither felt that much was to be gained from talking.

The German had convinced them of the seriousness of their position, and Abbershaw was overcome with self-reproach for what he could only feel was his own fault. Meggie was terrified but much too plucky to show it.

As the utter silence of the darkness descended upon them, however, the girl laid her hand on Abbershaw's arm. "We'll be all right," she murmured. "It was wonderful of you to come and get me out like that."

Abbershaw laughed bitterly. "I didn't get you very far," he said.

The girl peered at him through the shadow.

"Oh, I don't know," she said. "It's better up here than it was down there."

Abbershaw took her hand and spoke with unusual violence. "My God, they didn't hurt you?" he said.

"Oh no, nothing much."

It was evident from her voice that she was trying to make light of a terrible experience. "I was frightened more than hurt," she said, "but it was good to see you. Who are they, George? What are they doing here? What's it all about?"

Abbershaw covered his face with his hands and groaned in the darkness.

"I could kick myself," he said. "It's all my fault. I did an absurd, a foolhardy, lunatic thing when I destroyed those papers. I didn't realize whom we were up against."

The girl caught her breath.

"Then what you said was true?" she said. "You did destroy what they are looking for?"

"Yes." Abbershaw spoke savagely. "I've behaved like an idiot all the way through," he said. "I've been too clever by half, and now I've got you, of all people—the person I'd rather die than see any harm come to—into this appalling situation. I hit on the truth," he went on, "but only half of it, and like a fool I acted upon my belief without being sure. Oh, my God, what a fool I've been!"

The girl stirred beside him and laid her head on his shoulder, her weight resting in the hollow of his arm. "Tell me," she said.

Abbershaw was only too glad to straighten out his own thoughts in speech, and he began softly, keeping his voice down lest there should be listeners on the landing behind the bolted door.

"It was Colonel Coombe's murder that woke me up," he said. "And then, when I saw the body and realized that the plate across his face was unneeded and served as a disguise, I realized then that it was crooks we had to deal with, and casting about in my mind I arrived at something— not quite the truth—but very near it."

He paused and drew the girl closer to him.

"It occurred to me that Dawlish and Gideon might very well be part of the famous Simister gang—the notorious bank thieves of the States. The descriptions of two of the leaders seemed to tally very well, and like a fool I jumped to the conclusion that they were the Simister gangsters. So that when the documents came into my hands I guessed what they were."

The girl looked at him. "What were they?" she said.

Abbershaw hesitated.

"I don't want to lay down the law this time," he said, "but I don't see how I can be wrong. In these big gangs of crooks the science of thieving has been brought to such perfection that their internal management resembles a gigantic business concern more than anything else. Modern criminal gangs are not composed of amateurs—each man has his own particular type of work at which he is an expert. That is why the police experience such difficulty in bringing to justice the man actually responsible for a crime, and not merely capturing the comparatively innocent catspaw who performs the actual thieving."

He paused, and the girl nodded in the darkness. "I see," she said.

Abbershaw went on, his voice sunk to a whisper.

"Very big gangs, like Simister's, carry this cooperative spirit to an extreme," he continued, "and in more cases than one a really big robbery is planned and worked out to the last detail by a man who may be hundreds of miles away from the scene of the crime when it is committed. A man with an ingenious criminal brain, therefore, can always sell his wares without being involved in any danger whatsoever. The thing I found was, I feel perfectly sure, a complete crime, worked out to the last detail by the hands of a master. It may have been a bank robbery, but of that I'm not sure. It was written in code, of course, and it was only from the few plans included in the mass of written matter—and my suspicions—that I got a hint of what it was."

Meggie lifted her head.

"But would they write it down?" she said. "Would they risk that?"

Abbershaw hesitated.

"I admit that worried me at first," he said, "but consider the circumstances. Here is an organization, enormous in its resources, but every movement of which is bound to be carried out in absolute secrecy. A lot of people sneer at the efficiency of Scotland Yard, but not those who have ever had cause to come up against it. Imagine an organization like this, captained by a mind simple, forceful, and eminently sensible. A mind that only grasps one thing at a time, but which deals with that one thing down to the last detail, with the thoroughness of a Hun."

"Dawlish?" said Meggie.

Abbershaw nodded in the darkness.

"Yes," he said. "Mr. Benjamin Dawlish is one of his

names." He paused, and then went on again with new enthusiasm, "Then imagine the brains of his gang," he continued, "the man with the mind of a genius plus just that one crooked kink which makes him a criminal instead of a diplomat. It is most important that this one man of all others shall evade the police."

Meggie nestled closer to him.

"Go on," she said.

Abbershaw continued, his voice hardly raised above a whisper, but intense and vehement in the quietness.

"He must be kept away from the gang then, at all costs," he said. "So why not let him live at some out-of-the-way spot in the guise of an innocent old gentleman, an invalid, going out for long drives in his ramshackle old car for his health's sake; but in reality changing his personality on the road and becoming for a few hours an entirely different person? Not always the same man, you understand," he explained, "but adopting whatever guise seemed most suitable for the actual detail in hand. A respectable suburban householder eager to open a small account when it was necessary to inspect a certain bank manager's office; an insurance man when a watchman was to be interviewed; a jovial, open-handed man-about-town when clerks were to be pumped. And all these different personalities vanishing into thin air as soon as their work was done, each one of them merging into the quiet inoffensive old invalid driving about in his joke of a car."

His voice died away in the darkness, and Meggie stiffened.

"The Colonel," she whispered

"Yes," murmured Abbershaw. "I'm sure of it. He was the designer of the crimes. Dawlish organized them, and a carefully trained gang carried them out. The arrangements had to be written out," he went on, "because otherwise it would entail the Colonel spending some considerable time with the gang explaining his schemes, whereas it was much better that they should not know him, or he them. You see," he went on suddenly, "that's what Dawlish had to guard against—double-crossing. Old Coombe's plans had a definite market value. They were worth money to any criminal gang who could get hold of them, and, as I have said, to minimize any danger of this, Coombe was kept here, practically as a prisoner, by Dawlish. I dare say the only time he saw any member of the gang was when Gideon and some other member as witness came down here to collect the finished scheme for one robbery, or to discuss the next. On such occasions it was Coombe's practice to invite Wyatt to bring down a house-party as a blind to distract attention from any of his other visitors, who may in some cases have been characters 'known to the police.'" He stopped and sighed. "So far," he said, "I was practically right, but I had made one tremendous error."

"And that?" The girl's voice quivered with excitement.

"That," said Abbershaw gravely, "was the fatal one of taking Dawlish for Simister. Simister is a rogue about whom there are as many pleasant stories as unpleasant ones, but about Eberhard von Faber no one ever laughs. He is, without exception, the most notorious, unsavoury villain this era has produced. And I have pitched us all—you too—into his hands."

The girl repressed a shudder, but she clung to Abbershaw confidently.

"But why," she said suddenly, "why didn't they succeed? Why didn't the Colonel give Dawlish the papers and the whole thing work out according to plan?"

Abbershaw stirred.

"It would have done," he said, "but there *was* double-crossing going on. The Colonel, in spite of his bodyguard—Whitby and the butler—must have got into communication with Simister's gang and made some arrangement with them.

I'm only guessing here, of course, but I should say that the Colonel's plans were never allowed outside the house and that his attitude towards Simister must have been, 'I will sell them if you can get them without implicating me.' So Simister employed our friend, Mr. Campion, to smuggle himself into Wyatt's party without being recognized by Dawlish."

Meggie sat up. "I see," she said, "but then, George, who murdered the Colonel?"

"Oh, one of the gang, of course—evidently. When they discovered that he had double-crossed them."

The girl was silent for a moment, then:

"They were very quick," she said thoughtfully.

Abbershaw jerked his chin up. This was a point which it had never occurred to him to question.

"What do you mean?" he demanded.

Meggie repeated her former observation.

"They were very quick," she said. "If the Colonel didn't have a heart attack he was murdered when we were playing with the dagger. Before I had the thing in my hand, in fact. Did they see the old man part with the papers? And if so, why did they kill him and not Albert Campion?"

Abbershaw was silent. This point of view had not occurred to him. As far as he knew, apart from the single affair on the landing, they had not spotted Albert Campion at all.

"Besides," said Meggie, "if you remember, Dawlish seemed to be surprised when something you said suggested that Coombe had double-crossed them."

Abbershaw nodded: the incident returned to his mind. Meggie went on speaking, her voice very low.

"So Albert Campion was the murderer," she said.

Abbershaw started.

"Oh, no," he said. "I don't think that for a moment. In fact I'm sure of it," he went on, as he remembered the scene—it seemed incredible that it was only that afternoon—when Mr. Campion had heard of the Colonel's murder.

"I'm sure of it," he repeated, "and besides," he added, as the extenuating circumstances occurred to him, "why should von Faber have taken all those precautions to conceal someone else's crime?"

Meggie was silent at this, and Abbershaw continued. "There's no doubt that the Colonel intended to cheat the gang," he said. "The documents were exquisite pieces of work, written on the finest paper in a hand so small that it would have taken a reading glass to follow the words. It was in code—not one I know, either—and it was only the tiny plans that gave the clue to what it was. All sewn into the lining of a pocket-book which Dawlish didn't recognize when I showed it to him. Oh, what a fool I was to destroy it!"

The regret in his tone was very poignant, and for some seconds the girl did not speak. Then she moved a little nearer to him as if to compensate him for any embarrassment her question might cause him.

"Why did you?" she said at last.

Abbershaw was silent for some time before he spoke. Then he sighed deeply.

"I was a crazy, interfering, well-meaning fool," he said, "and there's no more dangerous creature on the face of the earth. I acted partly on impulse and partly because it really seemed to me to be the best thing to do at the moment. I had no idea whom we were up against. In the first place I knew that if I destroyed it I should probably be preventing a crime at least; you see, I had no means, and no time to decipher it and thereby obtain enough information to warn Scotland Yard. I didn't even know where the bank to be robbed was situated, or if indeed it was a bank. I knew we were up against pretty stiff customers, for one man had already been murdered, presumably on account of the papers, but I had no idea that they would dream of attempting anything so wholesale as this."

He paused and shook his head.

"I didn't realize then," he continued, "that there had been any double-crossing going on, and I took it for granted that the pocket-book would be recognized instantly. Situated as we were then, too, it was reasonable to suppose that I could not hold out against the whole gang, and it was ten chances to one that they would succeed in getting back their plans and the scheme would go forward with me powerless to do anything. Acting entirely upon the impulse of the moment, therefore, I stuffed the plans into the grate and set fire to them. That was just before I went down to speak to you in the garden. Now, of course, Dawlish won't believe me, and if he did, I'm inclined to believe he would take his revenge upon all of us. In fact, we're in a very nasty mess. If we get out of here we can't get out of the house, and that Hun is capable of anything. Oh, my dear, I wish you weren't here."

The last words broke from him in an agony of self-reproach. Meggie nestled closer to his shoulder.

"I'm very glad I am," she said. "If we're in for trouble let's go through it together. Look, we've been talking for hours—the dawn's breaking. Something may turn up today. Don't these people ever have postmen or milkmen or telegram-boys or anything?"

Abbershaw nodded.

"I've thought of that," he said, "but I think everyone like that is stopped at the lodge, and anyhow today's Sunday. Of course," he added brightly, "in a couple of days there'll be inquiries after some of us, but it's what von Faber may do before then that's worrying me."

Meggie sighed.

"I don't want to think," she said. "Oh, George," she added pitifully, "I'm so terribly tired."

On the last word her head lolled heavily against his breast, and he realized with sudden surprise that she was still a child who could sleep in spite of the horror of the situation. He sat there with his back against the wall supporting her in his arms, staring out across the fast-brightening room, his eyes fixed and full of apprehension.

Gradually the room grew lighter and lighter, and the sun, pale at first, and then brilliant, poured in through the high window with that warm serenity that is somehow peculiar to a Sunday morning. Outside he heard the far-away lowing of the cattle and the lively bickering of the birds.

He must have dozed a little in spite of his disturbing thoughts, for he suddenly came to himself with a start and sat up listening intently, his ears strained, and an expression of utter bewilderment on his face.

From somewhere close at hand, apparently in the room with the bolted door, there proceeded a curious collection of sounds. It was a hymn, sung with a malicious intensity, unequalled by anything Abbershaw had ever heard in his life before. The voice was a feminine one, high and shrill; it sounded like some avenging fury. He could make out the words, uttered with a species of ferocious glee underlying the religious fervour.

"Oh vain all outward signs of grief,
And in vain the form of prayer,
Unless the heart implore relief
And Penitence be there."

And then with still greater emphasis:

"We smite the breast, we weep in vain,
In vain in ashes mourn,
Unless with penitential pain—"

The quavering crescendo reached a pinnacle of self-righteous satisfaction that can never be known to more forgiving spirits.

"Unless with penitential pain
The smitten soul be torn."

The last note died away into silence, and a long drawn-out "Ah-ha-Ha-men" followed it.

Then all was still.

CHAPTER SIXTEEN

The Militant Mrs. Meade

"GOOD HEAVENS, what was that?"

It was Meggie who spoke. The noise had awakened her and she sat up, her hair a little wilder than usual and her eyes wide with astonishment.

Abbershaw started to his feet.

"We'll darned soon find out," he said, and went over to the second door and knocked upon it softly.

"Who's there?" he whispered.

"The wicked shall perish," said a loud, shrill, feminine voice, in which the broad Suffolk accent was very apparent. "The earth shall open and they shall be swallowed up. And you won't come into this room," it continued brightly. "No, not if you spend a hundred years a-tapping. And why won't you come in? 'Cause I've bolted the door."

There was demoniacal satisfaction in the last words, and Abbershaw and Meggie exchanged glances.

"It's a lunatic," whispered Abbershaw.

Meggie shuddered.

"What a horrible house this is," she said. "But talk to her, George. She may know how to get us out."

"Her chief concern seems to be not to let us in," said Abbershaw, but he returned to the door and spoke again.

"Who's there?" he said, and waited, hardly hoping for an answer, but the voice replied with unexpected directness:

"That's a thing I won't hide from anybody," it said vigorously. "Daisy May Meade's my name. A married woman and respectable. A church-going woman too, and there's some that's going to suffer for what's been going on in this house. Both here, *and* in the next world. The pit shall open and swallow them up. Fire and brimstone shall be their portion. The Lord shall smite them."

"Very likely," said Abbershaw dryly. "But who are you? How did you get here? Is it possible for you to get us out?"

Apparently his calm, matter-of-fact voice had a soothing effect upon the vengeful lady in the next room, for there was silence for some moments, followed by an inquisitive murmur in a less oracular tone.

"What be you doing of?"

"We're prisoners," said Abbershaw feelingly. "We've been shut up here by Mr. Dawlish, and are most anxious to get out. Can you help us?"

Again there was silence for some moments after he had spoken, then the voice said considerately, "I've a good mind to have the door open and have a look at ye."

"Good heavens!" said Abbershaw startled out of his calm. "Do you mean to say that you can open this door?"

"That I can," said the voice complacently. "Didn't I bolt it myself? I'm not having a lot of foreigners running round me. I told the German gentleman so. Oh, they shall be punished. 'To the devil you'll go,' I told them. 'Fire and brimstone and hot irons,' I said."

"Yes, I know," said Abbershaw soothingly, "but have you any idea how we can get out?"

A grunt of consideration was clearly audible through the

door. "I will have a look at ye," said the voice with sudden decision, and thereupon there began a fearsome noise of chains, bolts, and the scraping of heavy furniture, which suggested that Mrs. Meade had barricaded herself in with a vengeance. Soon after there was a creaking and the door swung open an inch or two, a bright black eye appearing in the crack. After a moment or so, apparently satisfied, Mrs. Meade pushed the door open wide and stood upon the threshold looking in on them.

She was a striking old woman, tall and incredibly gaunt, with a great bony frame on which her clothes hung skimpily. She had a brown puckered face in which her small eyes, black and quick as a bird's, glowed out at the world with a religious satisfaction at the coming punishment of the wicked. She was clothed in a black dress, green with age, and a stiff white apron starched like a board, which gave her a rotundity of appearance wholly false. She stood there for some seconds, her bright eyes taking in every nook and corner of the room. Apparently satisfied, she came forward.

"That'll be your sister, I suppose," she said, indicating Meggie with a bony hand, "seeing you've both red hair."

Neither of the two answered, and taking their silence for assent, she went on.

"You're visitors, I suppose?" she demanded. "It's my belief the devil's own work is going on in this house. Haven't I seen it with me own eyes? Wasn't I permitted— praise be the Lord!—to witness some of it? It's four shall swing from the gallows, their lives in the paper, before there's an end of this business."

The satisfaction in her voice was apparent, and she beamed upon them, the maliciousness in her old face truly terrible to see. She was evidently bursting with her story, and they found it was not difficult to get her to talk.

"Who are you?" demanded Abbershaw. "I know your

name, of course, but that doesn't make me much wiser. Where do you live?"

"Down in the village, three miles away," said the redoubtable Mrs. Meade, beaming at him. "I'm not a regular servant here, and I wouldn't be, for I've no need, but when they has company up here I sometimes come in for the week to help. My time's up next Wednesday, and when I don't come home my son'll come down for me. That's the time I'm waiting for. Then there'll be trouble!"

There was grim pleasure in her tone, and she wagged her head solemnly.

"He'll have someone to reckon with then, the German gentleman will. My son don't hold with foreigners nohow. What with this on top of it, and him being a murderer too, there'll be a fight, I can tell you. My son's a rare fighter."

"I shouldn't think the Hun would be bad at a scrap," murmured Abbershaw, but at the same time he marvelled at the complacency of the old woman who could time her rescue for four days ahead and settle down peacefully to wait for it.

There was one phrase, however, that stuck in his mind.

"Murderer?" he said.

The old woman eyed him suspiciously and came farther into the room.

"What do you know about it?" she demanded.

"We've told you who we are," said Meggie, suddenly sitting up, her clever pale face flushing a little and her narrow eyes fixed upon her face.

"We're visitors. And we've been shut up here by Mr. Dawlish, who seems to have taken over charge of the house ever since Colonel Coombe had his seizure."

The old woman pricked up her ears.

"Seizure?" she said. "That's what they said it was, did they? The fiery furnace is made ready for them, and they shall be consumed utterly. I know it wasn't no seizure. That was murder, that was. A life for a life, and an eye for an eye, a tooth for a tooth, that's the law, and they shall come to it."

"Murder? How do you know it was murder?" said Abbershaw hastily. The fanatical forebodings were getting on his nerves.

Once again the crafty look came into the little black eyes and she considered him dubiously, but she was much too eager to tell her story to be dissuaded by any suspicions.

"It was on the Friday night," she said, dropping her voice to a confidential monotone. "After dinner had been brought out, Mrs. Browning, that's the housekeeper, sent me upstairs to see to the fires. I hadn't been up there more than ten minutes when I come over faint." She paused and eyed the two defiantly.

"I never touch liquor," she said, and hesitated again. Abbershaw was completely in the dark, but Meggie had a flash of intuition, born of long experience of Mrs. Meade's prototypes.

"But as you weren't well you looked about for something to revive you?" she said. "Of course. Why not?"

Mrs. Meade's dubious expression faded.

"Of course," she said. "What else was I to do?"

"What else indeed?" said Meggie encouragingly.

"What did I do?" said the old woman, lapsing once more into the rhetorical form she favoured. "I remembered that in the Colonel's study—that's through his bedroom, you know—there was a little cupboard behind the screen by the window, where he kept a drop of Scotch whisky. That's soothing and settling to the stomach as much as anything is. So, coming over faint, and being in the Colonel's bedroom, I went into the study, and had just poured myself out a little drop when I heard voices, and the German gentleman with his friend Mr. Gideon and Dr. Whitby come in." She stopped again and looked at Meggie.

"I didn't holler out," she said, "because it would have looked so bad—me being there in the dark."

Meggie nodded understandingly, and Mrs. Meade continued.

"So I just stayed where I was behind the screen," she said. "Mr. Gideon was carrying a lamp and he set it down on the desk. They was all very excited, and as soon as Dr. Whitby spoke I knew something was up. 'What an opportunity,' he said, 'while they're playing around with that dagger he'll just sit where he is. We're safe for fifteen minutes at least.' Then the German gentleman spoke. Very brusque he is. 'Get on with it,' says he. 'Where does he keep the stuff?'"

Mrs. Meade paused, and her little black eyes were eloquent. "Imagine the state I was in, me standing there with the bottle in me 'and," she said. "But the next moment Dr. Whitby set me at peace again. 'In the secret drawer at the back of the desk,' he said. I peeked round the edge of the screen and saw 'im fiddling about with the master's desk." She fixed Meggie with a bright black eye. "I *was* upset," she said. "If it hadn't been for the whisky and the way it would have looked I'd 'ave gone out, but as it was I couldn't very well, and so I stayed where I was, but I listened. For I said to myself, 'The humblest of us are sometimes the ministers of the Lord,' and I realized someone would have to be brought to justice."

Her self-righteousness was so sublime that it all but carried her hearers away with it, and she went on, whilst they listened to her, fascinated.

"I saw them open the drawer and then there was such a swearing set-out that I was ashamed. 'It's gone,' said Mr. Gideon, and Dr. Whitby he started moaning like an idiot. 'He always kept them here,' he kept saying over and over again. Then the German, him that's for Hell Fire as sure as I'll be with the Lambs, he got very angry. 'You've played the fool enough,' he said, in such a loud voice that I nearly cried out and gave myself away. 'Go and fetch him,' he said. 'Bring him up here. I've had enough of this playing.' "

Mrs. Meade paused for breath.

"Dr. Whitby's rather a sullen gentleman," she continued, "but he went off like a child. I stood there, my knees knocking together, wishing me breathing wasn't so heavy, and praying to the Lord to smite them for their wickedness, while the German gentleman and Mr. Gideon were talking together in a foreign language. I couldn't understand it, of course," she added regretfully, "but I'm not an old fool, like you might imagine. Though I'm sixty-two I'm pretty spry, and I could tell by the way they was waving their hands about and the look on their faces and the sound of their voices that the German gentleman was angry about something or other, and that Mr. Gideon was trying to soothe 'im. 'Wait,' he said at last, in a Christian tongue, 'he'll have it on him, I tell you.' Well!...." She paused and looked from one to the other of her listeners, her voice becoming more dramatic and her little black eyes sparkling. Clearly she was coming to the cream of her narrative.

"Well," she repeated, when she was satisfied that they were both properly on edge, "at that moment the door was flung open and Dr. Whitby came back, white as a sheet, and trembling. 'Chief! Gideon!' he said. 'He's been murdered! Stabbed in the back!' "

Mrs. Meade stopped to enjoy the full effect of her announcement.

"Were they surprised?"

Abbershaw spoke involuntarily.

"You be quiet and I'll tell 'ee," said Mrs. Meade, with sudden sternness. "They was struck silly, I can tell you. The German gentleman was the first to come to his senses. 'Who?'

he said. Mr. Gideon turned on him then. 'Sinisters?' he says, as if asking a question."

Meggie and Abbershaw exchanged significant glances, while Mrs. Meade hurried on with her narrative, speaking with great gusto, acting the parts of the different speakers, and investing the whole gruesome story with an air of self-righteous satisfaction that made it even more terrible.

"The German gentleman wasn't pleased at that," she continued, "but it was he who kept his head, as they say. 'And the papers,' said he. 'Were they on him?' 'No,' says the doctor. 'Then,' said the German gentleman, 'get him upstairs. No one must leave the house till we get back the papers.' 'Don't let anyone know he's dead, then,' said Mr. Gideon. 'Say it's heart attack—anything you like.' 'There's blood about,' said Dr. Whitby—'bound to be.' 'Then clear it up,' says Mr. Gideon. 'I'll help you. We must hurry before the lights go up.'"

On the last word her voice sank to a whisper, but the stagey horror with which she was trying to invest the story did not detract from the real gruesomeness of the tale. Rather it added to it, making the scene down in the lamplit panelled room seem suddenly clear and very near to them.

Meggie shuddered and her voice was subdued and oddly breathless when she spoke.

"What happened then?"

Mrs. Meade drew herself up, and her little black eyes burned with the fire of righteousness.

"Then I could hold my tongue no longer," she said, "and I spoke out. 'Whoso killeth any person, the murderer shall be put to death by the mouth of witnesses,' I said, and stepped out from behind the screen."

Abbershaw's eyes widened as the scene rose up in his mind—the fanatical old woman, her harsh voice breaking in upon the three crooks in that first moment of their bewilderment.

"They were terrified, I suppose," he said.

Mrs. Meade nodded, and an expression of grim satisfaction spread over her wrinkled old face.

"They *was*," she said. "Mr. Gideon went pale as a sheet, and shrank away from me like an actor on the stage—Dr. Whitby stood there stupid like, his eyes gone all fishy and his mouth hanging open..." She shook her head. "You could see there was guilt there," she said, "if not in deed, in the *heart*—the German gentleman was the only one to stay his natural colour."

"And then?" Meggie hardly recognized her own voice, so toneless was it.

"Then he come up to me," the old woman continued, with a return of indignation in her voice. "Slowly he come and put his great heavy face close to mine. 'You be off,' said I, but that didn't stop him. 'How much have you heard?' said he. 'All of it,' says I, 'and what's more I'm going to bear witness.' "

Mrs. Meade took a deep breath.

"That did it," she said. "He put his hand over my mouth and the next moment Dr. Whitby had jumped forward and opened the cupboard by the fire-place. 'Put her in here,' said he; 'we can see to her after we've got *him* upstairs.'

"You struggled, of course," said Abbershaw. "It's extraordinary someone in the house didn't hear you."

Mrs. Meade regarded him with concentrated scorn.

"Me struggle, young man?" she said. "Not me. If there's going to be any scrabbling about, I said to myself, better leave it to my son who knows something about fighting, so as soon as I knew where I was I hurried up the stairs and shut myself in here. 'You can do what you like,' I said to the German gentleman through the door, 'but I'm staying here until Wednesday if needs be, when my son'll come for me—then there'll be summat to pay, I can tell you!'"

She paused, her pale cheeks flushing with the fire of

battle, as she remembered the incident. "He soon went away after that," she went on, wagging her head. "He turned the key on me, but that didn't worry me—I had the bolts on my side."

"But you couldn't get out?" interrupted Meggie, whose brain failed before this somewhat peculiar reasoning.

"O' course I couldn't get out," said Mrs. Meade vigorously. "No more'n could he come in. As long as my tongue's in my head someone'll swing for murder, and I'm quite willing to wait for my son on Wednesday. They won't get in to me to kill me, I reckon," she continued, with a flicker of pleasure in her eyes, "and so when my son comes along there'll be someone to help cast out the wicked. I ain't a-holding my tongue, not for nobody."

"And that's all you know, then?" said Meggie.

"All?" Mrs. Meade's tone was eloquent. "Some people'll find it's quite enough. Those three didn't actually do the murder, but there's someone in the house who did, and—" She broke off sharply and glanced from one to the other. "Why're you two lookin' at one 'nother so?" she demanded.

But she got no reply to her question. Meggie and Abbershaw were regarding each other fixedly, the same phrase in the old woman's remark had struck both of them, and to each it bore the same terrible significance. "Those three didn't actually do the murder, but there's someone in the house who did." Dawlish, Gideon, Whitby were cleared of the actual crime in one word; the servants were all confined in their own quarters—Albert Campion insisted that he locked the door upon them. Who then could be responsible? Albert Campion himself—or one of their own party? Neither spoke—the question was too terrifying to put into words.

CHAPTER SEVENTEEN

In the Evening

THE DISTURBING DISCOVERY which Meggie and Abbershaw had made in Mrs. Meade's story silenced them for some time. Until the old woman's extraordinary announcement ten minutes before, the division between the sheep and the goats had been very sharply defined. But now the horrible charge of murder was brought into their own camp. On the face of it, either Albert Campion or one of the young people in the house-party must be the guilty person.

Of course there was always the saving hope that in his haste Campion had locked one of the servants out instead of confining them all to their quarters as he had intended. But even so, neither Abbershaw nor the girl could blind themselves to the fact that in the light of present circumstances the odds were against the murderer lying in that quarter.

The entire staff of the house was employed by von Faber or his agents, that is to say that they were actually of the gang themselves. Coombe was an asset to them—it was not in their interest to kill him.

And yet, on the other hand, if the gang had not committed the murder they certainly covered up all traces of it. Mrs. Meade's story had deepened the mystery instead of destroying it.

Meggie looked at Abbershaw.

"If we could only get out," she murmured. Abbershaw nodded briskly. Conjectures and theories could wait until afterwards; the main business in hand at the moment was escape, if not out of the house at least back to the others.

He turned to the old woman.

"I don't suppose there's any chance of getting out through there?" he suggested, indicating the inner room in the doorway of which she still stood.

She shook her head.

"There's nobbut a fire-place and a door," she said, "and you'll not get through the door because I've bolted it and he's locked it. You can have a look at the fire-place if you like, but the chimney'll only land you up on the roof even if you could get up it; best wait till Wednesday till my son comes."

Abbershaw was inclined to enlighten her on the chances her son was likely to have against the armed Herr von Faber, but he desisted, and contented himself by shaking his head. Meggie, ever practical, came forward with a new question.

"But do you eat? Have you been starved all this time?" she said.

Mrs. Meade looked properly aggrieved.

"Oh, they bring me my victuals," she said; "naturally."

Apparently the event of her being starved out of her stronghold had not occurred to her. "Lizzie Tiddy brings me up a tray night and morning."

"Lizzie Tiddy?" Abbershaw looked up inquiringly. "Who's that?"

A smile, derisive and unpleasant, spread over the wrinkled face. "She's a natural," she said, and laughed.

"A natural?"

"She's not right in her head. All them Tiddy' s are a bit crazed. Lizzie is the wust."

"Does she work here?" Meggie's face expressed her disapproval.

Mrs. Meade's smile broadened into a grin, and her quick eyes rested on the girl.

"That's right. No one else wouldn't ha' had her. She helps Mrs. Browning, the housekeeper, washes up and such-like."

"And brings up the food?" There was an eagerness in Abbershaw's tone. An idiot country girl was not likely to offer much resistance if they made an attempt to escape as soon as she opened the door.

Mrs. Meade nodded.

"Ah, Lizzie brings up the tray," she said. "She sets it on the floor while she unlocks my door, then I pull the bolts back and open it ever such a little, and then I pull the tray in."

It was such a simple procedure that Abbershaw's spirits rose.

"When does this happen?" he said. "What time of day?"

"Half after eight in the morning and half after eight at night."

He glanced at his watch.

"She's due now, then, practically?"

Mrs. Meade glanced up at the window. "Shouldn't be at all surprised," she agreed. "Light looks about right. I'll go back to my own room, then, if you don't mind. Best not to let anybody know that I've been havin' any truck wi' you."

On the last word she turned her back on him, and after closing the door, connecting the two rooms, silently, they heard her softly pressing the bolts home.

"What an extraordinary old woman," whispered Meggie. "Is she mad, do you think?"

Abbershaw shook his head.

"No," he said. "I almost wish she were. But she's certainly not crazy, and I believe every word of her story is absolutely true.

My dear girl, consider—she certainly hasn't the imagination to invent it."

The girl nodded slowly.

"That's true," she said, and added suddenly, "but, George you don't really believe that those dreadful men didn't kill Colonel Coombe?"

Abbershaw looked at her seriously.

"I don't see why they should, do you?" he asked. "Think of it in the light of what we know."

"Then that means that either Albert Campion or—oh, George, it's horrible!"

Abbershaw's face grew even more serious.

"I know," he said, and was silent for a minute or so. "But that is not what is worrying me at the moment," he went on suddenly, as though banishing the thought from his mind. "I've got you into this appalling mess, and I've got to get you out of it—and that, unless I'm mistaken, is Lizzie Tiddy coming up the stairs now."

The girl held her breath, and for a moment or two they stood silent, listening. There was certainly the sound of footsteps on the stone landing outside, and the uneasy rattle of crockery on an unsteady tray. Abbershaw's hand closed round the girl's arm.

"Now," he whispered, "keep behind me, and at your first opportunity nip out of here into the room immediately on your left and go straight for the chest I told you of. You can't miss it. It's in the corner and enormous. I'll follow you."

The girl nodded, and at the same moment the key turned in the lock, and whatever hopes Abbershaw had entertained vanished immediately. The door opened some two inches, and there appeared in the aperture the muzzle of a revolver.

Abbershaw groaned. He might have known, he told himself bitterly, that their captors were not absolute fools. The girl clung to him and he could feel her heart beating against his arm. Gradually the door opened wider, and a face appeared above the gun. It was the stranger whom Dawlish had addressed as Wendon on the day before. He stood grinning in at them, the gun levelled directly at Meggie.

"Any monkey-tricks and the girl goes first," he said. "It's the Guvnor's orders. He's reserving you, mate, for 'is own personal attention. That's one of the reasons why he's feeding you. Now then, my girl, push the tray under and hurry about it."

The last remark was addressed to someone behind him, although he never for a moment took his eyes off Abbershaw and the girl. There was a scuffling in the passage outside, and then a narrow tray appeared upon the floor. It came sliding towards them through the crack in the door, and Abbershaw was suddenly conscious of a pair of idiot eyes, set in a pale, vacant face, watching him from behind it.

His impulse was to leap forward and risk the revolver, but the man had him helpless since it was Meggie whom he covered. Slowly the door closed, and on the moment that the gun disappeared Abbershaw sprang forward fiercely, but it was a forlorn hope. The heavy door slammed to, and they heard the lock shoot home.

There was food on the tray: a pile of sandwiches, and a jug of water. Meggie stood listening for a moment, then she whispered sharply:

"George, they don't take the same precautions with her. Perhaps if we got in there we could get past them."

Abbershaw darted across the room to the other door, then his face changed.

"She's bolted us out, of course," he said, "and besides, we're too late now. We must wait till they come this evening. Oh, my dear, I'm so sorry I got you into all this."

The girl smiled at him, but she did not reply, and presently, since in spite of their precarious position they were very hungry, they sat down and began to eat.

And then the long weary day dragged on. Mrs. Meade did not seem to be inclined for further conversation, and they knew that sooner or later Dr. Whitby and the man who had driven him must return, and the red-leather wallet be identified. What would happen then they could only conjecture, but since Dawlish was already prejudiced against Abbershaw he was not likely to be unmoved when he discovered the story of the burning of the papers to be true.

But it was Meggie's position that chiefly disturbed Abbershaw. Whatever they did to him, they were not likely to let her return to civilization knowing what she did about them. The others, after all, so far as Dawlish knew, realized little or nothing of the true position. Campion had succeeded in convincing them that he was no more than the fool he looked, and they knew nothing of his disclosures to Abbershaw and Prenderby.

The chances, therefore, were against them releasing the girl, and Abbershaw's brain sickened at the thought of her possible fate. Escape was impossible, however, and there was nothing in the room that could in any way be manufactured into a weapon. The window, even had it been large enough to permit a man's climbing through it, looked out on to a sheer drop of seventy feet on to the flags below.

There seemed nothing for it but to settle down and wait for Dawlish to make the next move.

As the morning passed and then afternoon without any change, save for a few martial and prophetic hymns from Mrs. Meade, their spirits sank deeper than ever; and it grew dark.

Clearly Whitby had not yet returned, and Abbershaw reflected that he might quite possibly have experienced some trouble with the cremation authorities, in which case there were distinct chances of the police coming to their rescue. He wondered, if that occasion should arise, what Dawlish would do—if he would remove Meggie and himself, or simply make a dash for it with his own gang, risking detection afterwards.

On the face of it, he reflected, as he considered what he knew of the man, both from what he had heard and his own experience, the chances were against Meggie and himself being left to tell their story. The prospects looked very black.

And then, quite suddenly, something happened that set his heart beating wildly with new hope, and made him spring to his feet with Meggie at his side, their eyes fixed upon the door, their ears strained to catch every sound.

From inside the room where Mrs. Meade had fortified herself, there came an extraordinary sound.

A gentle scraping followed by a burst of shrill indignation from the old woman herself, and the next moment, clear and distinct, a slightly nervous falsetto voice said briskly, "It's all right, my dear madam, I'm not from the assurance company."

Meggie grasped Abbershaw's arm.

"Albert Campion!" she said.

Abbershaw nodded: the voice was unmistakable, and he moved over to the inner door and tapped upon it gently.

"Campion," he called softly, "we're in here."

"That's all right, old bird, I'm coming. You couldn't call the old lady off, could you?"

Campion's voice sounded a little strained.

"She seems to think I'm not the sort of person you ought to know. Can't you tell her that many a true heart beats beneath a ready-made suit?"

"Mrs. Meade."

Abbershaw raised his voice a little.

"Mr. Campion is a friend of ours. Could you let him in to us?"

"You keep strange company," came the woman's strident voice from the other side of the door. "A man that creeps down a chimney upon a body isn't one that I'd put up with."

Abbershaw and Meggie exchanged glances. Apparently Mr. Campion had descended from the skies.

Then the absurd voice came out to them again, raised a little in indignation.

"But even if your son is coming, my dear old bird," he was saying, "there's really no reason why my friends and I should not meet before that happy moment. After all, I too have a mother." The exact significance of his last remark was not apparent, but it seemed to work like a charm upon the old woman, and with a few mumbled words she opened the door, and Albert Campion stood upon the threshold, beaming at them.

"I don't think I'll come in," he said cheerfully. "This lady seems crazy for me to meet her son and I'm afraid that she may compel me to do so by locking me in with you if I get far enough out of the room for her to shut this door. And as the laddie is not expected to call till Wednesday, I don't want him to get his diploma from me in person. I think if you're both ready, we'll all go back the way I came."

"Down the chimney?" said Meggie, in some trepidation.

"Through the chimney," corrected Campion, with pride. "I've been fooling about all day trying to find the 'money-back' handle—and now I've got the two coppers," he added brightly, grinning at the two red-headed young people before him. "You can't possibly dislike puns more than I do," he went on hastily. "Let's get back, shall we? This is an unhealthy spot."

They followed him into the old woman's room. She stood glaring at them suspiciously with her little bright eyes.

"Where are you going?" she demanded. "I don't know as 'ow I ought to let ye go."

"Aren't you coming with us?" said Meggie quickly. "Surely you want to get away from those dreadful men at once? You'll be much safer with us."

"What? And miss seeing my son beat 'em up?" said Mrs. Meade contemptuously. "Not me, miss. Besides," she added sharply, "I don't know as I'm not safer with the German gentleman than I am with a natural." She pointed to Campion suggestively. "Lizzie Tiddy's not the only half-wit in this house. Chimney-climbing—!" Her remark reminded them, as they turned to where an old stone fire-place, wide and primitive, stood on one side of the small room. It seemed at first utterly impracticable as a means of exit, but Campion led them over to it with a certain pride.

"Look," he said. "It's so simple when you think of it. The same chimney serves for both this room and the room behind it, which is no other, ladies and gentlemen, than the one which Mr. Campion performed his now famous disappearing trick in. Admission fourpence. Roll up in your hundreds. In fact," he went on more seriously, "virtually speaking, both rooms have the same fire-place separated only by this little wall arrangement—quite low, you see—to divide the two grates, and topped by a thin sheet of iron to separate the flames."

He paused, and surveyed them owlishly through his horn-rimmed spectacles. "I discovered, all by myself and with no grown-up aid, that this natty device was removable. I lifted it out, and stepped deftly into the presence of this lady on my right, whose opening remark rather cooled my ardour."

"I said 'The wicked shall be cast into hell,' " put in Mrs. Meade, "and so they shall. Into a burning fiery furnace, same as if that grate there was piled up with logs and you atop of them."

This remark was addressed to Abbershaw, but she turned

with tremendous agility upon Campion. "*And* the fools," she said, "the Lord 'isself couldn't abide fools."

Campion looked a little hurt.

"Something tells me," he said in a slightly aggrieved tone, "that I am not, as it were, a popular hero. Perhaps it might be as well if we went. You'll bolt your door again, won't you?" he added, turning to the old woman.

"You may lay I will," said she meaningly.

"Are you sure you won't come with us?"

It was Meggie who spoke, and the old woman eyed her less fiercely than she had done the others.

"Thank you, I'll bide where I am," she said. "I know what I'm up to, which is more than you do, I reckon, trapezing round with a pair of gorbies."

Campion touched the girl's arm.

"Come," he said softly. "I thought I heard someone. I'll go first, then you follow me."

He stepped up on the stone hob as he spoke, and then swung his leg over the brick back of the grate which they now saw was little over three feet high, and disappeared out of sight. Meggie followed him, and Abbershaw sprang after her. Within three minutes they had emerged into the box-room and Campion raised the lid of the chest in the far corner.

Meggie suffered herself to be led down the dusty passage, Campion in front of her, and Abbershaw behind.

As they went, they heard the cracked voice of Mrs. Meade chanting vigorously to herself:

"While the wicked are confounded
Doomed to flames of woe unbounded,
Call me with Thy saints surrounded.
Ah–ha–Ha–ha–men."

CHAPTER EIGHTEEN

Mr. Kennedy's Council

When ALBERT CAMPION AND HIS TWO REFUGEES crawled out at the far end of the passage, they found the cupboard door open and the entire crowd assembled in the bedroom without, waiting for them. Anne Edgeware threw herself across the room towards Meggie with a little squeaky cry that was part sympathy, part relief. Prenderby's little Jeanne had not been a reassuring companion.

The strain of the last twenty-four hours had told upon them all. The atmosphere in the wide, old-fashioned room was electric, and Campion's somewhat foolish voice and fatuous expression struck an incongruous note.

"Goods as per instructions," he said brightly, as he scrambled out of the cupboard. "Sign along the dotted line please."

As soon as they were all in the room, however, he shut the cupboard door carefully; betraying that he was especially anxious that no sound should percolate through into the little box-room they had just left.

Chris Kennedy was the first to speak. He was a little flushed, and there was an air of suppressed excitement about him that showed that his wounded arm no longer damped his spirits.

"Now we're all here," he said, "we can get right down to this thing and work out a scheme to get us out of here and those customers what they deserve. I'm for a fight."

"Here, I say, hold on a minute, my son," drawled Martin Watt, "let's all start fair. What have you two lost souls been up to first of all?" he went on, turning to Meggie and Abbershaw. "How did our little Albert get hold of you? No bickering, I hope?"

"No, all done by kindness," said Mr. Campion cheerfully; "there was only one dragon in my path, a female of the species, and full of good words. Most of them new to me," he added thoughtfully. The portion of Abbershaw's story which the little doctor felt inclined to tell did not take very long. The others also had had their adventures; Martin Watt seemed to have instituted himself spokesman, and as soon as the other had finished he began.

"We've had sport, too, in our own way. Old Dachshund Dawlish has had us up one at a time, you know, heard our catechism and our family history, searched our pockets and let us go again. He has also locked us all up in the central big hall and had another go at our rooms. Old Prenderby tried to square a servant and got the business end of a gun in his tummy by way of retort. The girls have been overhauled by a ghastly old housekeeper woman and a loony maid. And last but not least, we had a confidential lecture from Gideon, who gave us the jolliest little character-sketch of his pal that one can imagine."

He paused, and a faint smile at the recollection passed over his indolent face.

"According to him, the old boy is a cross between Mr. Hyde, Gilles de Rais, and Napoleon, but without the finesse of any of the three. On the whole I'm inclined to agree with him," he continued, "but a fat lot of good it's doing him or us, for that matter, because he can't find his package and we can't get home to our mommas. I told him that, but he didn't seem to see the argument. I'm afraid he's rather a stupid man."

Abbershaw nodded.

"Perhaps he is," he said, "but at the same time he's a very dangerous one. I may as well tell you fellows," he went on, with sudden determination in his grey eyes, "there's something that's on my conscience. I had those papers—they were papers, as a matter of fact—the first morning we were down here, and I burnt them. I told him what I'd done when I went in to see him yesterday, but he wouldn't believe me."

He paused and looked round him. Campion's pale eyes were goggling behind his enormous spectacles, and Wyatt met Abbershaw's appealing glance sympathetically. The rest were more surprised than anything else, and, on the whole, approving.

Campion voiced the general thought.

"Do you know what they were—the papers, I mean?" he said, and there was something very like wonderment in his tone. Abbershaw nodded.

"They were all written in code, but I had a pretty shrewd idea," he said, and he explained to them the outline of his ideas on the subject.

Campion listened to him in silence, and when he had finished glanced across and spoke softly.

"You burnt them?" he said dreamily, and then remarked, as if he had switched on to an entirely new subject, "I wonder if the smoke from five hundred thousand pounds in notes looks any different from any other sort of firing."

Abbershaw glanced at him sharply.

"Five hundred thousand pounds?" he said.

"Why not?" said Campion lightly. "Half a crown here, half a crown there, you know. It soon tells up."

The others turned to him, attributing the remark to his usual fatuity, but Abbershaw met the pale eyes behind the big spectacles steadily and his apprehension increased. It was not likely that Mr. Campion would be far out in his estimation since he knew so much about the affair.

Five hundred thousand pounds. The colossal sum brought home to him the extent of the German's loss, and he understood the crook's grim determination to recover the lost plans. He had not thought that the men were playing for such great stakes. In a flash he saw the situation as it really was, and his next words were sharp and imperative.

"It's more important than I can say that we should get out of here," he said. "In fact we've *got* to get out of here at once. Of course I know it's been the idea all along, but now it's imperative. At any moment now Whitby may return, and Dawlish will be convinced that I told him the truth yesterday. And then heaven only knows what he will do. Our one hope is to get out before Whitby comes back."

"There's only one way, I've been saying it all along." It was Chris Kennedy who spoke. He was seated on the end of the bed, his knees crossed, and his young face alert and eager. "We shall have to make a straight fight for it," he said. "It's our only hope. No one trying to sneak out on his own to inform the local Bobby would have an earthly. I've thought of that. They'd spot us and we know they don't mind shooting."

"There's a suit of armour in the hall," suggested Campion suddenly. "I'll put it on and toddle forth into the night, if you like. They could pot at me as much as they pleased. How about that?"

Abbershaw glanced at him sharply, but there was no trace of a sneer on the pleasant vacuous face, and he looked abashed when Kennedy spoke a little brutally.

"Sorry," he said, without looking round, "we haven't got time for that sort of stuff now. We're in a devilish unpleasant situation and we've got to get the girls and ourselves out of it. I tell you, a straight fight is the only thing for it. Look here, I've got it all taped. We've got our first chance coming in a moment. We've had dinner every night so far, so I expect we can reasonably suppose that we'll get it again tonight. Two fellows wait on us then. They're both armed, we know, and judging from the way they treated Michael they know how to use their guns all right."

"Why, they're not very tricky, are they?" said Mr. Campion, a faint expression of surprise appearing in his face. "I understood you just pressed the trigger and—pop!—off it went."

Chris Kennedy granted him one withering look and went on with his scheme.

"There's only one way to handle these customers, therefore," he said. "The first thing is to overpower those two and get their guns. Six of us ought to be able to do that. Then the two best shots had better take those revolvers and scout round for the others. The important thing is, of course, that the first bit of work is done in absolute silence. I believe that once we get those two guns we can lay 'em all by the heels. We shall be prepared, we shall be organized—they won't. What do you say?"

There was a moment or two of silence. Martin Watt was the first to speak.

"Well, I'm for it," he said.

"So am I," said Wyatt quietly.

Abbershaw hesitated, and Prenderby too was silent, whilst Albert Campion remained mild and foolish-looking as if he were looking in on the scene from outside.

Abbershaw was thinking of Meggie. Prenderby too had his fiancée clinging to his arm. Mr. Campion appeared to be thinking of nothing at all.

"After all, it does seem to be our only chance."

It was Prenderby who spoke, and the words stirred Abbershaw.

What the boy said was perfectly true. He turned to Kennedy.

"All right," he said, "I'm with you."

Kennedy looked pointedly at Albert.

"And you?" he said.

Albert shook his head. "Oh, I'm not standing out," he said. "I don't like these rough games, but I don't shirk them when they're thrust on me. What do we all do?"

Mr. Kennedy appeared to have the whole plan clear in his mind.

"It's quite simple," he said, leaning his chin in his unwounded hand and bending forward, an intent expression in his eyes.

"Let *me* shape your career for you!" quoted Mr. Campion brightly. Kennedy reddened angrily and dropped the pose, but he went on doggedly.

"My idea," he said, "is that three go down to dinner with the girls. I'm afraid they'll have to come or the men will smell a rat. They start food, and the other three fellows wait outside the door until one of their laddies is at work on the side table and the other serving the dishes at the big table. At that moment someone knocks a glass on to the flags. That's the signal. Then the blokes outside the door charge in and seize the carver. One of 'em gets his arm. Another stuffs a hanky in his mouth, and the third stands by to slog him over the head if necessary. Hang it, we can't go wrong like that. The only thing is they mustn't suspect us. We've got to take them by surprise. It's the simplest thing going as long as we don't make a row."

"Yes," said Mr. Campion, standing up with sudden solemnity. "A very clever idea, but what we have to ask ourselves is: Is it quite fair? Three men on to one. Come, come, we must remember that we are British, and all that. Perhaps we could each tie a hand behind our backs—or shall I offer them single combat instead?"

Chris Kennedy rose to his feet, and walking across to Mr. Campion spoke quietly but vigorously.

Mr. Campion blushed.

"I didn't think you'd take it like that. You will have it your own way, of course. I shan't say anything."

"You'd better not," said Kennedy, and walked back to his seat. "Abbershaw, you, Michael, and Mr. Campion had better go down with the girls, and Wyatt, Martin, and I will wait for the signal of the broken glass. Who's going to do that? It had better be a girl. Miss Oliphant, will you do it?"

Meggie nodded.

"As soon as one man is at the carving-table and the other serving us," she said.

Kennedy smiled at her. "That's it," he said. "Now is that clear?" he went on, glancing around him, his eyes dancing with excitement. "Abbershaw, you get the bloke's arms, Prenderby, you're responsible for gagging the sportsman!—"

"Yes?" said Campion, who was apparently gibbering with excitement. "And what can I do?"

"You stand by," said Kennedy, with something suspiciously like a sneer on his handsome young face.

"Oh, very well," said Mr. Campion, looking considerably disappointed. "I'll stand ready to dot the fellow with a bottle if necessary."

"That's the idea," agreed Chris Kennedy somewhat grudgingly, and returned to the others. "Of course," he said, "it'll be a bit of a shock for the two lackey-thugs to see you all turning up bright and happy after your adventures; still, I think the idea is to walk in as if nothing had ever happened. You can indulge in a certain amount of bright conversation if you like, to put them off the scent. That's where you'll come in useful," he added, turning to Campion. "Talk as much as you like. That's the time to be funny."

"Righto," said Mr. Campion, brightening visibly. "I'll show them my two-headed penny. I'll be awfully witty. 'They laughed when I sat down at the piano, but when I began to play they knew at once that I had taken Kennedy's Patent Course. How they cheered me on—' "

"Oh, shut up," said Martin Watt, grinning good-naturedly. "The fun starts at dinner, then. Oh, and by the way, when we've pinched these fellows' guns, what do we do with the laddies? Leave them lying about?"

"I've thought of that," said the indefatigable Kennedy; "we tie 'em up. I've been collecting portmanteau straps. That'll do it, you'll find. We'll lash 'em both into chairs and leave 'em there."

"Yes," said Martin, "and next? When we've fixed up all that, what happens next?"

"Then somebody takes charge of the girls," said Kennedy. "They lock themselves in some safe room—Miss Oliphant's bedroom just at the head of the stairs, for instance. Then the rest of us form into two parties with a revolver each and storm the servants' quarters, where, with a certain amount of luck, we shall get another gun or two. Then we can let out at some of these lads who amble round keeping an eye on us after dinner. We'll tie 'em up and raid old Dawlish's quarters."

He paused and looked round him, smiling.

"As soon as we've got everyone accounted for, we get the girls and sheer out of the house in a body. How's that?"

"Sounds lovely," said Mr. Campion, adding after a pause, "so simple. It'll be rather awkward if someone makes a noise, though, won't it? I mean you might have the entire gang down on you at the one-gun-per-three-men stage."

Kennedy snapped at him. He was thoroughly tired of Mr. Campion's helpful suggestions.

"There just hasn't got to be any noise," he said, "that's the point.

And by the way, I think you're the man to stay with the girls."

There was no mistaking his inference, but to Abbershaw's surprise Mr. Campion seemed to jump at the idea.

"Righto," he said, "I shall be delighted."

Chris Kennedy's answering remark was cut short, rather fortunately, Abbershaw felt, by a single and, in the circumstances, highly dramatic sound—the deep booming of the dinner gong.

CHAPTER NINETEEN

Mr. Campion's Conjuring Trick

THE SIX YOUNG PEOPLE went down to the big dining-hall with a certain amount of trepidation. Jeanne clung to Prenderby, the other two girls stuck together, and Abbershaw was able to have a word or two with Mr. Campion.

"You don't like the idea?" he murmured.

The other shrugged his shoulders.

"It's the risk, my old bird," he said softly. "Our pugilistic friend doesn't realize that we're not up against a gang of racecourse thugs. I tried to point it out to him but I'm afraid he just thought I was trying to be funny. People without humor always have curious ideas on that subject. However, it may come off. It'll be the last thing he'll expect us to do, anyway, and if you really have burnt that paper it's the best thing we could do."

"I suppose you think I'm a fool," said Abbershaw, a little defiantly. Campion grinned.

"On the contrary, young sir, I think you're a humorist. A trifle unconscious, perhaps, but none the worse for that."

Their conversation ended abruptly, for they had reached the foot of the staircase and were approaching the dining-room.

The door stood open, and they went in to find the table

set for all nine of them, and the two men who had acted as footmen during the week-end awaiting their coming. They sat down at the table. "The others won't be a moment, but we'll start, please," said Campion, and the meal began.

For some minutes it seemed as if the funereal atmosphere which surrounded the whole house was going to damp any attempt at bright conversation that anyone might feel disposed to make, but Mr. Campion sailed nobly into the breach.

Abbershaw was inclined to wonder at him until he realized with a little shock that considering the man's profession the art of talking rubbish in any circumstances might be one of his chief stock-in-trades.

At the moment he was speaking of food. His high voice worked up to a pitch of enthusiasm, and his pale eyes widened behind his horn-rimmed spectacles.

"It all depends what you mean by eating," he was saying. "I don't believe in stuffing myself, you know, but I'm not one of those people who are against food altogether. I knew a woman once who didn't believe in food—thought it was bad for the figure—so she gave it up altogether. Horrible results, of course; she got so thin that no one noticed her around—husband got used to being alone—estrangement, divorce—oh, I believe in food. I say, have you seen my new trick with a napkin and a salt-cellar—rather natty, don't you think?"

He covered a salt-cellar with his napkin as he spoke, made several passes over it, a solemn expression on his face, and then, whisking the napery away, disclosed nothing but shining oak beneath.

His mind still on Mr. Campion's profession, Abbershaw was conscious of a certain feeling of apprehension. The salt-cellar was antique, probably worth a considerable sum.

Mr. Campion's trick was not yet over, however. A few more passes and the salt-cellar was discovered issuing from the waistcoat of the man-servant who happened to be attending to him at the time.

"There!" he said. "A pretty little piece of work, isn't it? All done by astrology. For my next I shall require two assistants, any live fish, four aspidistras, and one small packet of Gold Flake." As he uttered the last words he turned sharply to beam around the table, and his elbow caught Meggie's glass and sent it crashing to the floor.

A little breathless silence would have followed the smash had not he bounded up from his chair immediately and bent down ostensibly to gather up the fragments, jabbering the whole time. "What an idiot! What an idiot! Have I splashed your dress, Miss Oliphant? All over the floor! What a mess, what a mess! Come here, my man, here: bring a dust-pan and broom with you." He was making such a fuss and such a noise that no one had noticed the door open, and the somewhat self-conscious entry of Chris Kennedy's little band. No one, that is, save Campion, who from his place of vantage half-way under the table had an excellent view of the feet.

At the moment when Martin Watt leapt forward at the man by the carving table, Campion threw his arms round the other man-servant's legs just below the knees, and jerked him back on to the flags with an almost professional neatness. Within two seconds he was seated astride the man's chest, his knees driven into the fleshy part of his arms, whilst he stuffed a handkerchief into his mouth. Abbershaw and Prenderby hurried to his assistance and between them they strapped the man into a chair, where he sat glaring at them, speechless and impotent.

Kennedy's party, though less neat, had been quite as successful, and Chris himself, flushed with excitement, now stood with his man's loaded revolver in his hand.

"Have you got his gun?" he said, in a voice which sounded hoarse even to himself, as he indicated Campion's captive.

"No," said Abbershaw, and began his search. Two minutes later he looked up, disappointed.

"He hasn't one," he said at last, and even the man himself seemed surprised.

Kennedy swore softly and handed the gun which he held to Martin.

"You'd better have it," he said. "I'm hopeless with my right arm gone. Now, then, Campion, will you go upstairs with the girls? Abbershaw, you'd better go with them. As soon as you've seen them safely locked in the room, come back to us. We're making for the servants' quarters."

They obeyed in silence, and Abbershaw led Campion and the three girls quietly out of the room, across the hall, and up the wide staircase. On the first landing they paused abruptly. Two figures were looming towards them through the dimness ahead. It was Jesse Gideon and the heavy, red-faced man whom Abbershaw had encountered outside Dawlish's door in his search for Meggie. They would have passed in silence had not Gideon spoken suspiciously in his smooth silken voice.

"Dinner is over early?" he said, fixing his narrow glittering eyes on Meggie.

She replied coldly that it was, and made as if to pass on up the stairs, but Gideon evidently intended to prolong the conversation, for he glided in front of her so that he and the surly ruffian beside him barred her progress up the stairs from the step above the one on which she was standing.

"You are all so eager," Gideon continued softly, "that it almost looks like an expedition to me. Or perhaps it is one of your charming games of hide-and-seek which you play so adroitly," he added, and the sneer on his unpleasant face was very obvious. "You will forgive me saying so I am sure," he went on, still in the same soothing obsequious voice, "but don't you think you are trying Mr. Dawlish's patience a little too much by being so foolish in your escapades? If you are wise you will take my advice and keep very quiet until it pleases him to release you."

He spoke banteringly, but there was no mistaking the warning behind his words, and it was with some eagerness that Abbershaw took Meggie's arm and piloted her between the two men. His one aim at the moment was to get the girl safely to her room.

"We understand you perfectly, Mr. Gideon," he murmured. Gideon's sneer deepened into a contemptuous smile and he moved aside a little to let them pass. Abbershaw deliberately ignored his attitude. He wanted no arguments till the girls were safe. They were passing silently, therefore, when suddenly from somewhere beneath them there sounded, ugly and unmistakable, a revolver shot.

Instantly Gideon's smiling contempt turned to a snarl of anger as all his suspicions returned—verified.

"So it is an expedition, is it?" he said softly. "A little explanation, if you please."

Abbershaw realized that once again they were caught, and a feeling of utter dejection passed over him.

Suddenly from the darkness behind him a high, rather foolish voice that yet had a certain quality of sternness in it said quickly, "Don't talk so much. Put 'em up!"

While Abbershaw stood looking at them, Gideon and his burly companion, with mingled expressions of rage and amazement on their faces, raised their hands slowly above their heads.

"Quick, man, get their guns!"

The words were uttered in Abbershaw's ear by a voice that was still vaguely foolish. He obeyed it instantly, removing a small, wicked little weapon from Gideon's hip pocket and a heavy service revolver from the thug's.

"Now then, turn round. Quick march. Keep 'em right up. I'm a dangerous man and I shoot like hell."

Abbershaw glanced round involuntarily, and saw what Gideon and his companions must have done some minutes before—Albert Campion's pleasant, vacuous face, pale and curiously in earnest in the faint light, as he peered at them from behind the gleaming barrel of a heavy Webley.

"Shove the girls in their room. Give Miss Oliphant the little pistol, and then come with me," he murmured to Abbershaw, as the strange procession set off up the stairs.

"Steady," he went on in a louder voice to the two men in front of him. "No fancy work. Any noise either of you makes will be voluntary suicide for the good of the cause. It'll mean one man less to tie up, anyway. I'm taking them up to my room," he murmured to Abbershaw. "Follow me there. They're slippery beggars and two guns are better than one."

Abbershaw handed Gideon's little revolver to Meggie, which she took eagerly.

"We'll be all right," she whispered. "Go on after him. They're terrible people."

"For God's sake wait here till we come, then," he whispered back. She nodded, and for a moment her steady brown eyes met his.

"We will, old dear. Don't worry about us. We're all right."

She disappeared into the room with Jeanne and Anne Edgeware, and Abbershaw hurried after Campion considerably reassured. Meggie was a wonderful girl.

He reached Campion just in time to get the bedroom door open and to assist him to get the two into the room. "Now," said Campion, "it's getting infernally dark, so we'll have to work fast. Abbershaw, will you keep watch over these two gentlemen. I'm afraid you may have to fire at the one on the right, he's swearing so horribly—while I attend to Mr. Gideon's immediate needs. That worthy enthusiast, Chris Kennedy, has pinched all my straps, and though I hate to behave as no guest should, I'm afraid there's no help for it. The Black Dudley linen will have to go."

As he spoke he stripped the clothes from the great four-poster bed, and began to tear the heavy linen sheets into wide strips. "If you could persuade Mr. Gideon to stand with his back against the post of this bed," he remarked at length, "I think something might be done for him. Hands still up, please."

Ten minutes later, a silent mummy-like figure, stretched against the bedpost, arms bandaged to the wood high above his head, an improvised gag in his mouth, was all that remained of the cynical little foreigner.

Mr. Campion seemed to have a touch of the professional in all he did. He stood back to survey his handiwork with some pride, then he glanced at their other captive.

"Heavy, unpleasant-looking bird," he remarked. "I'm afraid he's too heavy for the bed. Isn't there something we can shove him into?"

He glanced round the room as he spoke, and their captive fancied that Abbershaw's eyes followed his, for he suddenly lunged forward and caught the doctor, who was unused to such situations, round the ankles, sending him sprawling. The heavy gun was thrown out of Abbershaw's hand and the thug reached out a great hairy fist for it.

He was quick, but Campion was before him. With a sudden cat-like movement he snatched up the weapon, and as the other came for him, lunging forward, all his ponderous weight behind his fist, Campion stepped back lightly and then, raising his arm above his head, brought down the butt of the pistol with all his strength upon the close-shaven skull.

The man went down like a log as Abbershaw scrambled to his feet, breathless and apologetic.

"My dear old bird, don't lose your Organizing Power, Directive Ability, Self-Confidence, Driving Force, Salesmanship, and Business Acumen," chattered Mr. Campion cheerfully. "In other words, look on the bright side of things. This fruity affair down here, for instance, has solved his own problem. All we have to do now is to stuff him in a cupboard and lock the door. He won't wake up for a bit yet."

Abbershaw, still apologetic, assisted him to lift the heavy figure into a hanging cupboard, where they deposited him, shutting the door and tuning the key.

"Well, now I suppose we'd better lend a hand with the devilry downstairs," said Mr. Campion, stretching himself. "I haven't heard any more shots, have you?"

"I don't know," said Abbershaw. "I fancied I heard something while you were dealing with—er—that last customer. And I say, Campion, I haven't liked to ask you before now, but where the devil did you get that gun from?"

Mr. Campion grinned from behind his enormous spectacles. "Oh, that," he said, "that was rather fortunate as it happened. I had a notion things might be awkward, so I was naturally anxious that the guns, or at least one of them, should fall into the hands of someone who knew something about bluff at any rate."

"Where did you get it from?" demanded Abbershaw. "I thought only one of those men in the dining-room had a gun?"

"Nor had they when we tackled 'em," agreed Mr. Campion. "I relieved our laddie of this one earlier on in the meal, while I was performing my incredible act with the salt-cellar, in fact. It was the first opportunity I'd had, and I couldn't resist it."

Abbershaw stared at him.

"By Jove," he said, with some admiration, "while you were doing your conjuring trick you picked his pocket."

Mr. Campion hesitated, and Abbershaw had the uncomfortable impression that he reddened slightly.

"Well," he said at last, "in a way, yes, but if you don't mind—let's call it *léger de main*, shall we?"

CHAPTER TWENTY

The Round-Up

As ABBERSHAW AND CAMPION MADE THEIR WAY SLOWLY
DOWN THE STAIRCASE to the first floor, the house seemed to be
unnaturally silent. The candles in the iron sconces had not been
lighted, and the corridors were quite dark save for a faint greyness
here and there when the open doors of a room permitted the faint
light of the stars to penetrate into the gloom.

Abbershaw touched his companion's arm.

"How about going through the cupboard passage to the
box-room and then down the staircase into Dawlish's room
through the fire-place door?" he whispered. "We might take
him by surprise." Mr. Campion appeared to hesitate. Then his
voice, high and foolish as ever, came softly through the thick
darkness.

"Not a bad notion, doctor," he said, "but we're too late
for that, I'm afraid. Hang it all, our friends' target practice
downstairs must have given the old boy a hint that something
was up. It's only natural. I think we'd better toddle downstairs
to see how the little ones progress. Walk softly, keep your gun
ready, and for heaven's sake don't shoot unless it's a case of life
or sleep perfect sleep."

On the last word he moved forward so that he was a pace or two ahead of Abbershaw, and they set off down the long corridor in single file.

They reached the head of the staircase without hindrance and paused for a moment to listen.

All beneath them was silent, the husky, creaky quiet of an old house at night, and Abbershaw was conscious of an uneasy sensation in the soles of his feet and a tightening of his collar band.

After what seemed an interminable time Campion moved on again, hugging the extra shadow of the wall, and treading so softly that the ancient wood did not creak beneath him. Abbershaw followed him carefully, the gun clenched in his hand. This sort of thing was manifestly not in his line, but he was determined to see it through as creditably as he was able. He might lack experience, but not courage.

A sudden stifled exclamation from Mr. Campion a pace or so ahead of him made him start violently, however; he had not realized how much the experience of the past forty-eight hours had told on his nerves.

"Look out!" Campion's voice was barely audible. "Here's a casualty."

He dropped silently as he spoke, and the next moment a little pin-prick of light from a minute electric torch fell upon the upturned face of the body upon the stairs.

Abbershaw felt the blood rise and surge in his ears as he looked down and recognized Chris Kennedy, very pale from a gash over his right temple.

"Dotted over the beam with the familiar blunt instrument," murmured Campion sadly. "He was so impetuous. Boys will be boys, of course, but—well, well, well."

"Is he dead?" Abbershaw could not see the extent of the damage, and he hardly recognized his own voice, it was so strained and horror-stricken.

"Dead?" Mr. Campion seemed to be surprised. "Oh, dear me, no—he's only out of action for a bit. Our friends here are artists in this sort of thing, and I rather fancy that so far Daddy Dawlish has decided against killing off his chicks. Of course," he went on softly, "what his attitude will be now that we've taken up the offensive deliberately I don't like to suggest. On the whole I think our present policy of complete caution is to be maintained. Hop over this—he's as safe here as anywhere—and come on."

Abbershaw stepped carefully over the recumbent figure, and advanced softly after the indefatigable Mr. Campion.

They had hardly reached the foot of the staircase, and Abbershaw was speculating upon Campion's plan of campaign, when their direction was suddenly decided for them. From the vicinity of the servant's quarters far below them on their left there came a sudden crash which echoed dully over the entire house, followed by a volley of shots and a hoarse scream as of a man in pain or terror.

Albert Campion paused abruptly.

"That's done it!" he said. "Now we've *got* to lick 'em! Come on, Doc." On the last word he darted forward, Abbershaw at his heels. The door in the recess under the stairs was shut but unlocked, and on opening it they found themselves in a narrow stone corridor with a second door at the far end.

The noise was increasing; it sounded to Abbershaw as if a pitched battle were taking place somewhere near at hand.

The second door disclosed a great stone kitchen lit by two swinging oil lamps. At first Abbershaw thought it was deserted, but a smothered sound from the far end of the room arrested him, and he turned to see a heavy, dark-eyed woman and an hysterical weak-faced girl gagged and bound to wooden kitchen chairs in the darkest corner of the room.

These must be Mrs. Browning and Lizzie Tiddy; the thought flitted through his mind and was forgotten, for

Mr. Campion was already at the second door, a heavy iron-studded structure behind which pandemonium seemed to have broken loose.

Mr. Campion lifted the iron latch, and then sprang aside as the door shot open to meet him, precipitating the man who had been cowering against it headlong into the room. It was Wendon, the man who had visited Meggie and Abbershaw in their prison room early that morning.

He struggled to his feet and sprang at the first person he caught sight of, which unfortunately for him was Campion himself. His object was a gun, but Mr. Campion, who seemed to have a peculiar aversion to putting a revolver to its right use, extricated himself from the man's hold with an agility and strength altogether surprising in one of such a languid appearance, and, to use his own words, "dotted the fellow."

It was a scientific tap, well placed and of just adequate force; Wendon's eyes rolled up, he swayed forward and crashed. Abbershaw and Campion darted over him into the doorway.

The scene that confronted them was an extraordinary one.

They were on the threshold of a great vaulted scullery or brewhouse, in which the only light came from a single wall lamp and a blazing fire in the sunken hearth. What furniture there had been in the room, a rickety table and some benches, was smashed to firewood, and lay in splinters all over the stone floor.

There were seven men in the room. Abbershaw recognized the two he had last seen bound and gagged in the dining-hall, two others were strangers to him, and the remaining three were of his own party.

Even in the first moment of amazement he wondered what had happened to their guns.

The two prisoners of the dining-room had been relieved of theirs, he knew, but then Martin Watt should be armed. Wendon, too, had had a revolver that morning, and the other two, quick-footed Cockneys with narrow suspicious eyes, should both have had weapons, surely.

Besides, there were the shots he had just heard. There was evidence of gunfire also. Michael Prenderby lay doubled up on a long, flat stone sink which ran the whole length of the place some three feet from the floor. Martin Watt, every trace of his former languidness vanished, was fighting like a maniac with one of the erstwhile prisoners in the shadow at the extreme end of the room; but it was Wyatt who was the central figure in the drama.

He stood balanced on the edge of the sink in front of Michael. The flickering firelight played on the lines of his lank figure, making him seem unnaturally tall. His longish hair was shaken back from his forehead, and his clothes were blood-stained and wildly dishevelled; but it was his face that most commanded attention. The intellectual, clever, and slightly cynical scholar had vanished utterly, and in its place there had appeared a warrior of the Middle Ages, a man who had thrown his whole soul into a fight with fanatical fury.

In his two hands he wielded a wooden pole tipped at the end with a heavy iron scoop, such as are still used in many places to draw water up out of wells. It was clearly the first thing that had come to his hand, but in his present mood it made him the most formidable of weapons. He was lashing out with it with an extraordinary fury, keeping the three men at bay as if they had been yelping dogs, and as an extra flicker from the fire lit up his face afresh it seemed to Abbershaw that it was transformed; he looked more like the Avenging Angel than a scholar with a well scoop.

Campion whipped out his gun, and his quiet high voice sounded clearly through the noise.

"Now then, now then! Put 'em up!" he said distinctly. "There's been enough fun here for this evening. Put 'em up!

I'm firing," he added quietly, and at the same moment a bullet flashed past the head of the man nearest Wyatt and struck the stone wall behind him. The effect was instantaneous. The noise ceased, and slowly the four members of Dawlish's gang raised their hands above their heads.

Gradually Wyatt's uplifted weapon sank to the ground and he dropped down off the sink and collapsed, his head between his knees, his arms hanging limply by his sides.

Martin Watt came reeling into the circle of light by the fire, somewhat battered and dishevelled but otherwise unhurt.

"Thank God you've come," he said breathlessly, and grinned. "I thought our number was up."

Mr. Campion herded his captives into a straight line along one wall.

"Now if you fellows will hold them up," he said pleasantly, "I will repeat my celebrated rope trick. For this performance I shall employ nothing less than actual rope, which I see is all ready waiting for me."

As he spoke he was unfastening the hank of clothes line which hung ready for use near the fire. He handed Martin his gun, while Abbershaw, more alert this time, held up their captives. As he corded up the four, Martin Watt, still breathless, recounted briefly the events which had led up to the scene they had just witnessed.

"We got into the kitchen first," he said. "There didn't seem to be a soul about except the women. They started to scream the place down though, so we tied 'em up. It wasn't till we'd done that that we realized that Chris wasn't with us. We guessed he'd met trouble, so we started to go back. We hadn't got half-way across the room, though, before the door burst open and a man came in."

He paused and took a deep breath.

"I told him to put up his hands or I'd fire at him," he went on jerkily, "but he didn't. He just came for me, so I did fire. I didn't hit him, of course—I didn't mean to—but the noise seemed to start things up generally. There seemed to be footsteps all round us. We didn't know where to shove the cove. The door into here seemed handy and we'd just got him inside when these four charged in on us from the kitchen passage. Michael had got the first fellow's gun by that time. He lost his head a bit, I guess, and blazed at them—shooting wildly over their heads most of the time. Then one of the fellows got him and he curled up on the sink over there with his gun underneath him. By this time, however, I'd got 'em fairly well under control, God knows how."

The boy spoke modestly, but there were indications of "how" upon the faces of their captives.

"I got them to stick up their hands," he continued, "and then I yelled to Wyatt to get their guns."

He paused, and glanced at the silent figure hunched up on the flags.

"Poor old chap," he said. "I think he went barmy— almost ran amok. He got the guns all right—there were only two of them—and before I could stop him or yell at him even, he had chucked them into that bricked-in place over there. See what it is? A darn great well—I heard them splash ages after they went in. I bawled at him, but he yelled out what sounded like "Sweet Seventeen" or something equally potty, grabbed that scoop, and began to lay about with it like a loony." He shook his head and paused for breath. "Then a foul thing happened," he went on suddenly. "One of them came for me—and I warned him I'd shoot, and finally I tried to, but the thing only clicked in my hand. The shot I had already fired must have been the last. Then we closed. When you came in the other three were trying to get at Prenderby for his gun—he was knocked out, you know—and old Wyatt was lashing round like the flail of the Lord. Then, of course, you just finished things off for us."

"A very pretty tale of love and war," murmured Mr. Campion, some of his old inanity returning. " 'Featuring Our Boys. Positively for One Night Only.' I've finished with the lads now, Doc—you might have a look at the casualties."

Abbershaw lowered his revolver, and approached Prenderby with some trepidation. The boy lay on the stone sink dangerously doubled up, his face hidden. A hasty examination, however, disclosed only a long superficial scalp wound. Abbershaw heaved a sigh of relief.

"He's stunned," he said briefly. "The bullet grazed along his temple and put him out. We ought to get him upstairs, though, I think."

"Well, I don't see why we shouldn't," said Martin cheerfully. "Hang it, our way is fairly clear now. Gideon and a thug are upstairs, you say, safely out of the way; we have four sportsmen here and one outside; that's seven altogether. Then the doctor lad and his shover are still away presumably, so there's only old Dawlish himself left. The house is ours."

"Not so eager, not so eager!" Albert Campion strolled over to them as he spoke. "Old Daddy Dawlish is an energetic bit of work, believe me. Besides, he has only to get going with his Boy Scout's ever-ready, self-expanding, patent pocketknife and the fun will begin all over again. No, I think that the doc had better stay here with his gun, his patient and the prisoners, while you come along with me. I'll take Prenderby's gun."

"Righto," said Martin. "What's the idea, a tour of the works?"

"More or less," Campion conceded. "I want you to do a spot of ambulance work. The White Hope of our side is draped tastefully along the front stairs. While you're gathering up the wreckage I'll toddle round to find Poppa von Faber, and on my way back after the argument I'll call in for the girls, and we'll all make our final exit *en masse*. Dignity, Gentlemen, and British Boyhood's Well-known Bravery, Coolness, and Distinction are the passwords of the hour."

Martin looked at him wonderingly. "Do you always talk bilge?" he said.

"No," said Mr. Campion lightly, "but I learnt the language reading advertisements. Come on."

He led the way out of the brewhouse into the kitchen, Martin following. On the threshold he paused suddenly, and an exclamation escaped him.

"What's happened?" Abbershaw darted after them, and the next moment he, too, caught his breath.

Wendon, the man Campion had laid out not ten minutes before, and left lying an inert mass on the fibre matting, had vanished utterly. Campion spoke softly, and his voice was unusually grave.

"He didn't walk out of here on his own," he said. "There's not a skull on earth that would withstand that tap I gave him. No, my sons, he was fetched." And while they looked at him he grinned.

"To be continued—evidently," he said, and added lightly, "Coming, Martin?"

Abbershaw returned to his post in the brewhouse, and, after doing all he could for the still unconscious Prenderby, settled down to await further developments.

He had given up reflecting upon the strangeness of the circumstances which had brought him, a sober, respectable London man, into such an extraordinary position, and now sat staring ahead, his eyes fixed on the grey stone wall in front of him.

Wyatt remained where he had collapsed; the others had not addressed him, realizing in some vague subconscious way that he would rather that they left him alone.

Abbershaw had forgotten him entirely, so that when he raised himself suddenly and staggered to his feet the little red-haired doctor was considerably startled. Wyatt's face was unnaturally pale, and his dark eyes had become lacklustre and without expression.

"I'm sorry," he said quietly. "I had a brain storm, I think—I must get old Harcourt Gieves to overhaul me if we ever get back to London again."

"If we ever get back?" The words started out of Abbershaw's mouth. "My dear fellow, don't be absurd! We're bound to get back some time or other." He heard his own voice speaking testily in the silence of the room, and then with a species of forced cheerfulness foreign to him. "But now I think we shall be out of the house in an hour or so, and I shall be delighted to inform the county police of this amazing outrage."

Even while he spoke he wondered at himself. The words and the voice were those of a small man speaking of a small thing—he was up against something much bigger than that.

Further conversation was cut short by the arrival of Martin with the now conscious but still dazed Kennedy. The four prisoners remained quiet, and after the first jerky word of greeting and explanation there was no sound in the brewhouse, save the crackling of the fire in the great hearth.

It was Abbershaw himself who first broke the silence. It seemed that they had waited an age, and there was still no audible movement in the house above them.

"I hope he's all right," he said nervily.

Martin Watt looked up.

"An extraordinary chap," he said slowly. "What is he?"

Abbershaw hesitated. The more he thought about Mr. Albert Campion's profession the more confused in mind he became. It was not easy to reconcile what he knew of the man with his ideas on con-men and that type of shady character in general. There was even a possibility, of course, that Campion was a murderer, but the farther away his interview with Mrs. Meade became, the more ridiculous and absurd that supposition seemed. He did not answer Martin's question, and the boy went on lazily, almost as if he were speaking to himself.

"The fellow strikes one as a congenital idiot," he said. "Even now I'm not sure that he's not one; yet if it hadn't been for him we'd all be in a nasty mess at the present moment. It isn't that he suddenly stops fooling and becomes serious, though," he went on, "he's fooling the whole time all right—he *is* a fool, in fact."

"He's an amazing man," said Abbershaw, adding as though in duty bound, "and a good fellow." But he would not commit himself further, and the silence began again.

Yet no one heard the kitchen door open, or noticed any approach, until a shadow fell over the bright doorway, and Mr. Campion, inoffensive and slightly absurd as ever, appeared on the threshold.

"I've scoured the house," he murmured, "not a soul about. Old Daddy Hun and his pal are not the birds I took them for. They appear to have vamoosed—I fancy I heard a car. Ready?"

"Did you get the women?" It was Abbershaw who spoke. Campion nodded. "They're here behind me, game as hell. Bring Prenderby over your shoulder, Watt. We'll all hang together, women in the centre, and the guns on the outside; I don't think there's anyone around, but we may as well be careful. Now for the wide open spaces!"

Martin hoisted the unconscious boy over his shoulder and Abbershaw and Wyatt supported Kennedy, who was now rapidly coming to himself, between them. The girls were waiting for them in the kitchen. Jeanne was crying quietly on Meggie's shoulder, and there was no trace of colour in Anne Edgeware's round cheeks, but they showed no signs of panic. Campion marshalled the little force into advancing order, placing himself at the head, Meggie and Jeanne behind him, with Abbershaw on one side and Martin and Anne on the other, while Wyatt and Kennedy were behind.

"The side door," said Campion. "It takes us nearest the garage—there may be some juice about now. If not, we must toddle of course. The tour will now proceed, visiting the Albert Memorial, Ciro's, and the Royal Ophthalmic Hospital..."

As he spoke he led them down the stone passage-way, out of the door under the stairs, and down the corridor to the side door, through which Abbershaw had gone to visit the garage on the fateful night of the Dagger Ritual.

"Now," he said, as with extraordinarily silent fingers he manoeuvred the ponderous bars and locks on the great door, "this is where the orchestra begins to play soft music and the circle shuffles for its hats as we fall into one another's arms— that's done it!"

On the last word the hinges creaked faintly as the heavy door swung inwards. The night was pitch dark but warm and pleasant, and they went out eagerly on the gravel, each conscious of an unspeakable relief as the realization of freedom came to them.

"My God!" The words were uttered in a sob as Campion started forward.

At the same moment the others caught a shadowy glimpse of the radiator of a great car not two yards ahead of them. Then they were enveloped in the glare of enormous headlights, which completely blinded them.

They stood dazed and helpless for an instant, caught mercilessly and held by the glare.

A quiet German voice spoke out of the brightness, cold, and inexplicably horrible in its tonelessness.

"I have covered the girl with red hair with my revolver; my assistant has the woman on the left as his aim. If there is any movement from anybody other than those I shall command, we shall both fire. Put your hands over your heads. Every-body!…So."

CHAPTER TWENTY-ONE

The Point of View of Benjamin Dawlish

IT WAS ALL OVER very quickly.

There was no way of telling if the cold merciless voice behind the blinding lights was speaking truth or no, but in the circumstances it was impossible not to regard it.

The little party stood there, hands raised above their heads; then hurrying footsteps echoed down the stone corridor behind them and their erstwhile prisoners surrounded them.

The German had lied when he spoke of his assistant, then. The man must have slipped into the house by the other door and released the men in the brewhouse.

"You will now go up to a room on the top floor to which my men will lead you. Anyone who makes the least attempt to escape will be shot instantly. By 'shot' I mean shot dead."

The voice of Benjamin Dawlish came clearly to them from behind the wall of light. The icy tonelessness which had made the voice so terrible on the first hearing was still there and Abbershaw had a vision of the expressionless face behind it, heavy and without life, like a mask.

The spirit of the little group was momentarily broken.

They had made their attempt and failed in the very moment when their success seemed assured.

Again unarmed, they were forced back into the house and placed in a room on the top floor at the far end of the long gallery where Albert Campion had had his fight with the butler. It was a long narrow room, oak-panelled, but without a fire-place, and lighted only from a single narrow iron-barred window.

Even as Abbershaw entered it, a feeling of misgiving overcame him. Other rooms had possibilities of escape; this held none.

It was completely empty, and the door was of treble oak, iron-studded. It had doubtless been used at one time as a private chapel, possibly in those times when it was wisest to hold certain religious ceremonies behind barred doors.

The only light came from a hurricane lantern which one of the men had brought up with him. He set it on the floor now so that the room was striped with grotesque shadows. The prisoners were herded down to the end of the room, two men keeping them covered the whole time.

Martin Watt set Prenderby down in a corner, and Jeanne, still crying quietly, squatted down beside him and took his head in her lap.

Abbershaw darted forward towards their captors.

"This is absurd," he said bitterly. "Either let us interview Mr. Dawlish downstairs or let him come up to us. It's most important that we should come to a proper understanding at last."

One of the men laughed.

"I'm afraid you don't know what you're talking about," he said in a curiously cultured voice. "As a matter of fact I believe Mr. Dawlish is coming up to talk to you in a moment or so. But I'm afraid you've got a rather absurd view of the situation altogether. You don't seem to realize the peculiar powers of our chief."

Wyatt leaned against the oak panelling, his arms folded

and his chin upon his breast. Ever since the incident in the brewhouse he had been peculiarly morose and silent. Mr. Campion also was unusually quiet, and there was an expression on his face that betrayed his anxiety. Meggie and Anne stood together. They were obviously very frightened, but they did not speak or move. Chris Kennedy fumed with impotent rage, and Martin Watt was inclined to be argumentative.

"I don't know what the damn silly game is," he said, "but whatever it is it's time we stopped playing. Your confounded 'Chief' may be the great Pooh-Bah himself for all I care, but if he thinks he can imprison nine respectable citizens for an indefinite period on the coast of Suffolk without getting himself into serious trouble he's barmy, that's all there is to it. What's going to happen when inquiries start being made?"

The man who had spoken before did not answer, but he smiled, and there was something very unpleasant and terrifying about that smile.

Further remarks from Martin were cut short by steps in the corridor outside and the sudden appearance of Mr. Benjamin Dawlish himself, followed by Gideon, pale and stiff from his adventure, but smiling sardonically, his round eyes veiled, and his wicked mouth drawn all over to one side in the "O" which so irritated Abbershaw.

"Now look here, sir." It was Martin Watt who spoke. "It's time you had a straight talk with us. You may be a criminal, but you're behaving like a lunatic, and—"

"Stop that, young man."

Dawlish's deep unemotional voice sounded heavily in the big room, and instantly the boy found that he had the muzzle of a revolver pressed against his ribs.

"Shut up," a voice murmured in his ear, "or you'll be plugged as sure as hell."

Martin relapsed into helpless silence, and the German continued. He was still unblinking and expressionless, his heavy red face deeply shadowed in the fantastic light. He looked at them steadily from one to the other as if he had been considering them individually, but there was no indication from his face or his manner to betray anything of his conclusions.

"So," he said, "when I look at you I see how young you all are, and it does not surprise me any longer that you should be so foolish. You are ignorant, that is why you are so absurd."

"If you've come here to be funny—" Martin burst out, but the gun against his ribs silenced him, and the German went on speaking in his inflexible voice as if there had been no interruption.

"Before I explain to you what exactly I have ordained shall happen," he said, "I have decided to make everything quite clear to you. I do this because it is my fancy that none of you should consider I have behaved in any way unreasonably. I shall begin at the beginning. On Friday night Colonel Coombe was murdered in this house while you were playing in the dark with that ancient dagger which hangs in the hall. It was with that dagger that he was killed."

This announcement was news to some of his hearers, and his quick eyes took in the expressions of the little group before him. "I concealed that murder," he continued deliberately, "because at that time there were several very excellent reasons why I should do so. It would have been of very great inconvenience to me if there had been an inquest upon Coombe, as he was in my employ, and I do not tolerate any interference, private or official, in my affairs. Apart from that, however, the affair had very little interest for me, but I should like to make it clear now that although I do not know his identity, the person who killed Gordon Coombe is in this room facing me. I say this advisedly because I know that no one entered the house from outside that night, nor has any stranger left it since, and even had they not perfect alibis there is no reason why I should credit it to one of my own people."

His inference was clear, and there was a moment of resentment among the young people, although no one spoke. The German went on with inexorable calm.

"But as I have said," he repeated, in his awkward pedantic English, "that does not interest me. What is more important to me is this. Either the murderer stole a packet of papers off the body of his victim, or else Colonel Coombe handed them at some time or other in that evening to one of you. Those papers are mine. I think I estimate their value to me at something over half one million pounds. There is one other man in the world to whom they would be worth something approaching the same value. I assume that one of you here is a servant of that man."

Again he paused, and again his small round eyes scrutinized the faces before him. Then, apparently satisfied, he continued. "You will admit that I have done everything in my power to obtain possession of these papers without harming anyone. From the first you have behaved abominably. May I suggest that you have played hide-and-seek about the house like school-children? And at last you have annoyed me. There are also one or two among you"—he glanced at Abbershaw—"with whom I have old scores to settle. You have been searched, and you have been watched, yet no trace of my property has come to light. Therefore I give you one last chance. At eleven o'clock tomorrow morning I leave this house with my staff. We shall take the side roads that will lead us on to the main Yarmouth motor way without passing through any villages. If I have my property in my possession when I go, I will see that you can contrive your release for yourselves. If not—"

He paused, and they realized the terrible thing that was coming a full second before the quiet words left his lips.

"I shall first set fire to the house. To shoot you direct would be dangerous—even charred skeletons may show traces of bullet fractures. No, I am afraid I must just leave you to the fire."

In the breathless silence that followed this announcement Jeanne's sobs became suddenly very audible, and Abbershaw, his face pale and horror-stricken, leapt forward.

"But I told you," he said passionately. "I told you. I burnt those papers. I described them to you. I burnt them—the ashes are probably in my bedroom grate now."

A sound that was half a snarl, half a cry, broke from the German, and for the second time they saw the granite composure of his face broken, and had a vision of the livid malevolence behind the mask.

"If I could believe, Dr. Abbershaw," he said, "that you could ever be so foolish—so incredibly foolish—as to destroy a packet of papers, a portion of whose value must have been evident to you, then I could believe also that you could deserve no better fate than the singularly unpleasant death which most certainly awaits you and your friends unless I am in possession of my property by eleven o'clock tomorrow morning. Good night, ladies and gentlemen. I leave you to think it over."

He passed out of the room on the last words, the smirking Gideon on his heels. His men backed out after him, their guns levelled. Abbershaw dashed after them just as the great door swung to. He beat upon it savagely with his clenched fists, but the oak was like a rock.

"Burn?" Martin's voice broke the silence, and it was almost wondering. "But the place is stone—it can't burn."

Wyatt raised his eyes slowly.

"The outer walls are stone," he said, and there was a curious note in his voice which sent a thrill of horror through everyone who heard it. "The outer walls are stone, but the rest of it is oak, old, well-seasoned oak. It will burn like kindling wood in a grate."

CHAPTER TWENTY-TWO

The Darkest Hour

"THE TIME," said Mr. Campion, "is nine o'clock."

Chris Kennedy stretched himself wearily.

"Six hours since that swine left us," he said. "Do you think we've got an earthly?"

There was a stir in the room after he had spoken, and almost everybody looked at the pale-haired bespectacled young man who sat squatting on his haunches in a corner. Jeanne and Prenderby were alone unconscious of what was going on. The little girl still supported the boy's head in her lap, with her timid little figure crouched over him, her face hidden.

Albert Campion shook his head.

"I don't know," he said, but there was no hopefulness in his tone, and once again the little group relapsed into the silence that had settled over them after the first outburst which had followed von Faber's departure.

Whatever their attitude had been before, they were all now very much alive to the real peril of their position.

Von Faber had not been wasting his time when he had spoken to them, and they had each been struck by the stark callousness which had been visible in him throughout the entire interview.

At last Campion rose to his feet and came across to where Meggie and Abbershaw were seated. Gravely he offered Abbershaw his cigarette-case in which there was a single cigarette neatly cut into two pieces.

"I did it with a razor blade," he said. "Rather neat, don't you think?"

Abbershaw took the half gratefully and they shared a match.

"I suppose," said Campion suddenly, speaking in a quiet and confidential tone, "I suppose you did really burn that junk, Doc."

Abbershaw glanced at him sharply.

"I did," he said. "God forgive me. When I think what I'm responsible for I feel I shall go mad."

Mr. Campion shrugged his shoulders.

"My dear old bird," he said, "I shouldn't put too much stress on what our friend von Faber says. He doesn't seem to me to be a person to be relied upon."

"Why? Do you think he's just trying to frighten us?"

Abbershaw spoke eagerly, and the other shook his head.

"I'm afraid not, in the sense you mean," he said. "I think he's set his heart on this little conflagration scene. The man is a criminal loony, of course. No, I only meant that probably, had someone handed over his million-dollar book of the words, the Guy Fawkes celebrations would have gone forward all the same. I'm afraid he's just a nasty vindictive person."

Meggie shuddered, but her voice was quite firm. "Do you mean to say that you really think he'll burn the house down with us up here?" she said.

Campion looked up at her, and then at Abbershaw.

"Not a nice type is he?" he murmured. "I'm afraid we're for it, unless by a miracle the villagers see the bonfire before we're part of it, or the son of our friend in the attic calls earlier than was expected."

Meggie stiffened.

"Mrs. Meade," she said. "I'd forgotten all about her. What will Mr. Dawlish do about her, do you suppose?"

Mr. Campion spoke grimly.

"I could guess," he said, and there was silence for a while after that.

"But how terrible!" Meggie burst out suddenly. "I didn't believe that people like this were allowed to exist. I thought we were civilized. I thought this sort of thing couldn't happen."

Mr. Campion sighed.

"A lot of people believe things like that," he said. "They imagine the world is a well-ordered nursery with Scotland Yard and the British Army standing by to whack anybody who quarrels or uses a naughty word. I thought that at one time, I suppose everybody does, but it's not like that really, you know. Look at me, for example—who would dream of the cunning criminal brain that lurks beneath my inoffensive exterior?"

The other two regarded him curiously. In any other circumstances they would have been embarrassed. Abbershaw was the first to speak.

"I say," he said, "if you don't mind my asking such a thing, what on earth made you take up your—er—present profession?"

Mr. Campion regarded him owlishly through his enormous spectacles.

"Profession?" he said indignantly. "It's my vocation. It seemed to me that I had no talent for anything else, but in this line I can eke out the family pittance with tolerable comfort. Of course," he went on suddenly, as he caught sight of Meggie's face, "I don't exactly 'crim,' you know, as I told the doc here. My taste is impeccable. Most of my commissions are more secret than shady. I occasionally do a spot of work for the Government, though, of course, that isn't as lucrative as honest crime. This little affair, of course, was perfectly simple. I had only to join this house-party, take a packet of letters from the old gentleman, toddle back to the Savoy, and my client would be waiting for me. A hundred guineas, and all clean fun—no brain-work required." He beamed at them. "Of course I knew what I was in for," he went on. "I knew that more or less as soon as I got down here. I didn't expect anything quite like this, though, I admit. I'm afraid the Gay Career and all that is in the soup."

He spoke lightly, but there was no callousness in his face, and it suddenly occurred to Abbershaw that he was doing his best to cheer them up, for after a moment or two of silence he remarked suddenly:

"After all, I don't see why the place should burn as he says it will, and I know people do escape from burning houses because I've seen it on the pictures."

His remarks were cut short by a thundering blow upon the door, and in the complete silence that followed, a voice spoke slowly and distinctly so that it was audible throughout the entire room.

"You have another hour," it said, "in which to restore Mr. Dawlish's property. If it is not forthcoming by that time there will be another of these old country-mansion fires which have been so frequent of late. It is not insured and so it is not likely that anyone will inquire into the cause too closely."

Martin Watt threw himself against the door with all his strength, and there was a soft amused laugh from outside.

"We heard your attempts to batter down the door last night," said the voice, "and Mr. Dawlish would like you to know that although he has perfect faith in it holding, he has taken the precaution to reinforce it considerably on this side. As you have probably found out, the walls, too, are not negotiable and the window won't afford you much satisfaction."

"You dirty swine!" shouted Chris Kennedy weakly from his corner, and Martin Watt turned slowly upon his heel and came back into the center of the room, an expression of utter hopelessness on his face.

"I'm afraid we're sunk," he said slowly and quietly and moved over towards the window, where he stood peering out between the bars.

Wyatt sat propped up against the wall, his chin supported in his hands, and his eyes fixed steadily upon the floor in front of him. For some time he had neither moved nor spoken. As Abbershaw glanced at him he could not help being reminded once again of the family portraits in the big dining-hall, and he seemed somehow part and parcel of the old house, sitting there morosely waiting for the end.

Meggie suddenly lifted her head.

"How extraordinary," she said softly, "to think that everything is going on just the same only a mile or two away. I heard a dog barking somewhere. It's incredible that this fearful thing should be happening to us and no one near enough to get us out. Think of it," she went on quietly. "A man murdered and taken away casually as if it were a light thing, and then a criminal lunatic"—she paused and her brown eyes narrowed—"I hope he's a lunatic—calmly proposes to massacre us all. It's unthinkable."

There was silence for a moment after she had spoken, and then Campion looked at Abbershaw.

"That yarn about Coombe," he said quietly. "I can't get over it. Are you sure he was murdered?"

Abbershaw glanced at him shrewdly. It seemed unbelievable that this pleasant, inoffensive-looking young man could be a murderer attempting to cast off any suspicion against himself, and yet, on the face of Mrs. Meade's story, the evidence looked very black against him.

As he did not reply, Campion went on.

"I don't understand it at all," he said. "The man was so valuable to them…he must have been."

Abbershaw hesitated and then he said quietly:

"Are you sure he was—I mean do you *know* he was?"

Campion's pale eyes opened to their fullest extent behind his enormous glasses.

"I know he was to be paid a fabulous sum by Simister for his services," he said, "and I know that on a certain day next month there was to be a man waiting at a big London hotel to meet him. That man is the greatest genius at disguise in Europe, and his instructions were to give the old boy a face-lift and one or two other natty gadgets and hand him a ticket for the first transatlantic liner, complete with passport, family history, and pretty niece. Von Faber didn't know that, of course, but even if he did I don't see why he should stick the old gentleman in the gizzard, do you? The whole thing beats me. Besides, why does he want to saddle us with the nasty piece of work? It's the sort of thing he'd never convince us about. I don't see it myself. It can't be some bright notion of easing his own conscience."

Abbershaw remained silent. He could not forget the old woman's strangely convincing story, the likelihood of which was borne out by Campion's own argument, but the more he thought about the man at his side, the more absurd did an explanation in that direction seem.

A smothered cry of horror from Martin at the window brought them all to their feet.

"The swine," he said bitterly, turning to them, his face pale and his eyes glittering. "Look. I saw Dawlish coming out of the garage towards the house. He was carrying petrol cans. He intends to have a good bonfire."

"Good God!" said Chris Kennedy, who had taken his place at the window. "Here comes a lad with a faggot. Oh, why can't I get at 'em!"

"They're going to burn us!"

For the first time the true significance of the situation seemed to dawn upon little Jeanne, and she burst into loud hysterical sobbing which was peculiarly unnerving in the tense atmosphere. Meggie crossed over to her and attempted to soothe her, but her self-control had gone completely and she continued to cry violently.

Anne Edgeware, too, was crying, but less noisily, and the tension became intolerable.

Abbershaw felt for his watch, and was about to draw it out when Albert Campion laid a hand over his warningly. As he did so his coat sleeve slipped up and Abbershaw saw the dial of the other's wrist-watch. It was five minutes to eleven.

At the same moment, however, there were footsteps outside the door again, and this time the voice of Jesse Gideon spoke from without.

"It is your last chance," he said. "In three minutes we leave the house. You know the rest. What shall I say to Mr. Dawlish?"

"Tell him to burn and to be damned to him!" shouted Martin.

"Very appropriate!" murmured Mr. Campion, but his voice had lost its gaiety, and the hysterical sobs of the girl drowned the words.

And then, quite suddenly, from somewhere far across the fields there, came a sound which everybody in the room recognized. A sound which brought them to their feet, the blood returning to their cheeks, and sent them crowding to the window, a new hope in their eyes.

It was the thin far-off call of a hunting horn.

Martin, his head jammed between the bars of the narrow window, let out a whoop of joy.

"The Hunt, by God!" he said. "Yes—Lord! There's the pack not a quarter of a mile away! Glory be to God, was that a splodge of red behind that hedge? It was! Here he comes!"

His voice was resonant with excitement, and he struggled violently as if he would force himself through the iron bars.

"There he is," he said again; "and yes, look at him—look at him! Half the county behind him! They're in the park now. Gosh! They're coming right for us. Quick! Yell to 'em! God! They mustn't go past! How can we attract them! Yell at 'em! Shout something! They'll be on us in a minute."

"I think," murmured a quiet, rather foolish voice that yet had a note of tension in its tone, "that in circumstances like this a 'view-halloo' would be permissible. Quickly! Now, are you ready, my children? Let her go!"

There was utter silence after the shout died away upon the wind, and then Campion's voice behind them murmured again:

"Once more. Put your backs into it."

The cry rang out wildly, agonizingly, a shout for help, and then again there was stillness.

Martin suddenly caught his breath.

"They've heard," he said in a voice strangled with excitement. "A chap is coming over here now."

CHAPTER TWENTY-THREE

An Error in Taste

"WHAT SHALL I SHOUT to him?" said Martin nervously, as the solitary horseman came cantering across the turf towards the house. "I can't blab out the whole story."

"Yell, 'We're prisoners,'" suggested Kennedy, "and, 'Get us out for the love of Mike.'"

"It's a young chap," murmured Martin. "Sits his horse well. Must be a decent cove. Here goes."

He thrust his head as far out of the window as the bars would permit, and his clear young voice echoed out across the grass.

"Hello! Hello! Hell-o! Up here—top window! Up here! I say, we're prisoners. A loony in charge is going to burn the house down. For God's sake give the alarm and get us out."

There was a period of silence, and then Martin spoke over his shoulder to the others:

"He can't hear. He's coming closer. He seems to be a bit of an ass."

"For heaven's sake get him to understand," said Wyatt. "Everything depends on him."

Martin nodded, and strained out of the window again.

"We're locked in here. Prisoners, I tell you. We—" he broke off suddenly and they heard him catch his breath.

"Dawlish!" he said. "The brute's down there talking to him quietly as if nothing were up."

"We're imprisoned up here, I tell you," he shouted again. "That man is a lunatic—a criminal. For heaven's sake don't take any notice of him."

He paused breathless, and they heard the heavy German voice raised a little as though with suppressed anger.

"I tell you I am a doctor. These unfortunate people are under my care. They are poor imbeciles. You are exciting them. You will oblige me by going away immediately. I cannot have you over my grounds."

And then a young voice with an almost unbelievable county accent spoke stiffly:

"I am sorry. I will go away immediately, of course. I had no idea you—er—kept lunatics. But they gave the 'view-halloo' and naturally I thought they'd seen."

Martin groaned.

"The rest of the field's coming up. The pack will be past in a moment."

Mr. Campion's slightly falsetto voice interrupted him. He was very excited. "*I* know that voice," he said wildly. "That's old 'Guffy' Randall. Half a moment."

On the last word he leapt up behind Martin and thrust his head in through the bars above the boy's.

"Guffy!" he shouted. "Guffy Randall! Your own little Bertie is behind these prison bars in desperate need of succour. The old gentleman on your right is a fly bird— look out for him."

"That's done it!"

Martin's voice was triumphant.

"He's looking up. He's recognized you, Campion. Great Scott! The Hun is getting out his gun."

At the same moment the German's voice, bellowing now in his fury, rose up to them.

"Go away. You are trespassing. I am an angry man, sir. You are more than unwise to remain here."

And then the other voice, well bred and protesting.

"My dear sir, you have a friend of mine apparently imprisoned in your house. I must have an explanation."

"Good old Guff—" began Mr. Campion, but the words died on his lips as the German's voice again sounded from the turf beneath them.

"You fool! Can none of you see when I am in earnest? Will that teach you?"

A pistol shot followed the last word, and Martin gasped.

"Good God! He hasn't shot him?" The words broke from Abbershaw in horror.

Martin remained silent, and then a whisper of horror escaped the flippant Mr. Campion.

"Shot him?" he said. "No. The unmitigated arch-idiot has shot one of the hounds. Just caught the tail end of the pack. Hullo! Here comes the huntsman with the field bouncing up behind him like Queen Victoria rampant. Now he's for it."

The noise below grew to a babel, and Albert Campion turned a pink, excited face towards the anxious group behind him.

"How like the damn fool Guffy," he said. "So upset about the hound he's forgotten me."

He returned to his look-out and the next moment his voice resounded cheerfully over the tumult.

"I think they're going to lynch Poppa von Faber. I say, I'm enjoying this."

Now that the danger was less imminent, the spirits of the whole party were reviving rapidly.

There was an excited guffaw from Martin.

"Campion," he said, "look at this."

"Coo!" said Mr. Campion idiotically, and was silent.

"The most militant old dear I've ever seen in all my life," murmured Martin aloud. "Probably a Lady Di-something-or-other. Fourteen stone if she weighs an ounce, and a face like her own mount. God, she's angry. Hullo! She's dismounting."

"She's coming for him," yelped Mr. Campion. "Oh, Inky-Pinky! God's in His Heaven, all's right with the world. She's caught him across the face with her crop. Guffy!" The last word was bellowed at the top of his voice, and the note of appeal in it penetrated through the uproar.

"Get us out! And take care for yourselves. They're armed and desperate."

"With you, my son."

The cheering voice from outside thrilled them more than anything had done in their lives before, and Martin dropped back from the window, breathless and flushed.

"What a miracle," he said. "What a heaven-sent glorious miracle. Looks as if our Guardian Angel had a sense of humour."

"Yes, but will they be able to get to us?" Meggie spoke nervously. "After all, they are armed, and—"

"My dear girl, you haven't seen!" Martin turned upon her. "He can't murder half the county. There's a crowd outside the house that makes the place look like the local horse show. Daddy Dawlish's stunt for putting the fear of God into Campion's little friend has brought the entire Hunt down upon him thirsting for his blood. Looks as if they'll get it now, too. Hullo! Here they come."

His last words were occasioned by the sound of footsteps outside, and then a horrified voice said clearly:

"Good heavens! What's the smell of kerosene?"

Several heavy blows outside followed. Then there was the grating of bolts and the heavy door swung open.

On the threshold stood Guffy Randall, a pleasant, horsy young man with a broken nose and an engaging smile. He was backed by half a dozen or so eager and bewildered horsemen.

"I say, Bertie," he said, without further introduction, "what's up? The passage out here is soaked with paraffin, and there's a small mountain of faggots on the stairs."

Martin Watt grasped his arm.

"All explanations later, my son," he said. "The one thing we've got to do now is to prevent Uncle Bosche from getting away. He's got a gang of about ten, too, but they're not so important. He's the lad we want, and a little sheeny pal of his."

"Righto. We're with you. Of course the man's clean off the bean. Did you see that hound?"

"Yes," said Martin soothingly. "But it's the chappie we want now. He'll make for his car."

"He won't get to it yet awhile," said the new-comer grimly. "He's surrounded by a tight hedge composed of the oldest members, and they're all seeing red—but still, we'll go down."

Campion turned to Abbershaw.

"I think the girls had better come out," he said. "We don't want any mistakes at this juncture. Poor old Prenderby too, if we can bring him. The place is as inflammable as gun-cotton. I'll give you a hand with him."

They carried the boy downstairs between them.

As Randall had said, the corridors smelt of paraffin and there were enormous faggots of dry kindling wood in advantageous positions all the way down to the hall. Clearly Herr von Faber had intended to leave nothing to chance.

"What a swine!" muttered Abbershaw. "The man must be crazy, of course."

Albert Campion caught his eye.

"I don't think so, my son," he said. "In fact I shouldn't be at all surprised if at this very moment our friend Bosche wasn't proving his sanity pretty conclusively...Did it occur to you that his gang of boy friends have been a little conspicuous by their absence this morning?"

Abbershaw halted suddenly and looked at him.

"What are you driving at?" he demanded.

Mr. Campion's pale eyes were lazy behind his big spectacles. "I thought I heard a couple of cars sneaking off in the night," he said. "We don't know if old Whitby and his Dowager Daimler have returned—see what I mean?"

"Are you suggesting Dawlish is here *alone*?" said Abbershaw.

"Not exactly alone," conceded Campion. "We know Gideon is still about, and that county bird with the face like a thug also, but I don't expect the others are around. Consider it! Dawlish has us just where he wants us. He decides to make one last search for his precious package, which by now he realizes is pretty hopelessly gone. Then he means to make the place ready for his firework display, set light to it and bunk for home and mother; naturally he doesn't want all his pals standing by. It's not a pretty bit of work even for those lads. Besides, even if they do use the side roads, he doesn't want three cars dashing from the scene at the same time, does he?"

Abbershaw nodded.

"I see," he said slowly. "And so, now—"

The rest of his sentence was cut short by the sound of a shot from the turf outside, followed by a woman's scream that had more indignation than fear in it. Abbershaw and Campion set down their burden in the shadow of the porch and left him to the tender ministrations of Jeanne while they dashed out into the open.

The scene was an extraordinary one.

Spread out in front of the gloomy, forbidding old house was all the colour and pageantry of the Monewdon Hunt. Until a moment or two before, the greater part of the field had kept back, leaving the actual interviewing of the offender to the

Master and several of the older members, but now the scene was one of utter confusion.

Apparently Herr von Faber had terminated what had proved to be a lengthy and heated argument with a revolver shot which, whether by accident or by design, had pinked a hole through the Master's sleeve, and sent half the horses in the field rearing and plunging; and then, under cover of the excitement, had fled for the garage, his ponderous form and long grey hair making him a strange, grotesque figure in the cold morning sun.

When Abbershaw and Campion burst upon the scene the first moment of stupefied horror was barely over.

Martin Watt's voice rang out clearly above the growing murmur of anger.

"The garage...quickly!" he shouted, and almost before the last word had left his lips there was the sound of an engine "revving" violently. Then the great doors were shattered open, and the big Lanchester dived out like a torpedo. There were three men in it, the driver, Dawlish, and Gideon. Guffy Randall sprang into his saddle, and followed by five or six of the younger spirits, set off at a gallop across the turf. Their intention was obvious. With reasonable luck they could expect to cut off the car at a point some way up the drive.

Campion shouted to them warningly, but his voice was lost in the wind of their speed, and he turned to Abbershaw, his face pale and twisted with horror.

"They don't realize!" he said, and the doctor was struck with the depth of feeling in his tone. "Von Faber won't stop for anything—those horses! God! Look at them now!"

Guffy Randall and his band had drawn their horses up across the road in the way of the oncoming car.

Campion shouted to them wildly, but they did not seem to hear. Every eye in the field was upon them as the great grey car shot on, seeming to gather speed at every second.

Campion stood rigidly, his arm raised above his head.

"He'll charge 'em," he murmured, and suddenly ducked as though unable to look any longer. Abbershaw, too, in that moment when it seemed inevitable that men and horse-flesh must be reduced to one horrible bloody mêlée blinked involuntarily. They had reckoned without horsemanship, however; just when it seemed that no escape were possible the horses reared and scattered, but as the car swept between them Guffy's lean young form shot down and his crop caught the driver full across the face.

The car leapt forward, swerved over the narrow turf border into a small draining ditch, and, with a horrible sickening grind of smashing machinery, overturned.

CHAPTER TWENTY-FOUR

The Last of Black Dudley

"**I**'M SORRY to 'ave 'ad to trouble you, sir."

Detective-Inspector Pillow, of the County Police, flapped back a closely written page of his notebook and resettled himself on the wooden chair which seemed so small for him as he spoke. Abbershaw, who was bending over the bed in which Prenderby lay, now conscious and able to take an interest in the proceedings, did not speak.

The three of them were alone in one of the first-floor rooms of Black Dudley, and the Inspector was coming to the end of his inquiry.

He was a sturdy, red-faced man with close-cropped yellow hair, and a slow-smiling blue eye. At the moment he was slightly embarrassed, but he went on with his duty doggedly.

"We're getting everybody's statements—in their own words," he said, adding importantly and with one eye on Abbershaw, "The Chief is not at all sure that Scotland Yard won't be interested in this affair. 'E is going to acquaint them with the facts right away, I believe…I know there's no harm in me telling *you* that, sir."

He paused, and cast a wary glance at the little red-haired doctor.

"Oh, quite," said Abbershaw hastily, adding immediately: "Have you got everything you want now? I don't want my patient here disturbed more than I can help, you understand, Inspector."

"Oh, certainly not, sir—certainly not. I quite understand." The Inspector spoke vehemently, but he still fingered his notebook doubtfully.

"There's just one point more, sir, I'd like to go into with you, if you don't mind," he said at last. "Just a little discrepancy 'ere. Naturally we want to get everything co'erent if we can, you understand. This is just as a matter of form, of course. Only you see I've got to hand my report in and—"

"That's all right, Inspector. What is it?" said Abbershaw encouragingly.

The Inspector removed his pencil from behind his ear and, after biting the end of it reflectively for a moment, said briskly: "Well, it's about this 'ere tale of a murder, sir. Some of the accounts 'ave it that the accused, Benjamin Dawlish, believed to be an alias, made some rather startling accusations of murder when you was all locked up together on the evening of the 27th, that is, yesterday."

He paused and looked at Abbershaw questioningly. The doctor hesitated.

There were certain details of the affair which he had decided to reserve for higher authorities since he did not want to risk the delay which a full exposure now would inevitably cause.

Whitby and the driver of the disguised Rolls had not returned. Doubtless they had been warned in time.

Meanwhile the Inspector was still waiting.

"As I take it, sir," he said at length, "the story was a bit of 'colour,' as you might say, put in by the accused to scare the ladies. Perhaps you 'ad some sort of the same idea?"

"Something very much like that," agreed Abbershaw, glad to have evaded the awkward question so easily. "I signed the cremation certificate for Colonel Coombe's body, you know."

"Oh, you did, did you, sir. Well, that clears that up."

Inspector Pillow seemed relieved. Clearly he regarded Abbershaw as something of an oracle since he was so closely associated with Scotland Yard, and incidentally he appeared to consider that the affair was tangled enough already without the introduction of further complications.

"By the way," said Abbershaw suddenly, as the thought occurred to him, "there's an old woman from the village in one of the attics, inspector. Has she been rescued yet?"

A steely look came into the Inspector's kindly blue eyes. "Mrs. Meade?" he said heavily. "Yes. The party 'as been attended to. The local constable 'as 'er in charge at the moment." He sniffed. *"And* 'e's got 'is 'ands full," he added feelingly. "She seems to be a well-known character round 'ere. A regular tartar," he went on more confidentially. "Between you and me, sir"—he tapped his forehead significantly—"she seems to be a case for the County Asylum. It took three men half an hour to get 'er out of the 'ouse. Kept raving about 'ell-fire and 'er son comin' of a Wednesday or something, I dunno. 'Owever, Police-Officer Maydew 'as 'er in 'and. Seems 'e understands 'er more or less. 'Er daughter does 'is washing, and it's well known the old lady's a bit queer. We come acrost strange things in our work, sir, don't we?"

Abbershaw was properly flattered by this assumption of colleagueship.

"So you expect Scotland Yard in on this, inspector?" he said.

The policeman wagged his head seriously.

"I shouldn't be at all surprised, sir," he said. "Although," he added, a trifle regretfully, "if they don't hurry up I shouldn't wonder if there wasn't much for them to do except to attend the inquest. Our Dr. Rawlins thinks 'e may pull 'em round, but 'e can't say yet for certain."

Abbershaw nodded.

"It was Dawlish himself who got the worst of it, wasn't it?" he said.

"That is so," agreed the Inspector. "The driver, curiously enough, seemed to get off very lightly, I thought. Deep cut acrost his face, but otherwise nothing much wrong with 'im. The Chief's been interviewing 'im all the morning. Jesse Gideon, the second prisoner, is still unconscious. 'E 'as several nasty fractures, I understand, but Dawlish got all one side of the car on top of 'im and the doctor seems to think that if he keeps 'im alive 'is brain may go. There's not much sense in that, I told 'im. Simply giving everybody trouble, I said. Still, we 'ave to be 'umane, you know. How about Mr. Prenderby, sir? Shall I take 'is statement later?"

Prenderby spoke weakly from the bed.

"I should like to corroborate all Dr. Abbershaw has told you," he said. "Do you think you could make that do, Inspector?"

"It's not strictly in accordance with the regulations," murmured Pillow, "but I think under the circumstances we might stretch a point. I'll 'ave your name and address and I won't bother you two gentlemen no more."

After Prenderby's name, age, address, and telephone number had been duly noted down in the inspector's notebook, Abbershaw spoke.

"I suppose we may set off for Town when we like, then?" he said.

"Just whenever you like, sir."

The Inspector shut his notebook with a click, and picking up his hat from beneath his chair, moved to the door.

"I'll wish you good day, then, gentlemen," he said, and stalked out.

Prenderby looked at Abbershaw.

"You didn't tell him about Coombe?" he said.

Abbershaw shook his head.

"No," he said.

"But surely, if we're going to make the charge we ought to do it at once? You're not going to let the old bird get away with it, are you?"

Abbershaw looked at him curiously.

"I've been a damned fool all the way through," he said, "but now I'm on ground I understand, and I'm not going to live up to my record. You didn't hear what Dawlish said to us last night, but if you had, and if you had heard that old woman's story, I think you'd see what I'm thinking. He didn't murder Coombe."

Prenderby looked at him blankly.

"My head may be still batty," he said, "but I'm hanged if I get you. If the Hun or his staff aren't responsible, who is?"

Abbershaw looked at him fixedly, and Prenderby was moved to sarcasm.

"Anne Edgeware, or your priceless barmy crook who showed up so well when things got tight, I suppose," he suggested.

Abbershaw continued to stare at him, and something in his voice when he spoke startled the boy by its gravity.

"I don't know, Michael," he said. "That's the devil of it, I don't know."

Prenderby opened his mouth to speak, but he was cut short by a tap on the door. It was Jeanne and Meggie.

"This will have to wait, old boy," he murmured as they came in. "I'll come round and have a talk with you if I may, when we get back."

"May Michael be moved?" It was Meggie who spoke. "I'm driving Jeanne up to Town," she explained, "and we wondered if we might take Michael too."

Prenderby grinned to Abbershaw.

"As one physician to another," he said, "perhaps not. But speaking as man to man, I don't think the atmosphere of this house is good for my aura. I think with proper feminine care and light conversation only, the journey might be effected without much danger, don't you?"

Abbershaw laughed.

"I believe in the feminine care," he said. "I'd like to come with you, but I've got the old A.C. in the garage, so I must reconcile myself to a lonely trip."

"Not at all," said Meggie. "You're taking Mr. Campion. Anne and Chris are going up with Martin. Chris's car is hopeless, and Anne says she'll never drive again until her nerves have recovered. The garage man is taking her car into Ipswich, and sending it up from there."

"Where's Wyatt?" said Prenderby.

"Oh, he's staying down here—till the evening, at any rate." It was Jeanne who spoke. "It's his house, you see, and naturally there are several arrangements to make. I told him I thought it was very terrible of us to go off, but he said he'd rather we didn't stay. You see, the place is quite empty—there's not a servant anywhere—and naturally it's a bit awkward for him. You'd better talk to him, Dr. Abbershaw."

Abbershaw nodded.

"I will," he said. "He ought to get away from here pretty soon, or he'll be pestered to death by journalists."

Meggie slipped her arm through his.

"Go and find him then, dear, will you?" she said. "It must be terrible for him. I'll look after these two. Come and see me when you get back."

Abbershaw glanced across the room, but Jeanne and Michael were too engrossed in each other to be paying any attention to anything else, so he bent forward impetuously and kissed her, and she clung to him for a moment.

"You bet I will," he said, and as he went out of the room he felt himself, in spite of his problems, the happiest man alive.

He found Wyatt alone in the great hall. He was standing

with his back to the fire-place, in which the cold embers of yesterday's fire still lay.

"No, thanks awfully, old boy," he said, in response to Abber-shaw's suggestion. "I'd rather stay on on my own if you don't mind. There's only the miserable business of caretakers and locking up to be seen to. There are my uncle's private papers to be gone through, too, though Dawlish seems to have destroyed a lot of them. I'd rather be alone. You understand, don't you?"

"Why, of course, my dear fellow..." Abbershaw spoke hastily. "I'll see you in Town no doubt when you get back."

"Why, yes, I hope so. You do see how it is, don't you? I must go through the old boy's personalia."

Abbershaw looked at him curiously.

"Wyatt," he said suddenly, "do you know much about your uncle?"

The other glanced at him sharply.

"How do you mean?" he demanded.

The little doctor's courage seemed suddenly to fail him.

"Oh, nothing," he said, and added, somewhat idiotically, he felt, "I only wondered."

Wyatt let the feeble explanation suffice, and presently Abbershaw, realizing that he wished to be alone, made his adieux and went off to find Campion and to prepare for the oncoming journey. His round cherubic face was graver than its wont, however, and there was a distinctly puzzled expression in his grey eyes.

It was not until he and Campion were entering the outskirts of London late that evening that he again discussed the subject which perplexed him chiefly.

Mr. Campion had chatted in his own particular fashion all the way up, but now he turned to Abbershaw with something more serious in his face.

"I say," he said, "what *did* happen about old Daddy

Coombe? No one raised any row, I see. What's the idea? Dawlish said he was murdered; you said he was murdered; Prenderby said he was murdered. Was he?"

His expression was curious but certainly not fearful, Abbershaw was certain.

"I didn't say anything, of course, to the old Inspector person," Campion went on, "because I didn't know anything, but I thought you fellows would have got busy. Why the reticence? *You* didn't do it by any chance, did you?"

"No," said Abbershaw shortly, some of his old pompousness returning at the suggestion of such a likelihood.

"No offence meant," said Mr. Campion, dropping into the vernacular of the neighbourhood through which they were passing. "Nor none taken, I hope. No, what I was suggesting, my dear old bird, was this: Are you sleuthing a bit in your own inimitable way? Is the old cerebral machine ticking over? Who and what and why and wherefore, so to speak?"

"I don't know, Campion," said Abbershaw slowly. "I don't know any more than you do who did it. But Colonel Coombe was murdered. Of that I'm perfectly certain, and—I don't think Dawlish or his gang had anything to do with it."

"My dear Holmes," said Mr. Campion, "you've got me all of a flutter. You're not serious, are you?"

"Perfectly," said Abbershaw. "After all, who might not have done it, with an opportunity like that, if they wanted to? Hang it all, how do I know that you didn't do it?"

Mr. Campion hesitated, and then shrugged his shoulders.

"I'm afraid you've got a very wrong idea of me," he said. "When I told you that I never did anything in bad taste, I meant it. Sticking an old boy in the middle of a house-party parlour-game occurs to me to be the height of bad form. Besides, consider, I was only getting a hundred guineas. Had my taste been execrable I wouldn't have risked putting my neck in a noose for a hundred guineas, would I?"

Abbershaw was silent. The other had voiced the argument that had occurred to himself, but it left the mystery no clearer than before.

Campion smiled.

"Put me down as near Piccadilly as you can, old man, will you?" he said.

Abbershaw nodded, and they drove on in silence.

At last, after some considerable time, he drew up against the kerb on the corner of Berkeley Street. "Will this do you?" he said.

"Splendidly. Thanks awfully, old bird. I shall run into you some time, I hope."

Campion held out his hand as he spoke, and Abbershaw, overcome by an impulse, shook it warmly, and the question that had been on his lips all the drive suddenly escaped him.

"I say, Campion," he said, "who the hell are you?"

Mr. Campion paused on the running-board and there was a faintly puckish expression behind his enormous glasses.

"Ah," he said. "Shall I tell you? Listen—do you know who my mother is?"

"No," said Abbershaw, with great curiosity.

Mr. Campion leaned over the side of the car until his mouth was an inch or two from the other man's ear, and murmured a name, a name so illustrious that Abbershaw started back and stared at him in astonishment.

"Good God!" he said. "You don't mean that?"

"No," said Mr. Campion cheerfully, and went off striding jauntily down the street until, to Abbershaw's amazement, he disappeared through the portals of one of the most famous and exclusive clubs in the world.

CHAPTER TWENTY-FIVE

Mr. Watt Explains

AFTER DINNER one evening in the following week, Abbershaw held a private consultation on the affair in his rooms in the Adelphi.

He had not put the case before his friend, Inspector Deadwood, for a reason which he dared not think out, yet his conscience forbade him to ignore the mystery surrounding the death of Colonel Coombe altogether.

Since von Faber and his confederates were wanted men, the County Police had handed over their prisoners to Scotland Yard; and in the light of preliminary legal proceedings, sufficient evidence had been forthcoming to render the affair at Black Dudley merely the culminating point in a long series of charges. Every day it became increasingly clear that they would not be heard of again for some time.

Von Faber was still suffering from concussion, and there seemed every likelihood of his remaining under medical supervision for the term of his imprisonment at least.

Whitby and his companion had not been traced, and no one, save himself, so far as Abbershaw could tell, was likely to raise any inquiries about Colonel Coombe.

All the same, although he had several excellent reasons for wishing the whole question to remain in oblivion, Abbershaw had forced himself to institute at least a private inquiry into the mystery.

He and Meggie had dined together when Martin Watt was admitted.

The girl sat in one of the high-backed Stuart chairs by the fire, her brocade-shod feet crossed, and her hands folded quietly in her lap.

Glancing at her, Abbershaw could not help reflecting that their forthcoming marriage was more interesting to him than any criminal hunt in the world.

Martin was more enthusiastic on the subject of the murder. He came in excited, all trace of indolence had vanished from his face, and he looked about him with some surprise.

"No one else here?" he said. "I thought we were going to have a pukka consultation with all the crowd present—decorations, banners, and salute of guns!"

Abbershaw shook his head.

"Sorry! I'm afraid there's only Prenderby to come," he said. "Campion has disappeared, Anne Edgeware is in the South of France recuperating, Jeanne doesn't want to hear or think anything about Black Dudley ever again, so Michael tells me, and I didn't think we'd mention the thing to Wyatt, until it's a certainty at any rate. He's had his share of unpleasantness already. So you see there are only the four of us to talk it over. Have a drink?"

"Thanks." Martin took up the glass and sipped it meditatively. It was evident from his manner that he was bubbling with suppressed excitement. "I say," he said suddenly, unable to control his eagerness any longer, "have you folk twigged the murderer?"

Abbershaw glanced at him sharply.

"No," he said hesitatingly. "Why, have you?"

Martin nodded.

"Fancy so," he said, and there was a distinctly satisfied expression in his grey eyes. "It seems pretty obvious to me, why—"

"Hold hard, Martin."

Abbershaw was surprised at the apprehension in his own voice, and he reddened slightly as the other two stared at him.

Martin frowned.

"I don't get you," he said at last. "There's no special reason against suspecting Whitby, is there?"

"Whitby?"

Abbershaw's astonishment was obvious, and Meggie looked at him curiously, but Martin was too interested in his theory to raise any question.

"Why, yes," he said. "Whitby. Why not? Think of it in cold blood, who was the first man to find Colonel Coombe dead? Who had a better motive for murdering him than anyone else? It seems quite obvious to me." He paused, and as neither of them spoke went on again, raising his voice a little in his enthusiasm.

"My dear people, just think of it," he insisted. "It struck me as soon as it occurred to me that it was so obvious that I've been wondering ever since why we didn't hit on it at once. We should have done, of course, if we hadn't all been having fun in our quiet way. Look here, this is exactly how it happened."

He perched himself on an armchair and regarded them seriously.

"Our little friend Albert is the first person to be considered. There is absolutely no reason to doubt that fellow's word, his yarn sounds true. He showed up jolly well when we were in a tight place. I think we'll take him as cleared. His story is true, then. That is to say, during Act One of the drama when we were all playing 'touch' with the haunted dagger, little Albert stepped smartly up, murmured 'Abracadabra' in the old man's ear and collected the doings, leaving the Colonel hale and hearty. What happened next?" He paused and glanced at them eagerly. "See what I'm driving at? No? Well, see column two—'The Remarkable Story of the Aged and Batty Housemaid!' Now have you got it?"

Meggie started to her feet, her eyes brightening.

"George," she said, "I do believe he's got it. Don't you see, Mrs. Meade told us that she had actually seen Whitby come in with the news that the Colonel was stabbed in the back. Why—why it's quite clear—"

"Not so fast, not so fast, young lady, *if* you please. Let the clever detective tell his story in his own words."

Martin leant forward as he spoke and beamed at them triumphantly.

"I've worked it all out," he said, "and, putting my becoming modesty aside, I will now detail to you the facts which my superlative deductions have brought to light and which only require the paltry matter of proof to make them as clear as glass to the meanest intelligence. Get the scene into your mind. Whitby, a poor pawn in his chief's hands, a man whose liberty, perhaps his very life, hangs upon the word of his superior, von Faber; this man leads his chief to the Colonel's desk to find that precious income-tax form or whatever it was they were all so keen about, and when he gets there the cupboard is bare, as the classics have it." Martin, who had been gradually working himself up, now broke into a snatch of imaginary dialogue:

" 'It must be on Coombe himself,' growls the Hun," he began.

"'Of course,' agrees the pawn, adding mentally: 'Heaven pray it may be so,' or words to that effect. 'Go and see, *you*!" venoms the Hun, and off goes Whitby, fear padding at his heels."

He paused for breath and regarded them soberly.

"Seriously, though," he continued with sudden gravity. "The chap must have had a nasty ten minutes. He knew that if anything had gone wrong and old Coombe had somehow managed to double-cross the gang, as guardian he was for it with von Faber at his nastiest. Look now," he went on cheerfully, "this is where the deduction comes in; as I work it out, as soon as Whitby entered the darkened part of the house, someone put the dagger in his hand and then, I should say, the whole idea occurred to him. He went up to old Coombe in the dark, asked him for the papers; Coombe replied that he hadn't got them. Then Whitby, maddened with the thought of the yarn he was bound to take back to von Faber, struck the old boy in the back and, after making a rapid search, took the dagger, joined in the game for thirty seconds, maybe—just enough time to hand the thing on to somebody—and then dashed back to Faber and Gideon, with his news. How about that?"

He smiled at them with deep satisfaction—he had no doubts himself.

For some minutes his audience were silent. This solution was certainly very plausible. At last Abbershaw raised his head. The expression on his face was almost hopeful.

"It's not a bad idea, Martin," he said thoughtfully. "In fact, the more I think about it the more likely it seems to become."

Martin pressed his argument home eagerly.

"I feel like that too," he said. "You see, it explains so many things. First of all, it gives a good reason why von Faber thought that one of our crowd had done it. Then it also makes it clear why Whitby never turned up again. And then it has another advantage—it provides a motive. No one else had any *reason* for killing the old boy. As far as I can see he seems to have been very useful to his own gang and no harm to anybody else. Candidly now, don't you think I'm obviously right?"

He looked from one to the other of them questioningly.

Meggie was frowning.

"There is just one thing you haven't explained, Martin," she said slowly. "What happened to the dagger? When it was in my hand it had blood on it. Someone snatched it from me before I could scream, and it wasn't seen again until the next morning, when it was all bright and clean again and back in its place in the trophy."

Martin looked a little crestfallen.

"That had occurred to me," he admitted. "But I decided that in the excitement of the alarm whoever had it chucked it down where it was found next morning by one of the servants and put back."

Meggie looked at him and smiled.

"Martin," she said, "your mother has the most marvellous butler in the world. Plantagenet, I do believe, would pick up a blood-stained dagger in the early morning, have it cleaned, and hang it up on its proper nail, and then consider it beneath his dignity to mention so trifling a matter during the police inquiries afterwards. But believe me, that man is unique. Besides, the only servants there were members of the gang. Had they found it we should probably have heard about it. Anyway, they wouldn't have cleaned it and hung it up again."

Martin nodded dubiously, and the momentary gleam of hope disappeared from Abbershaw's face.

"Of course," said Martin, "Whitby may have put it back himself. Gone nosing around during the night, you know, and found it, and thinking, 'Well, we can't have this about,' put it back in its proper place and said no more about it." He brightened visibly. "Come to think of it, it's very likely. That makes my theory all the stronger, what?"

The others were not so easily convinced.

"He might," said Meggie, "but there's not much reason why he should go nosing about at night, as you say. And even so it doesn't explain who took it out of my hand, does it?"

Martin was shaken but by no means overwhelmed.

"Oh, well," he said airily, "all that point is a bit immaterial, don't you think? After all, it's the main motive and opportunity and questions that are important. Anyone might have snatched the dagger from you. It is one of those damn fool gallant gestures that old Chris Kennedy might have perpetrated. It might have been anyone playing in the game. However, in the main, I think we've spotted our man. Don't you, Abbershaw?"

"I hope so."

The fervency of the little doctor's reply surprised them.

Martin was gratified.

"I *know* I'm right," he said. "Now all we've got to do is to prove it."

Abbershaw agreed.

"That's so," he said. "But I don't think that will be so easy, Martin. You see, we've got to find the chap first, and without police aid that's going to be a well-nigh impossible job. We can't bring the Yard into it until we've got past theories."

"No, of course not," said Martin. "But I say," he added, as a new thought occurred to him, "there is one thing, though. Whitby was the cove who had the wind-up, wasn't he? No one else turned a hair, and if there was a guilty conscience amongst the gang, surely it was his?"

This suggestion impressed his listeners more than any of his other arguments. Abbershaw looked up excitedly.

"I do believe you're right," he said. "What do you think, Meggie?"

The girl hesitated. As she recollected Mrs. Meade's story of the discovery of the murder, Martin's theory became rapidly more and more plausible.

"Yes," she said again. "I believe he's hit it."

Martin grinned delightedly.

"That's fine," he said. "Now all we've got to do is to find the chap and get the truth out of him. This is going to be great. Now what's the best way to get on to the trail of those two johnnies? Toddle round to all the crematoriums in the country and make inquiries?"

The others were silent. Here was a problem which, without the assistance of Scotland Yard, they were almost powerless to tackle.

They were still discussing it when, fifteen minutes later, Michael Prenderby walked in. His pale face was flushed as if from violent exertion and he began to talk eagerly as soon as he got into the room.

"Sorry I'm late," he said; "but I've had an adventure. Walked right into it in the Lea Bridge Road. I stopped to have a plug put in and there it was staring at me. I stared at it—I thought I was seeing things at first—until the garage man got quite embarrassed."

Martin Watt regarded the new-comer coldly.

"Look here, Michael," he said with reproach. "We're here to discuss a murder, you know."

"Well?" Prenderby looked pained and surprised. "Aren't I helping you? Isn't this a most helpful point?"

Abbershaw glanced at him sharply.

"What are you talking about?" he said.

Prenderby stared at him.

"Why, *the* car, of course," he said. "What else could it be? The car," he went on, as they regarded him uncomprehendingly for a moment or so. "The car. The incredible museum specimen in which that precious medico carted off the poor old bird's body. There it was, sitting up looking at me like a dowager-duchess."

CHAPTER TWENTY-SIX

"Cherchez la Femme"

"IF YOU'D ONLY KEEP QUIET," said Michael Prenderby, edging a chair between himself and the vigorous Martin who was loudly demanding particulars, "I'll tell you all about it. The garage is half-way down the Lea Bridge Road, on the left-hand side not far past the river or canal or whatever it is. It's called 'The Ritz'—er—because there's a coffee-stall incorporated with it. It's not a very big place. The usual type—a big white-washed shed with a tin roof—no tiles or anything. While the chap was fixing the plug the doors were open, so I looked in, and there, sitting in a corner, a bit like 'Dora' and a bit like a duchess, but unmistakably herself, was Colonel Coombe's original mechanical brougham."

"But are you sure?"

Martin was dancing with excitement.

"Absolutely positive." Prenderby was emphatic. "I went and had a look at the thing. The laddie in the garage was enjoying the joke as much as anyone. He hadn't had time to examine it, he said, but he'd never set eyes on anything like it in his life. I didn't know what to do. I didn't think I'd wait and see the fellows without telling you because I didn't know what schemes you were hatching, so I told the garage man that I'd like to buy the bus as a museum piece. He told me that the people who brought it in were coming back for it some time tonight and he'd tell them. I thought we'd get down there first and be waiting for them as they came in. Of course the old car may have changed hands, but even so—"

"Rather!" Martin was enthusiastic. "We'll go down there right away, shall we? All of us?"

"Not Meggie," said Abbershaw quickly. "No," he added with determination, as she turned to him appealingly. "You had your share of von Faber's gang at Black Dudley, and I'm not going to risk anything like that again."

Meggie looked at him, a faintly amused expression playing round the corners of her mouth, but she did not attempt to argue with him: George was to be master in his own home, she had decided.

The three men set off in Prenderby's small Riley, Abbershaw tucked uncomfortably between the other two.

Martin Watt grinned.

"I've got a gun this time," he said. "Our quiet country week-end taught me that much."

Abbershaw was silent. He, too, had invested in an automatic, since his return to London. But he was not proud of the fact, since he secretly considered that its purchase had been a definite sign of weakness.

They wormed their way through the traffic, which was mercifully thin at that time of night, although progress was by no means easy. A clock in Shoreditch struck eleven as they went through the borough, and Martin spoke fervently.

"Good Lord, I hope we don't miss them," he said, and added with a chuckle, "I bet old Kennedy would give his ears to be on this trip. How far down is the place, Prenderby?"

"Not far now," said Michael, as he swung into the unprepossessing tram-lined thoroughfare which leads to the "Bakers' Arms" and Wanstead.

"And you say the garage man was friendly?" said Abbershaw.

"Oh, perfectly," said Prenderby, with conviction. "I think we can count on him. What exactly is our plan of campaign?"

Martin spoke airily.

"We just settle down and wait for the fellows, and when they come we get hold of them and make them talk."

Abbershaw looked dubious. Now that he was back in the civilization of London he was inclined to feel that the lawless methods of Black Dudley were no longer permissible, no matter what circumstances should arise. Martin had more of the adventurous spirit left in him, however. It was evident that he had made up his mind about their plan of campaign.

"The only thing these fellows understand is force," he said vigorously. "We're going to talk to 'em in their mother tongue."

Abbershaw would have demurred, but at this moment all conversation was suspended by their sudden arrival at the garage. They found "The Ritz" still open, though business even at the coffee-stall was noticeably slack.

As soon as the car came to a standstill, a loose-limbed, raw-boned gentleman in overalls and a trilby hat came out to meet them.

He regarded them with a cold suspicion in his eyes which even Prenderby's friendly grin did not thaw.

"I've come back to see about the old car I wanted to buy—" Prenderby began, with his most engaging grin.

"You did, did you?" The words were delivered with a burst of Homeric geniality that would have deceived nobody. "But, it's not for sale, see! You'd better back your car out, there's no room to turn here."

Prenderby was frankly puzzled; clearly this was the last reception he had expected.

"He's been told to hold his tongue," whispered Martin, and then, turning to the garage man, he smiled disarmingly. "You've no idea what a disappointment this is to me," he said.

"I collect relics of this sort and by my friend's description the specimen you have here seems to be very nearly perfect. Let me have a look at it at any rate."

He slipped hastily out of the car as he spoke and made a move in the direction of the darkened garage door.

"Oh no, you don't!" The words were attended by the suspicious and unfriendly gentleman in the overalls and at the same moment Martin found himself confronted with the whole six-foot-three of indignant aggressiveness, while the voice, dropping a few tones, continued softly, "There's a lot of people round here what are friends of mine. Very particular friends. I'd 'op it if I was you."

Martin stared at him with apparent bewilderment.

"My dear man, what's the matter?" he said. "Surely you're not the type of fellow to be unreasonable when someone asks you to show him a car. There's no reason why I should be wasting your time even."

He chinked some money in his pocket suggestively. The face beneath the trilby remained cold and unfriendly.

"Now look 'ere," he said, thrusting his hands into his trousers pockets through the slits in his overalls, "I'm telling you, and you can take it from me or not as you please. But if you do take it, and I 'ope for your sake you do, you'll go right away from this place. I've got my reasons for telling you—see?"

Martin still seemed bewildered.

"But this is extraordinary," he said, and added as if the thought had suddenly occurred to him, "I suppose this doesn't interest you?"

A crackle of notes sounded as he spoke and then his quiet lazy voice continued. "*So* attractive I always think. That view of the Houses of Parliament on the back is rather sweet—or perhaps you like this one better—or this? I've got two here printed in green as well. What do you say?"

For a moment the man did not answer, but it was evident that some of his pugnacity had abated.

"A fiver!" he said, and went on more reasonably after a considerable pause. "Look here, what *is* this game you're up to? What's your business is your business and I'm not interfering, but this I 'ope and arsk. I don't want any fooling around my garage. I've got 'undreds of pounds' worth of cars in 'ere and I've got my reputation to think of. So no setting fire to anything or calling of the police— see? If I let you in 'ere to 'ave a look at that car that's got to be understood."

"Why, of course not. Let us have a look at the car at any rate," said Martin, handing him the notes.

The man was still doubtful, but the money had a warming and soothing effect upon his temper.

"Are you all coming in?" he said at last. "Because if so you'd better hurry up. The owners may be back any time now."

This was a step forward at any rate. Abbershaw and Prenderby climbed out of the Riley and followed Martin with the visibly softening proprietor into the garage.

The man switched on the light and the three surveyed the miscellaneous collection of cars with interest.

"There she is," said Prenderby, his voice betraying his excitement. "Over in that corner there. Now, I ask you, could you miss her anywhere?"

The others followed the direction of his eyes and an exclamation broke from Martin.

"She certainly has IT," he said. "Once seen never forgotten." He turned to the garage proprietor. "Have you looked at her, Mr.—er—er—?" he hesitated, at a loss for the name.

"'Aywhistle," said the man stolidly, "and I ain't. I don't know anything about 'er nor don't want to. Now, 'ave you seen enough to keep you 'appy?"

Martin looked at him curiously.

"Look here, Captain," he said. "You come over here. I want to show you something if you haven't seen it already."

He moved over to the old car as he spoke, Mr. Haywhistle

following him unwillingly. Martin pulled up the bonnet and pointed to the engine.

"Ever seen anything like that before?" he said.

Mr. Haywhistle looked at the machinery casually and without interest at first. But gradually his expression changed and he dropped upon his knees and peered underneath the car to get a glimpse of the chassis. A moment or two later he lifted a red face towards them which wore an expression almost comic in its surprise.

"Gawd lumme!" he said. "A bloomin' Rolls."

Martin nodded and an explanation of these "Young Nob's" interest in the affair presented itself to the garage owner:

"Pinched it, did he?" he said. "Oh! I see now. But I pray and arsk you, sir, don't 'ave any rowin' in 'ere. I've 'ad a bit of trouble that way already—see?" He looked at them appealingly.

Martin turned to the others.

"I don't think we need do anything in here, do you?" he said. "If Mr. Haywhistle will let us wait in his yard at the side, with the gates open, as soon as Whitby comes out we can follow him. How's that?"

"That suits me fine," said Mr. Haywhistle, looking at them anxiously. "Now I'll tell you what," he went on, clearly eager to do all that he could to assist them now that he was not so sure of himself. "This is wot 'e says to me. Early this morning, about eight o'clock, 'e comes in 'ere with the car. My boy put 'er in for 'im, so I didn't 'ear the engine running. I came in just as 'e was leaving instructions. As far as I could gather he intended to meet a friend 'ere late tonight and they was going off together in the car as soon as this friend turned up. Well, about eight o'clock tonight, this gentleman 'ere,"—he indicated Prenderby—"'e calls in and spots the car and mentioned buying it. Of course I see where 'is artfulness comes in now," he added, beaming at them affably. " 'Owever, I didn't notice anything fishy at the time so when the owner of the car comes in about 'alf an hour ago I tells him that there was a gentleman interested in the old bus. Whereupon 'e went in the air—a fair treat. 'Tell me,' says 'e, 'was 'e anything like this?' Thereupon 'e gives a description of a little red-'eaded cove, which I see now is this gentleman 'ere."

He nodded at Abbershaw. "Perhaps it's your car, sir?" he suggested.

Abbershaw smiled noncommittally, and Mr. Haywhistle went on.

"Well, what eventually transpired," he said ponderously, "was this. I was not to show 'is property to anybody, and a very nasty way 'e said it too. 'E said 'e was coming back this side of twelve and if 'is friend turned up before him I was to ask 'im to wait."

Abbershaw looked at his watch.

"We'd better get into the yard straight away," he said.

Mr. Haywhistle glanced up at a big clock on the bare white-washed wall.

"Lumme, yes," he said. "'Alf a minute, I'll come and 'elp you."

With his assistance they backed the Riley into the dark yard by the side of "The Ritz" and put out their lights.

"You get into 'er and sit waiting. Then as soon as they come out on the road you can nip after them—see?" he said.

Since there was nothing better to do they took his advice and the three sat silent in the car, waiting.

Martin was grinning to himself. The promise of adventure had chased the lazy expression out of his eyes and he appeared alert and interested. Prenderby leant on the steering wheel, his thin pale face utterly expressionless.

Abbershaw alone looked a little perturbed. He had some doubts as to the Riley's capabilities as far as chasing the disguised Rolls were concerned. He was also a little afraid of Martin's gun. He realized that they were on a lawless errand since they were acting entirely without proof, and any casualties that might occur would be difficult to explain afterwards even to so obliging a person as Inspector Deadwood.

He was disturbed in his reflections by Martin's elbow gently prodded into his ribs. He looked up to see a tall burly figure, in a light overcoat and a cap pulled down well on his head, standing in the wedge of light cast through the open doorway of the garage.

"The butler," whispered Prenderby excitedly.

Abbershaw nodded; he too had recognized the man.

Mr. Haywhistle's manner was perfect.

"'Ere you are, sir," they heard him say cheerfully. "Your friend won't be long. Said 'e'd be round just before twelve. I shouldn't stand out there," he went on tactfully, as the man showed a disposition to look about him. "I'm always 'aving cars swing in 'ere without looking where they're going. I can't stop 'em. It's dangerous you know. That's right. Come inside."

As the two figures disappeared, a third, moving rapidly with quick, nervous steps, hurried in out of the darkness.

The three men in the car caught a glimpse of him as he passed into the garage. It was Whitby himself.

"Shall I start the engine?" murmured Prenderby. Martin put a warning hand on his.

"Wait till they start theirs," he said. "Now."

Michael trod softly on the starter and the Riley began to purr.

"Keep back, see which way they turn, and then after them," Martin whispered sharply. "Hullo! Here they come!"

Even as he spoke there was the soft rustle of wheels on the concrete and then the curious top-heavy old car glided softly and gently into the road, taking the direction of Wanstead, away from the city.

Prenderby dropped in the clutch and the Riley slipped out of its hiding-place and darted out in pursuit, a graceful silver fish amid the traffic.

CHAPTER TWENTY-SEVEN

A Journey by Night

For THE FIRST FEW MILES, while they were still in the traffic, Prenderby contented himself with keeping the disguised Rolls in sight. It would be absurd, he realized to overtake them while still in London, since they were acting in an unofficial capacity and he was particularly anxious not to arouse the suspicions of the occupants of the car in front of them.

He went warily, therefore, contriving always to keep a fair amount of traffic between them.

Martin was exultant. He was convinced by his own theory, and was certain that the last act of the Black Dudley mystery was about to take place.

Prenderby was too much absorbed by the details of the chase to give any adequate thought to the ultimate result.

Abbershaw alone was dubious. This, like everything else connected with the whole extraordinary business, appalled him by its amazing informality. He could not rid his mind of the thought that it was all terribly illegal—and besides that, at the back of his mind, there was always that other question, that problem which had caused him so many sleepless nights since his return to London. He hoped Martin was right in his theory, but he was sufficiently alarmed by his own secret thought to wish not to put Martin's idea to the test. He wanted to think Martin was right, to find out nothing that would make him look elsewhere for the murderer.

As they escaped from the tramway lines and came out into that waste of little new houses which separates the city from the fields, they and the grotesque old car in front were practically alone on the wide ill-lighted roads.

It was growing cold and there was a suggestion of a ground mist so that the car in front looked like a dim ghost returned from the early days of motoring.

As the last of the houses vanished and they settled down into that long straight strip of road through the forest, Prenderby spoke:

"How about now?" he said. "Shall I open out?"

Martin glanced at Abbershaw.

"What do you think?" he said.

Abbershaw hesitated.

"I don't quite see what you intend to do," he said. "Suppose you succeed in stopping them, what are you going to say? We have no proof against the man and no authority to do anything if we had."

"But we're going to get proof," said Martin cheerfully. "That's the big idea. First we stop them, then we sit on their heads while they talk."

Abbershaw shook his head.

"I don't think we'd get much out of them that way," he said. "And if we did it wouldn't be evidence. No, if you take my advice you'll run them to earth. Then perhaps we'll find something, although really, my dear Martin, I can't help feeling—"

"Let's kick him out, Prenderby," said Martin, "he's trying to spoil the party."

Abbershaw grinned.

"I think we're doing all we can do," he said. "After all it's no good letting them out of our sight."

Prenderby sighed.

"I wish you'd decided to overtake," he said. "This is a marvellous road. It wouldn't hurt us to be a bit nearer, anyway, would it?"

Martin nudged him gently.

"If you want to try your speed, my lad," he said, "here's your opportunity. The old lady has started to move."

The other two glanced ahead sharply. The Rolls had suddenly begun to move at something far beyond her previous respectable rate. The red tail-light was already disappearing into the distance.

Prenderby's share in the conversation came to an abrupt end. The Riley began to purr happily and they shot forward at an ever-increasing pace until the speedometer showed sixty.

"Steady!" said Martin. "Don't pass them in your excitement. We don't want them to spot us either."

"What makes you so sure that they haven't done so already?" said Abbershaw shrewdly, and added as they glanced at him inquiringly, "I couldn't help thinking as we came along that they were going very leisurely, taking their time, when there was plenty of other traffic on the road. As soon as we were alone together they began to move. I believe they've spotted us."

Prenderby spoke without looking round.

"He's right," he said. "Either that or they're suddenly in the deuce of a hurry. I'm afraid they're suspicious of us. They can't possibly know who we are with lights like these."

"Then I say," cut in Martin excitedly, "they'll try to dodge us. I'd get as near as you can and then sit on their tail if I were you."

Abbershaw said nothing and the Riley slowly crept up on the other car until she was directly in her head-lights. The Rolls swayed to the side to enable them to pass, but Prenderby did not avail himself of the invitation. Eventually the big car slackened speed but still Prenderby did not attempt to pass.

The next overture from the Rolls was as startling as it was abrupt. The little rear window opened suddenly and a bullet hit the road directly in front of them.

Prenderby swerved and brought the Riley almost to a full stop.

"A pot-shot at our front tire," he said. "If he'd got us we'd have turned over. Martin, I believe you're on the right tack. The cove is desperate."

"Of course I'm right," said Martin excitedly. "But don't let them get away, man, they'll be out of sight in a minute."

"Sorry," said Prenderby obstinately, "I'm keeping my distance. You don't seem to realize the result of a tire-burst at that pace."

"Oh, he won't do it again," said Martin cheerfully. "Besides, he's a rotten shot anyway."

Prenderby said no more, but he was careful to keep at a respectable distance from the Rolls.

"They'll start moving now," said Martin. "We shall have our work cut out if we're going to be in at the death. Look out for the side turnings. Do you know this road at all?"

"Pretty well," said Prenderby. "He's heading for Chelmsford, I should say, or somewhere round there. I think he'll have some difficulty in shaking us off."

The big car ahead was now speeding away from them rapidly and Prenderby had his hands full to keep them anywhere in sight. In Chelmsford they lost sight of it altogether and were forced to inquire of a policeman in the deserted High Street.

The placid country bobby took the opportunity of inspecting their licence and then conceded the information that a "vehicle of a type now obsolete, and bearing powerful lamps" had passed through the town, taking the Springfield road for Kelvedon and Colchester some three minutes before their own arrival.

The Riley sped on down the winding road through the town, Martin cursing vigorously.

"Now we're sunk," he said. "Missed them sure as Pancake-tide. They've only got to nip into a side road and shut off their lamps and we're done. In fact," he went on disconsolately, "I don't know if there's any point in going on at all now."

"There's only one point," cut in Abbershaw quietly. "If by chance they are going somewhere definite—I mean if they want to get to a certain spot in set time—they'll probably go straight on and trust to luck that they've shaken us off."

"That's right," said Martin. "Let's go on full tilt to Colchester and ask there. No one could miss a bus like that. It looks as if it ought not to be about alone. Full steam ahead, Michael."

"Ay, ay, sir," said Prenderby cheerfully and trod on the accelerator.

They went through Witham at a speed that would have infuriated the local authorities, but still the road was ghostly and deserted. At length, just outside Kelvedon, far away in the distance there appeared the faint haze of giant headlights against the trees.

Martin whooped.

"A sail, a sail, captain," he said. "It must be her. Put some speed into it, Michael."

"All right. If we seize up or leave the road, on your head be it," said Prenderby, through his teeth. "She's all out now."

The hedges on either side of them became blurred and indistinct. Finally, in the long straight strip between Marks Tey and Lexden, they slowly crept up behind the big car again.

"That's her all right," said Martin; "she's crawling, isn't she? Comparatively, I mean. I believe Abbershaw's hit it. She's keeping an appointment. Look here, let's drop down and shut off our head-lights—the sides will carry us."

"Hullo! Where's he off to now?"

It was Michael who spoke. The car ahead had taken a sudden turn to the right, forsaking the main road.

"After her," said Martin, with suppressed excitement. "Now we're coming to it, I do believe. Any idea where that leads to?"

"No," said Michael. "I haven't the least. There's only a lane there if I remember. Probably the drive of a house."

"All the better." Martin was enthusiastic. "That means we have located them anyway."

"Wait a bit," said Michael, as, dimming his lights, he swung round after the other car. "It's not a drive. I remember it now. There's a signpost over there somewhere which says, 'To Birch,' wherever 'Birch' may be. Gosh! No speeding on this road, my children," he added suddenly, as he steered the Riley round a concealed right-angle bend in the road.

The head-lights of the car they were following were still just visible several turns ahead. For the next few miles the journey developed into a nightmare. The turns were innumerable.

"God knows how we're going to get back," grumbled Michael. "I don't know which I prefer; your friend with the gun or an attempt to find our way back through these roads before morning."

"Cheer up," said Martin consolingly. "You may get both. Any idea where we are? Was that a church we passed just now?"

"I thought I heard a cow," suggested Abbershaw helpfully.

"Let's catch 'em up," said Martin. "It's time something definite happened."

Abbershaw shook his head.

"That's no good, my dear fellow," he said. "Don't you see our position? We can't stop a man in the middle of the night and accuse him of murder without more proof or more authority. We must find out where he is and that's all."

Martin was silent. He had no intention of allowing the adventure to end so tamely. They struggled on without speaking.

At length, after what had seemed to be an interminable drive, through narrow miry lanes with surfaces like ploughed fields, through forgotten villages, past ghostly churches dimly outlined against the sky, guided only by the glare ahead, the darkness began to grey and in the uncertain light of the dawn they found themselves on a track of short springy grass amid the most desolate surroundings any one of them had ever seen.

On all sides spread vast stretches of salting covered with clumps of rough, coarse grass with here and there a ragged river or a dyke-head.

Far ahead of them the old black car lumbered on.

Martin sniffed.

"The sea," he said. "I wonder if that old miracle ahead swims? A bus like that might do anything. That would just about sink us if we went to follow them."

"Just about," said Michael dryly. "What do we do now?"

"I suppose we go on to the bitter end," said Martin. "They may have a family house-boat out there. Hullo! Look at them now."

The Rolls had at last come to a full stop, although the head-lights were still streaming out over the turf.

Michael brought the Riley up sharply.

"What now?" he said.

"Now the fun begins," said Martin. "Get out your gun, Abbershaw."

Hardly had he spoken when an exclamation came down the morning to them, followed immediately by a revolver shot which again fell short of them.

Without hesitation Martin fired back. The snap of his automatic was instantly followed by a much larger explosion.

"That's their back tire," he said. "Let's get behind the car and play soldiers. They're sure to retaliate. This is going to be fun."

But in this he was mistaken. Neither Whitby nor his companion seemed inclined for further shooting. The two figures were plainly discernible through the fast-lightening gloom, Whitby in a long dust coat and a soft hat, and the other man taller and thinner, his cap still well down over his face.

And then, while they were still looking at him, Whitby thrust his handkerchief which he shook at them solemnly, waving it up and down. Its significance was unmistakable.

Abbershaw began to laugh. Even Martin grinned.

"That's matey, anyway," he said. "What happens next?"

CHAPTER TWENTY-EIGHT

Should a Doctor Tell?

STILL HOLDING THE HANDKERCHIEF well in front of him, Whitby came a pace or two nearer, and presently his weak, half-apologetic voice came to them down the wind.

"Since we've both got guns, perhaps we'd better talk," he shouted thinly. "What do you want?"

Martin glanced at Abbershaw.

"Keep him covered," he murmured. "Prenderby, old boy, you'd better walk behind us. We don't know what their little game is yet."

They advanced slowly—absurdly, Abbershaw could not help thinking—on that vast open salting, miles from anywhere.

Whitby was still the harassed, scared-looking little man who had come to ask Abbershaw for his assistance on that fateful night at Black Dudley. He was, if anything, a little more composed now than then, and he greeted them affably.

"Well, here we are, aren't we?" he said, and paused. "What do you want?"

Martin Watt opened his mouth to speak; he had a very clear notion of what he wanted and was anxious to explain it.

Abbershaw cut him short, however.

"A word or two of conversation, Doctor," he said.

The little man blinked at him dubiously.

"Why, yes, of course," he said, "of course. I should hate to disappoint you. You've come a long way for it, haven't you?"

He was so patently nervous that in spite of themselves they could not get away from the thought that they were very unfairly matched.

"Where shall we talk?" continued the little doctor, still timidly; "I suppose there must be quite a lot of things you want to ask me?"

Martin pocketed his gun.

"Look here, Whitby," he said, "that is the point—there are lots of things. That's why we've come. If you're sensible you'll give us straight answers. You know what happened at Black Dudley after you left, of course?"

"I—I read in the papers," faltered the little figure in front of them. "Most regrettable. Who would have thought that such a clever, intelligent man would turn out to be such a dreadful criminal?"

Martin shook his head.

"That's no good, Doc," he said. "You see, not everything came out in the papers."

Whitby sighed. "I see," he said. "Perhaps if you told me exactly how much you know I should see precisely what to tell you."

Martin grinned at this somewhat ambiguous remark.

"Suppose we don't make things quite so simple as that," he said. "Suppose we both put our cards on the table—all of them."

He had moved a step nearer as he spoke and the little doctor put up his hand warningly.

"Forgive me, Mr. Watt," he said. "But my friend behind me is very clever with his pistol, as you may have noticed, and we're right in his range now, aren't we? If I were you I really think I'd take my gun out again."

Martin stared at him and slowly drew his weapon out of his pocket.

"That's right," said Whitby. "Now we'll go a little farther away from him, shall we? You were saying—?"

Martin was bewildered. This was the last attitude he had expected a fugitive to take up in the middle of a saltmarsh at four o'clock in the morning.

Abbershaw spoke quietly behind him.

"It's Colonel Coombe's death we are interested in, Doctor," he said. "Your position at Black Dudley has been explained to us."

He watched the man narrowly as he spoke but there was no trace of surprise or fear on the little man's face.

He seemed relieved.

"Oh! I see," he said. "You, Doctor Abbershaw, would naturally be interested in the fate of my patient's body. As a matter of fact, he was cremated at Eastchester, thirty-six hours after I left Black Dudley. But, of course," he went on cheerfully, "you will want to know the entire history. After we left the house we went straight over to the registrar's. He was very sympathetic. Like everybody else in the vicinity he knew of the Colonel's weak health and was not surprised at my news. In fact, he was most obliging. Your signature and mine were quite enough for him. He signed immediately and we continued our journey. I was on my way back to the house when I received—by the merest chance—the news of the unfortunate incidents which had taken place in my absence. And so," he added with charming frankness, "we altered our number plates and changed our destination. Are you satisfied?"

"Not quite," said Martin grimly.

The nervous little doctor hurried on before they could stop him.

"Why, of course," he said, "I was forgetting. There must be a great many things that still confuse you. The exact import of the papers that you, Doctor Abbershaw, were so fool-hardy as to destroy? Never revealed, was it?"

"We know it was the detailed plan of a big robbery," said Abbershaw stiffly.

"Indeed it was," said Whitby warmly. "Quite the largest thing our people had ever thought of undertaking. Have you—er—any idea what place it was? Everything was all taped out so that nothing remained to chance, no detail left unconsidered. It was a complete plan of campaign ready to be put into immediate action. The work of a master, I assure you. Do you know the place?"

He saw by their faces that they were ignorant, and a satisfied smile spread over the little man's face.

"It wasn't my secret," he said. "But naturally I couldn't help hearing a thing or two. As far as I could gather von Faber's objective was the Repository of the Bullion for the Repayment of the American Debt."

The three were silent, the stupendousness of the scheme suddenly brought home to them.

"Then," continued Whitby rapidly, "there was Colonel Coombe's own part in von Faber's affairs. Perhaps you don't know that for the greater part of his life Colonel Coombe had been under von Faber's influence to an enormous extent, in fact I think I might almost say that he was dominated absolutely by von—"

"It's not Colonel Coombe's life, Doctor Whitby, which interests us so particularly," cut in Martin suddenly. "It's his death. You know as well as we do that he was murdered."

For an instant the nervous garrulousness of the little doctor vanished and he stared at them blankly.

"There are a lot of people interested in that point," he said at last. "I am myself, for one."

"So we gathered," murmured Martin, under his breath, while Abbershaw spoke hastily.

"Doctor Whitby," he said, "you and I committed a very grave offence by signing those certificates."

"Yes," said Whitby, and paused for a moment or so, after which he brightened up visibly and hurried on. "But really, my dear sir, in the circumstances I don't see that we could have done anything else, do you? We were the victims of a stronger force."

Abbershaw disregarded the other's smile and spoke steadily.

"Doctor Whitby," he said, "do you know who murdered Colonel Coombe?"

The little doctor's benign expression did not alter.

"Why, of course," he said. "I should have thought that, at least, was obvious to everybody—everybody, who knew anything at all about the case, that is."

Abbershaw shook his head.

"I'm afraid we must plead either great stupidity or peculiarly untrusting dispositions," he said. "That is the point on which we are not at all satisfied."

"But my dear young people—" for the first time during that interview the little man showed signs of impatience. "That is most obvious. Amongst your party—let us say, Mr. Petrie's party, as opposed to von Faber's—there was a member of the famous Simister gang of America. Perhaps you have heard of it, Doctor Abbershaw. Colonel Coombe had been attempting to establish relations with them for some time. In fact, that was the reason why I and my pugnacious friend behind us were placed at Black Dudley—to keep an eye upon him. During the progress of the Dagger Ritual, Simister's man eluded our vigilance and chose that moment not only to get hold of the papers, but also to murder the unfortunate Colonel. That, by the way, was only a title he adopted, you know."

The three younger men remained unimpressed.

Martin shook his head.

"Not a bad story, but it won't wash," he said. "If one of our party stabbed the old boy, why do you all go to such lengths to keep it so quiet for us?"

"Because, my boy," said Whitby testily, "we didn't want a fuss. In fact, the police on the scene was the last thing we desired. Besides, you seem to forget the extraordinary importance of the papers."

Again Martin shook his head.

"We've heard all this before," he said; "and it didn't sound any better then. To be perfectly frank, we are convinced that one of your people was responsible. We want to know who, and we want to know why."

The little doctor's face grew slowly crimson, but it was the flush of a man annoyed rather than a guilty person accused of his crime.

"You tire me with your stupidity," he said suddenly. "Good God, sir, consider it. Have you any idea how valuable the man was to us? Do you know what he was paid for his services? Twenty thousand pounds for this coup alone. Simister would probably have offered him more. You don't hear about these things. Government losses rarely get into the papers—certainly not with figures attached. Not the smallest member of our organization stood to gain anything at all by his death. I confess I was surprised at Simister's man unless he was double-crossing his own people."

For a moment even Martin's faith in his own theory was shaken.

"In that case," said Abbershaw unexpectedly, "it will doubtless surprise you to learn that the man employed by Simister to obtain the package had a complete alibi. In fact, it was impossible for him ever to have laid hands upon the dagger."

"Impossible?" The word broke from Whitby's lips like a

cry, but although they were listening to him critically, to not one of them did it sound like a cry of fear. He stared at them, amazement in his eyes.

"Have you proof of that?" he said at last.

"Complete proof," said Abbershaw quietly. "I think you must reconsider your theory, Doctor Whitby. Consider how you yourself stand, in the light of what I have just said."

An expression of mild astonishment spread over the insignificant little face. Then, to everybody's surprise, he laughed.

"Amateur detectives?" he said. "I'm afraid you've had a long ride for nothing, gentlemen. I confess that my position as accessory after the fact is a dangerous one, but then, so is Doctor Abbershaw's. Consider the likelihood of your suggestion. Have you provided me with a motive?"

"I suggest," said Martin calmly, "that your position when von Faber discovered that your prisoner had 'eluded your vigilance,' as you call it, would not have been too good."

Whitby paused thoughtfully.

"Not bad," he said. "Not bad at all. Very pretty. But"—he shook his head—"unfortunately not true. My position with Coombe dead was 'not good' as you call it. But had Coombe been alive he would have had to face the music, wouldn't he? It was von Faber's own fault that I ever left his side at all."

This was certainly a point which they had not considered. It silenced them for a moment, and in the lull a sound which had been gradually forcing itself upon their attention for the last few moments became suddenly very apparent—the steady droning of an aeroplane engine.

Whitby looked up, mild interest on his face.

It was now quite light, and the others, following his gaze, saw a huge Fokker monoplane flying low against the grey sky.

"He's out early," remarked Prenderby.

"Yes," said Whitby. "There's an aerodrome a couple of miles across here, you know. Quite near my house, in fact."

Martin pricked up his ears.

"Your house?" he echoed.

The little doctor nodded.

"Yes. I have a small place down here by the sea. Very lonely, you know, but I thought it suited my purpose very well just now. Frankly, I didn't like the idea of your following me and it made my friend quite angry."

"Hullo! He's in difficulties or something."

It was Prenderby who spoke. He had been watching the aeroplane, which was now almost directly above their heads. His excited cry made them all look up again, to see the great plane circling into the wind.

There was now no drone of the engine but they could hear the sough of the air through the wires, and for a moment it seemed as if it were dropping directly on top of them. The next instant it passed so near that they almost felt its draught upon their faces. Then it taxied along the ground, coming to a halt in the glow of the still burning head-lights of the big car.

Instinctively, they hurried towards it, and until they were within twenty yards they did not realize that Whitby's confederate had got there first and was talking excitedly to the pilot.

"Good God!" said Martin suddenly stopping dead in his tracks. The same thought struck the others at precisely the same instant.

Through the waves of mingled anger and amazement which overwhelmed them, Whitby's precise little voice came clearly.

"I observe that he carries a machine-gun," he remarked. "That's what I like about these Germans—so efficient. In view of what my excitable colleague has probably said to the pilot, I really don't think I should come any nearer. Perhaps you would turn off our head-lights when you go back, they have served their purpose. Take the car too if you like."

He paused and beamed on them.

"Good-bye," he said. "I suppose it would annoy you if I thanked you for coming to see me off? Don't do that," he added sharply, as Martin's hand shot to his side pocket. "Please don't do that," he repeated more earnestly. "For my friends would most certainly kill you without the least compunction, and I don't want that. Believe me, my dear young people, whatever your theories may be, I am no murderer. I am leaving the country in this melodramatic fashion because it obviates the inconveniences which might arise if I showed my passport here just at present. Don't come any nearer. Good-bye, gentlemen."

As they watched him go, Martin's hand again stole to his pocket.

Abbershaw touched his aim.

"Don't be a fool, old man," he said. "If he's done one murder, don't encourage him to do another, and if he hasn't why help him to?"

Martin nodded and made a remark which did nobody any credit.

They stood there watching the machine with the gun trained upon them from its cockpit until it began to move again; then they turned back towards the Riley.

"Right up the garden," said Martin bitterly. "Fooled, done brown, put it how you like. There goes Coombe's murderer and here are we poor muffs who listened trustingly while he told us fairy stories to pass the time away until his pals turned up for him. I wish we'd risked that machine-gun."

Prenderby nodded gloomily.

"I feel sick," he said. "We spotted him and then he got away with it."

Abbershaw shook his head.

"He got away certainly," he said. "But I don't think we've got much cause to regret it."

"What do you mean? Think he didn't kill him?"

They looked at him incredulously.

Abbershaw nodded.

"I know he didn't kill him," he said quietly.

Martin grunted.

"I'm afraid I can't agree with you there," he said. "Gosh! I'll never forgive myself for being such a fool!"

Prenderby was inclined to agree with him, but Abbershaw stuck to his own opinion, and the expression on his face as they drove silently back to Town was very serious and, somehow, afraid.

CHAPTER TWENTY-NINE

The Last Chapter

IN THE SIX WEEKS which followed the unsatisfactory trip to the Essex Marshes, Abbershaw and Meggie were fully occupied preparing for their wedding, which they had decided should take place as soon as was possible.

Prenderby seemed inclined to forget the Black Dudley affair altogether: his own marriage to Jeanne was not far distant and provided him with a more interesting topic of thought and conversation, and Martin Watt had gone back to his old haunts in the City and the West End.

Wyatt was in his flat overlooking St. James's, apparently immersed as ever in the obscurities of his reading.

But Abbershaw had not forgotten Colonel Coombe.

He had not put the whole matter before his friend, Inspector Deadwood of Scotland Yard, for a reason which he was unable to express in definite words, even to himself.

An idea was forming in his mind—an idea which he shrank from and yet could not wholly escape.

In vain he argued with himself that his thought was preposterous and absurd; as the days went on and the whole affair sank more and more into its true perspective, the more the insidious theory grew upon him and began to haunt his nights as well as his days.

At last, very unwillingly, he gave way to his suspicions and set out to test his theory.

His procedure was somewhat erratic. He spent the best part of a week in the reading-room of the British Museum; this was followed by a period of seclusion in his own library, with occasional descents upon the bookshops of Charing Cross Road, and then, as though his capacity for the tedium of a subject in which he was not naturally interested was not satiated, he spent an entire week-end in the Kensington house of his uncle, Sir Dorrington Wynne, one-time Professor of Archaeology in the University of Oxford, a man whose conversation never left the subject of his researches.

Another day or so at the British Museum completed Abbershaw's investigations, and one evening found him driving down Whitehall in the direction of the Abbey, his face paler than usual, and his eyes troubled.

He went slowly, as if loth to reach his destination, and when a little later he pulled up outside a block of flats, he remained for some time at the wheel, staring moodily before him. Every moment the task he had set himself became more and more nauseous.

Eventually, he left the car, and mounting the carpeted stairs of the old Queen Anne house walked slowly up to the first floor.

A man-servant admitted him, and within three minutes he was seated before a spacious fire-place in Wyatt Petrie's library.

The room expressed its owner's personality. Its taste was perfect but a little academic, a little strict. It was an ascetic room. The walls were pale-coloured and hung sparsely with etchings and engravings—a Goya, two or three moderns, and a tiny Rembrandt. There were books everywhere, but tidily, neatly kept, and a single hanging in one corner, a dully burning splash of old Venetian embroidery.

Wyatt seemed quietly pleased to see him. He sat down on the other side of the hearth and produced cigars and Benedictine.

Abbershaw refused both. He was clearly ill at ease, and he sat silent for some moments after the first words of greeting, staring moodily into the fire.

"Wyatt," he said suddenly, "I've known you for a good many years. Believe me, I've not forgotten that when I ask you this question."

Wyatt leaned back in his chair and closed his eyes, his liqueur glass lightly held in his long, graceful fingers. Abbershaw turned in his chair until he faced the silent figure.

"Wyatt," he said slowly and evenly, "why did you stab your uncle?"

No expression appeared upon the still pale face of the man to whom he had spoken. For some moments he did not appear to have heard.

At last he sighed and, leaning forward, set his glass down upon the little book-table by his side.

"I'll show you," he said.

Abbershaw took a deep breath. He had not been prepared for this; almost anything would have been easier to bear.

Meanwhile Wyatt crossed over to a small writing-desk let into a wall of bookshelves and, unlocking it with a key which he took from his pocket, produced something from a drawer; carrying it back to the fire-place, he handed it to his visitor.

Abbershaw took it and looked at it with some astonishment.

It was a photograph of a girl.

The face was round and childlike, and was possessed of that peculiar innocent sweetness which seems to belong only to a particular type of blonde whose beauty almost invariably hardens in maturity.

At the time of the portrait, Abbershaw judged, the girl must have been about seventeen—possibly less. Undeniably lovely, but in the golden-haired unsophisticated fashion of the medieval angel.

The last face in the world that he would have suspected Wyatt of noticing.

He turned the thing over in his hand. It was one of those cheap, glossy reproductions which circulate by the thousand in the theatrical profession.

He sat looking at it helplessly; uncomprehending, and very much at sea.

Wyatt came to the rescue.

"Her stage name was 'Joy Love,' " he said slowly, and there was silence again.

Abbershaw was still utterly perplexed, and opened his mouth to ask the obvious question, but the other man interrupted him, and the depth and bitterness of his tone surprised the doctor.

"Her real name was Dolly Lord," he said. "She was seventeen in that photograph, and I loved her—I do still love her—most truly and most deeply." He added simply, "I have never loved any other woman."

He was silent, and Abbershaw, who felt himself drifting further and further out of his depth at every moment, looked at him blankly. There was no question that the man was sincere. The tone in his voice, every line of his face and body proclaimed his intensity.

"I don't understand," said Abbershaw.

Wyatt laughed softly and began to speak quickly, earnestly, and all in one key.

"She was appearing in the crowd scene in *The Faith of St. Hubert,* that beautiful little semi-sacred opera that they did at the Victor Gordon Arts Theatre in Knightsbridge," he said. "That's where I first saw her. She looked superb in a snood and wimple. I fell in love with her. I found out who she was after considerable trouble. I was crazy about her by that time."

He paused and looked at Abbershaw with his narrow dark eyes in which there now shone a rebellious, almost fanatical light.

"You can call it absurd with your modern platonic-suitability complexes," he said, "but I fell in love with a woman as nine-tenths of the men have done since the race began and will continue to do until all resemblance of the original animal is civilized out of us and the race ends—with her face, and with her carriage, and with her body. She seemed to me to fulfill all my ideals of womankind. She became my sole object. I wanted her, I wanted to marry her."

He hesitated for a moment and looked at Abbershaw defiantly, but as the other did not speak he went on again. "I found out that in the ordinary way she was what they call a 'dancing instructress' in one of the night-clubs at the back of Shaftesbury Avenue. I went there to find her. From the manager in charge I discovered that for half a crown a dance and anything else I might choose to pay I might talk as long as I liked with her."

Again he hesitated, and Abbershaw was able to see in his face something of what the disillusionment had meant to him.

"As you know," Wyatt continued, "I know very little of women. As a rule they don't interest me at all. I think that is why Joy interested me so much. I want you to understand," he burst out suddenly with something akin to savagery in his tone, "that the fact that she was not of my world, that her accent was horrible, and her fingernails hideously over-manicured would not have made the slightest difference. I was in love with her: I wanted to marry her. The fact that she was stupid did not greatly deter me either. She was incredibly stupid—the awful stupidity of crass ignorance and innocence. Yes," he went on bitterly as he caught Abbershaw's involuntary expression, "innocence. I think it was that that broke me up. The girl was innocent with the innocence of a savage. She knew nothing. The elementary civilized code of right and wrong was an abstruse doctrine to her. She was horrible." He shuddered, and Abbershaw fancied that he began to understand. An incident that would have been ordinary enough to a boy in his teens had proved too much for a studious recluse of twenty-seven. It had unhinged his mind.

Wyatt's next remark therefore surprised him.

"She interested me," he said. "I wanted to study her. I thought her extraordinary mental state was due to chance at first—some unfortunate accident of birth and upbringing—but I found I was wrong. That was the thing that turned me into a particularly militant type of social reformer. Do you understand what I mean, Abbershaw?"

He leant forward as he spoke, his eyes fixed on the other man's face. "Do you understand what I'm saying? The state of that girl's mentality was not due to chance—it was *deliberate*."

Abbershaw started.

"Impossible," he said involuntarily, and Wyatt seized upon the word.

"Impossible?" he echoed passionately. "That's what everybody would say, I suppose, but I tell you you're wrong. I went right into it. I found out. That girl had been trained from a child. She was a perfect product of a diabolical scheme, and she wasn't the only victim. It was a society, Abbershaw, a highly organized criminal concern. This girl, my girl, and several others of her kind, were little wheels in the machinery. They were the catspaws— specially prepared implements with which to attract certain men or acquire certain information. The thing is horrible when the girl is cognizant of what she is doing—when the choice is her own— but think of it, trained from childhood, minds deliberately warped, deliberately developed along certain lines. It's driven me insane, Abbershaw."

He was silent for a moment or so, his head in his hands. Abbershaw rose to his feet, but the other turned to him eagerly.

"Don't go," he said. "You must hear it all."

The little red-haired doctor sat down immediately.

"I found it all out," Wyatt repeated. "I shook out the whole terrible story and discovered that the brains for this organization were bought, like everything else. That is to say, they had a special brain to plan the crime that other men would commit. That appalled me. There's something revolting about mass-production anyway, but when applied to crime it's ghastly. I felt I'd wasted my life fooling around with books and theories, while all around me, on my very doorstep, these appalling things were happening. I worked it all out up here. It seemed to me that the thing to be done was to get at those brains—to destroy them. Lodging information with the police wouldn't be enough. What's the good of sending brains like that to prison for a year or two when at the end of the time they can come back and start afresh? It took me a year to trace those brains and I found them in my own family, though not, thank God, in my own kin…my aunt's husband, Gordon Coombe. I saw that there was no point in simply going down there and blowing his brains out. *He* was only the beginning. There were others, men who could organize the thing, men who could conceive such an abominable idea as the one which turned Dolly Lord into Joy Love, a creature not quite human, not quite animal—a machine, in fact. So I had to go warily. My uncle was in the habit of asking me to take house-parties down to Black Dudley, as you probably know, to cover his interviews with his confederates. I planned what I thought was a perfect killing, and the next time I was asked I chose my house-party carefully and went down there with every intention of putting my scheme into action."

"You *chose* your house-party?"

Abbershaw looked at him curiously as he spoke.

"Certainly," said Wyatt calmly. "I chose each one of you deliberately. You were all people of blameless reputation. There was not one of you who could not clear himself with perfect certainty. The suspicion would therefore necessarily fall on one of my uncle's own guests, each of whom had done, if not murder, something more than as bad. I thought Campion was of their party until we were all prisoners. Until Prenderby told me, I thought Anne Edgeware had brought him, even then."

"You ran an extraordinary risk," said Abbershaw.

Wyatt shook his head.

"Why?" he said. "I was my uncle's benefactor, not he mine. I had nothing to gain by his death, and I should have been as free from suspicion as any of you. Of course," he went on, "I had no idea that things would turn out as they did. No one could have been more surprised than I when they concealed the murder in that extraordinary way. When I realized that they had lost something I understood, and I was desperately anxious that they should not recover what I took to be my uncle's notes for the gang's next coup. That is why I asked you to stay."

"Of course," said Abbershaw slowly, "you were wrong."

"In not pitching on von Faber as my first victim?" said Wyatt.

Abbershaw shook his head.

"No," he said. "In setting out to fight a social evil single-handed. That is always a mad thing to do."

Wyatt raised his eyes to meet the other's.

"I know," he said simply. "I think I am a little mad. It seemed to me so wicked. I loved her."

There was silence after he had spoken, and the two men sat for some time, Abbershaw staring into the fire, Wyatt leaning back, his eyes half-closed. The thought that possessed Abbershaw's mind was the pity of it—such a good brain, such a valuable idealistic soul. And it struck him in a sudden impersonal way that it was odd that evil should beget evil. It was as if it went on spreading in ever-widening circles, like ripples round the first splash of a stone thrown into a pond.

Wyatt recalled him from his reverie.

"It was a perfect murder," he said, almost wonderingly. "How did you find me out?"

Abbershaw hesitated. Then he sighed. "I couldn't help it," he said. "It was too perfect. It left nothing to chance. Do you know where I have spent the last week or so? In the British Museum."

He looked at the other steadily.

"I now know more about your family history than, I should think, any other man alive. That Ritual story would have been wonderful for your purpose, Wyatt, if it just hadn't been for one thing. It was not true."

Wyatt rose from his chair abruptly, and walked up and down the room. This flaw in his scheme seemed to upset him more than anything else had done.

"But it might have been true," he argued. "Who could prove it? A family legend."

"But it wasn't true," Abbershaw persisted. "It wasn't true because from the year 1100 until the year 1603—long past the latest date to which such a story as yours could have been feasible, Black Dudley was a monastery and not in the possession of your family at all. Your family estate was higher up the coast, in Norfolk, and I shouldn't think the dagger came into your possession until 1650 at least, when an ancestor of yours is referred to as having returned from the Papal States laden with merchandise."

Wyatt continued to pace up and down the room.

"I see," he said. "I see. But otherwise it was a perfect

murder. Think of it—Heaven knows how many fingerprints on the dagger handle, no one with any motive—no one who might not have committed the crime, and by the same reasoning no one who might. It had its moments of horror too, though," he said, pausing suddenly. "The moment when I came upon Miss Oliphant in the dark—I had to follow the dagger round, you see, to be in at the first alarm. I saw her pause under the window and stare at the blade, and I don't think it was until then that I realized that there was blood on it. So I took it from her. It was an impulsive, idiotic thing to do, and when the alarm did come the thing was in my own hand. I didn't see what they were getting at at first, and I was afraid I hadn't quite killed him, although I'd worked out the blow with a medical chart before I went down there. I took the dagger up to my own room. You nearly found me with it, by the way."

Abbershaw nodded.

"I know," he said. "I think it was instinct, but as you came in from the balcony I caught a glimpse of something in your hand, and although I didn't see what it was, I couldn't get the idea of the dagger out of my mind."

"Two flaws," said Wyatt, and was silent.

The atmosphere in the pleasant room had become curiously cold, and Abbershaw shivered. The sordid glossy photograph lay upon the floor, and the pretty childish face with the expression of innocence which had now become so sinister smiled up at him from the carpet.

"Well, what are you going to do?"

It was Wyatt who spoke, pausing abruptly in his feverish stride.

Abbershaw did not look at him.

"What are *you* going to do?" he murmured.

Wyatt hesitated.

"There is a Dominican Foundation in the rocky valley of El Puerto in the north of Spain," he said. "I have been in correspondence with them for some time. I have been disposing of all my books this week. I realized when von Faber passed into the hands of the police that my campaign was ended, but—"

He stopped and looked at Abbershaw; then he shrugged his shoulders.

"What now?" he said.

Abbershaw rose to his feet and held out his hand.

"I don't suppose I shall see you again before you go," he said. "Good-bye."

Wyatt shook the outstretched hand, but after the first flicker of interest which the last words had occasioned his expression had become preoccupied. He crossed the room and picked up the photograph, and the last glimpse Abbershaw had of him was as he sat in the deep armchair, crouching over it, his eyes fixed on the sweet, foolish little face.

As the little doctor walked slowly down the staircase to the street his mind was in confusion. He was conscious of a strong feeling of relief, even though his worst fears had been realized. At the back of his head, the old problem of Law and Order as opposed to Right and Wrong worried itself into the inextricable tangle which knows no unravelling. Wyatt was both a murderer and a martyr. There was no one who could decide between the two, in his opinion.

And in his thoughts, too, were his own affairs: Meggie, and his love for her, and their marriage.

❀ ❀ ❀

As he stepped out into the street, a round moon face, red and hot with righteous indignation, loomed down upon him out of the darkness.

"Come at last, 'ave yer?" inquired a thick sarcastic voice. "Your name and address, *if* you please."

Gradually it dawned upon the still meditative doctor

that he was confronted by an excessively large and unfriendly London bobby.

"This is your car, I suppose?" the questioner continued more mildly, as he observed Abbershaw's blank expression, but upon receiving the assurance that it was, all his indignation returned.

"This car's been left 'ere over an hour to my certain personal knowledge," he bellowed. "Unattended and drawn out a foot from the kerb, which aggravates the offence. This'll mean a summons, you know"—he flourished his notebook. "Name and address."

Abbershaw having furnished him with this information, he replaced the pencil in its sheath and, clicking the book's elastic band smartly, continued his homily. He was clearly very much aggrieved.

"It's people like you," he explained, as Abbershaw climbed into the driving seat, "wot gives us officers all our work. But we're not goin' to have these offences, I can tell you. We're making a clean sweep. Persons offending against the Law are not going to be tolerated."

He paused suspiciously. The slightly dazed expression upon the face of the little red-haired man in the car had suddenly given place to a smile.

"Splendid!" he said, and there was unmistakable enthusiasm in his tone. "Really, really splendid, Officer! You don't know how comforting that sounds. My fervent wishes for your success." And he drove off, leaving the policeman looking after him, wondering a little wistfully if the charge in his notebook should not perhaps have read, "Drunk in charge of a car."